HEROICS

A VILLANOUS HEROICS BOOK

LOU WILHAM

Midnight Tide
PUBLISHING

Copyright © 2022 by Lou Wilham

All rights reserved.

No part of this book may be reproduced in any form or by any electronic or mechanical means, including information storage and retrieval systems, without written permission from the author, except for the use of brief quotations in a book review.

❧ Created with Vellum

The people who make mistakes. The people learning who they are one day at a time. The constantly evolving.

This one is to you.

AUTHOR'S NOTE

Please note that this book contains issues of misgendering, ableism, discrimination, and violence. Please take care of yourself.

A VILLAINOUS HEROICS BOOK

HEROICS

LOU WILHAM

CHAPTER ONE

Rain pattered from above, soaking the black hoodie that J had forced Sol to wear for "stealth". Mythikos stretched out below them. The lights shimmering in the city's puddles and off raindrop-streaked windows, made it look magical, and ominous all in one go. Sol still didn't understand the strange desire to blend into the shadows that J had. It was like she thought if no one saw them then they wouldn't connect Sol back to the crime. Which was just plain silliness as Sol all but signed his work these days, and Soliel Tsuki was supposed to be dead besides. Killed in a failed attempt to flee while on the way to the hospital. The news said so, and the everyday citizen believed it—they all knew the news couldn't lie—not that they *cared*. What was one more dead Unseelie? But Sol wanted certain people to know he was still out there in the world, trying to set it to rights. He wanted the crooked politicians and the power tripping Hero Alliance to know that he was watching them. That he saw what they were doing, and he was going to expose them at any cost.

He wanted to *matter*. He would give *anything* to matter to this city, even his life, he supposed...

The billboard behind them fizzled and blacked out, casting Sol and J into darkness.

"Well, that wasn't supposed to happen," Sol said with a lightness to the words that didn't ring true. There had been a plan. There were fail safes. This stupid fucking billboard was the one right outside of Councilman Tor's big expensive penthouse. He'd see it from his window when he looked out while enjoying his midnight glass of overly expensive whiskey. Which tasted like absolute swill; Sol would know because he'd broken into the place to figure out which billboard was the best one to hit so they could scare the metaphorical, and probably literal, shit out of the man.

"I hate it when you say shit like that," J grumbled from where she crouched beside Sol. Her wide shoulders tensed up underneath the matching black hoodie she'd thrown on before they left.

"These things happen." They didn't. Not to Soliel Tsuki. Son of the late Adelia Tsuki. Partner in all things to Colette Jericho. Not to *him*. He was meticulous in his planning. He had always been exactly where he wanted to be, and nothing had ever gone wrong. *All right*, almost *nothing*, he amended, brushing his fingers over the scar that ran down the front of his throat. But that wasn't the point. Sol shrugged J's intense gaze off when it prickled at the back of his neck. "Just keep an eye on the street, and let me know if anyone notices."

"Maz and Dominic are down there. They'll let us know if anyone is staring up here for too long. Just fix the fucking thing before we wind up on the news." *Again*, went left unsaid, but Sol heard it anyway.

Sol grunted at the reprimand, his fingers tapping probably too hard against the tablet balanced on his knee. The rain made the touch screen slick, and his fingers were starting to prune from trying to get the damn billboard back online.

"It's 11:58," J's voice whispered too close to Sol's ear, and her breath was hot on his cheek.

"Okay well maybe if you weren't breathing down my *neck*, I could get this done."

"Is it the breathing down your neck that's the problem, or is it that you just don't know how to work that thing?" J snorted, the sound undeniably fond to Sol's ears.

"I'm turning off my fucking hearing aid if you don't shut up so I can work."

J made another sound in the back of her throat, like an annoyed puppy, and turned away to watch the window across the street. If they weren't in the middle of the cold rain, with Sol trying to figure out what the fuck had gone wrong with a simple billboard take over, he might have cuddled her into his chest, and pressed a kiss to her head. But they were in the rain, and this billboard was being an absolute bitch.

Sol reached into the pouch on his belt, pulling out a packet of glowing powder. "Take this and sprinkle it on that service panel over there," he said, sprinkling a little on the tablet.

"What is it?"

"It'll create a connection to the billboard so I can access the stupid thing directly, and get it back online. It looks like Pickle's virus has completely knocked it off the main server." The explanation was muttered mostly to himself, but Sol knew that J would hear it even over the sounds of traffic below, and the rain above—werewolf hearing and all that.

"What if it corrupts our network through your device?" J twirled the packet around in her fingers, watching the way the glowing contents shifted around in the envelope with narrowed green eyes.

"It won't. It's fine. I just need to see what error it's kicking back. Now, be quiet, and let me work. We've got like..."

"70 seconds," Maz supplied helpfully into the com on his hearing aid. "That gives you two idiots exactly ten seconds to get down off there before Tor sees and calls the heroes in." They did *not* want the heroes involved in this; Mythikos' "public safety" force would be less than thrilled to see one of their own hacking into a billboard alongside someone who they'd personally told the public was dead.

"No pressure," Dominic chimed in, his tone light.

"Right. No pressure." Sol rolled his eyes, before flapping his hand at J to do as she was told. She did, but there was a begrudging grumble in her throat that Sol didn't have to hear to know was there. "Thanks a lot, both of you."

"Anytime!" Dominic sounded like he was having a grand ol' time, and that just made the whole situation that much more frustrating as a little spinning wheel on the tablet spun and spun and spun. He'd rather be back at headquarters with Rachel, watching the feeds for the public's response, not that Sol could blame him. None of them wanted to be out in this rain. But as always, Dominic was making the best of it. So annoying.

"When did everyone on my fucking team become a bunch of critical ass—"

"50 seconds," Maz said.

"Shut *up*, Maz!" Sol's friend, and the first person he'd recruited to Eventide after it had formed could be a real pain sometimes. He loved her, but she just never seemed to realize when enough was enough.

The spinning wheel disappeared a second later, the backlit screen blinked, then a little pop-up window appeared that just said, '\/\/H1T3_R4BB1T'. Sol cocked his head, narrowing his eyes on the error message. "Huh. That's weird."

"I hate that one more than 'that wasn't supposed to happen'." J muttered, moving to peer over Sol's shoulder to look at the screen. Her hood slipped a little, long blond hair spilling down to brush at Sol's cheek.

"I'm with J, that one's worse." Dominic's tone was still light, like he was laughing despite the situation they were in.

Which might have been better than the sweat crawling down Sol's spine in spite of the cold rain soaking through his clothes and into his binder. It could be nothing, he reasoned. Just a weird system glitch. Magic and technology didn't always work together as nicely as people hoped they would. But... but Pickle didn't make mistakes like that. None of her viruses had ever kicked back an error code. Ildri's motto was "glitch-free is the way to be." And the pixie had had centuries of figuring out how to combine tech with magic, she wasn't an amateur. Sol tried to tell himself that there was a first time for everything. That even Pickle wasn't infallible. But his stomach twisted with unease. He pushed those thoughts aside. Now wasn't the time. He could deal with this \/\/H1T3_R4BB1T error later.

"Everyone's a fucking comedian in this organization, I swear." Sol breathed out slowly, forcing himself back to focus on what he was doing. He exited the error window, and went back to the program, then a couple of taps later and the billboard flickered back to life, nearly blinding him and J.

"Fucking hell," J cursed under her breath.

The slideshow started up quickly thereafter. Photos of Councilman Tor meeting with some shady looking folks, accepting gifts, smiling, and laughing, and looking all too chummy with someone that looked like they belonged to Mythikos' underground. And then documents. Nothing that anyone could read from the street, but Tor would see them from his window; he'd know that they knew. And any passersby could download the file to their own device if they so chose, just by clicking on an alert that would be sent from the infected billboard. It would be a real pain in the ass to undo, likely take at least an hour, and by then at least a couple hundred people could have seen the information packet.

Simply put, Councilman Tor was fucked.

"We're live, people!" Sol laughed, turning carefully where he squatted on the little ledge in front of the billboard to peer into Tor's window. He could just see the outline of the man silhouetted through the glass, but that shape wasn't moving, hardly looked like he was breathing in fact.

"Time to get gone." J came over to grab Sol by the collar of his hoodie, and pull him to his feet, readying to drag him back to the ladder down to the roof. All it really did was dislodge the hood from where it had kept Sol's face hidden.

Sol tilted his head at the figure on the other side of the glass, digging his heels into the metal beneath him so J couldn't pull him along. He lifted one hand, and blew the figure a kiss.

"Press is on their way," Pickle said into his ear. "The drone is just around the block, Dusk. Remember to smile!"

"Stop encouraging him!" J growled, her hand tightening in the fabric at the back of Sol's neck. But it was too late, Sol heard the buzzing of the drone as it rounded the building.

It stopped, idling before the billboard as it seemed to contemplate what was flashing before it. Sol gave the little camera a jaunty wave, then turned to bow, one arm extended to draw the drone's attention back to the billboard which had cycled to an email chain between Tor and some unnamed account.

"All right, they're on it. They've started downloading the packet off the billboard's system. Time for you guys to make your exit." Pickle's voice was just barely audible over the sound of her typing in the background.

"I hear sirens," Maz said.

"Fuck!" J tightened her hold on Sol, and dragged him back

to the ladder. Seemed she was done playing around. "Do we have a route, Pickle?"

"Working on it. Maz and Dominic are already on their way back, but I'll take you two the roundabout way."

Sol pulled the hood back up over his head, his eyes flicking around to see if the news drone had decided to follow them. It hadn't, it was still hovering in front of the billboard.

"Don't worry about that thing, I made sure the packet was big enough it'd give you a clean break." Pickle's words were soft, but sure. A comfort as Sol's heart started to race.

"We may have to split up." Sol moved to the edge of the roof, looking down at the street. The rooftops would be the quickest escape, but the heroes had started utilizing drones in the year since Jericho had broken Dusk out of a Hero run transport. Sol took no small pleasure knowing it was because of his own notoriety.

"No." J's teeth glinted in the lights of the surrounding buildings as she snarled at him.

"No need." Pickle assured in that soft, soothing tone of hers. The one that kept J in line, and Sol's nerves settled. "I've got you a route, and control of the cameras along the way. I sent it to your phone, just in case we get cut off."

"What if we need to diverge?" Sol crouched to jiggle a drainpipe to test its sturdiness. J glared at him, but didn't say anything against it. They both knew they couldn't go back down through the building. There was too much chance of them getting cornered in the enclosed space.

"Reboot is standing by on the other channel." Pickle sounded like she was smiling, but Sol decided he didn't have time to think about that. Nor did he have time to imagine Pickle and Reboot working back to back to get them the fuck out of there, and back home.

"Who's Reboot?" J asked, her voice a hiss through the

coms instead of right at his ear as Sol started shimmying his way down the drainpipe.

"You'll meet her," Pickle said with a choked off chuckle, "eventually."

And then the line fell silent so Sol and J could focus on getting down the side of the building into the shadowed alley without breaking anything or falling to their deaths. Sol pulled out his phone, and lead the way back to the street, where the heavy work traffic of Mythikos would hide them. He felt J's presence at his back, a few people behind. Separating them to add an air of casualness to their sedate pace.

The rain started down in earnest a moment later, and then everyone around them opened their umbrellas, and J and Sol disappeared entirely from the view of any drones or cameras above. It was almost too easy to escape after that, through the foot traffic, down a back alley, through a mostly empty shopping mall, and back out onto an abandoned street in Ilygroth.

J was pressed in close to Sol on the train back toward the outskirts of the city before Sol let himself breathe easily again. He reached out to thread his fingers through J's, and was happy to find J pressing her palm back into his. Letting warmth seep in from everywhere they were pushed together in the overcrowded train—a comfort he hadn't known he needed nor wanted before a little over a year ago when J came back into his life.

"I feel like we're playing fucking whack-a-mole," Sol mumbled under his breath, the words too soft for anyone but J, with the sharp hearing of a werewolf beside him to hear. He was heavy with them, weighed down by the certainty that this would never end. Because ultimately no one gave enough of a fuck to make it end. "We take one out, and two more pop out of the ground like fucking daisies. We'll never fix things this way."

J sighed, leaning over to rest her head on Sol's shoulder. She reached up to turn the com off, so the others wouldn't hear them, and waited for Sol to do the same.

"Here's the thing," J said when she was sure they were alone again, but for the hordes of Mythikos citizens obliviously going about their day around them. "It's probably going to be like that for a while."

Sol ignored the way the words seemed to drag him down, making him tired. It wouldn't matter, he knew what he needed to do. But... well, he *was* getting tired. It had been a long couple of years, and still the corruption of Mythikos was so thick, he was swimming in it. Like nothing he did made a difference.

"We can stay. We can stay and fight. Try to save them all. We can try to make this place better..." J let her words drift off, her breath slow, and even, calm. Sol slowed his own breathing to match hers, keeping the panic at bay for just a bit longer.

"Or?" he breathed, only half wanting to know the alternative, because it would be enticing. Whatever thing J thought they could do instead would sound a hundred times better than what they were currently doing. He didn't even have to hear it to know.

"Or, we say fuck 'em, and save ourselves." J shrugged, letting the words settle between them like they were a genuine offer. Like they were a choice that either of them had. Sol knew better though. That was never going to be an option, not for them. They wouldn't be leaving Mythikos, not until they were done.

"Is that really an option?" Sol asked, even as he knew that it wasn't.

"I'm good with whatever you choose." J leaned her head to brush her nose against his cheek, letting out a soft, pleased rumble. "We're a team"

"You're sweet." Sol smiled.

"You tell anyone that, and I'll fucking smother you in your sleep." J grumbled, but there was no heat behind the threat, and they settled for a long moment into the sway and the bustle of the train around them. The noise of people getting on and off the train, muttering about their day, and humming softly along to whatever was on their headphones lulled Sol into a daze, and J stayed silent, giving him the space he needed to truly consider her offer. Not that there was much to consider. It was a forgone conclusion that Sol would spend his life trying to save the people of Mythikos, or die trying, for all that they seemed to notice.

"So... what'll it be?"

"We're not going anywhere," Sol sighed, hating himself a little for his own resolve. "So long as Dusk can still make a difference—"

"Fine. No need to get all uppity about it. It was just a question." J shifted uncomfortably beside him on the hard train bench, but didn't say anything else. Instead she let Sol sit with the offer. Let him mull it over. He was still doing that when they reached the last stop on the line, almost to the wilds beyond Mythikos. They couldn't leave, no, but maybe there was something more they *could* do right where they were. He'd have to talk to Pickle about it once they'd cleaned up.

CHAPTER TWO

"There's got to be more we can be doing," Sol said, lifting his hand to push the teal hair back from his face as he paced in front of Pickle's workbench.

"We're doing what we can," Reboot's soft voice came from the phone on speaker next to Pickle. Sol wasn't sure why Pickle had decided to call her, but Pickle had said this was a conversation for the whole family, and he wasn't about to argue with either of them, it had only ever gotten him into trouble before. He'd learned early on that a person didn't argue with the people in charge of finding an exit, or erasing records; the tech crew was to be respected at all times, especially Reboot and Pickle.

"It's not enough!" Sol slammed his hands down onto the edge of the workbench, making all the metal bits and bobs clatter against its steel surface, in an attempt to hide the way they were starting to tremble. It didn't hide anything. If anything, it made it more obvious, he realized too late.

"Dusk, you need to calm down." Pickle's voice was sharp, her blue eyes following him as he paced from one end of the metal table laden in gadgetry to the other.

"I am calm!" She was right—of course she was, Pickle was always *right*—he needed to calm down, but he couldn't seem to. Every part of him was vibrating with the need to *do* something, fight back, attack, break something, anything!

"Soliel." Reboot's tone was soft, but reprimanding, making Sol stop in his tracks. "Take a breath."

Sol let out a long breath, his shoulders sinking with it, then ran his hands through his hair to get the bright teal stripe out of his face. "I'm sorry. I'm sorry. I didn't mean to yell."

"We understand that you're upset. And we understand why," Reboot said soft, and soothing, just as her voice had always been. Her tone gentle, and kind. It made the thing that had gripped Sol's chest in a vice, loosen. She was right. They needed to remain calm about this. They couldn't go rushing in unprepared. And he trusted Reboot and Pickle to help him come up with a plan that would get things moving. They had been at this much longer than him, after all.

"Now that everyone is done yelling." Pickle pushed her goggles up onto her head, brushing her pink and blue hair out of her face like a headband. "I have an idea."

"You do?" Reboot and Sol asked at the same time. Although Reboot sounded suspicious, and Sol, surprised.

"Of course I do."

"And you didn't bring this up to me before... why?" Reboot's tone turned sharp, and Sol could imagine her narrowing her brown eyes, nose crinkling with irritation.

"Don't get mad, love," Pickle offered placatingly. "I wanted to bring it up at a family meeting so I could get everyone's opinion."

"Uh huh." Reboot's tone had only grown more suspicious, and Sol didn't envy the dressing down Pickle would get for this little stunt later.

"And I knew if I brought it up to just you, you'd veto it

before Dusk could even hear it." Pickle winked at Sol, and Reboot let out a long breath that sounded like a groan. "Does that mean I'm not allowed to tell him?"

"Is there any way of stopping you?" Reboot grumble.

"Not really?" Pickle laughed, her face scrunching up with the happiness of it.

"Proceed," Reboot said, resigned.

"Perfect." Pickle perked up, grabbing a tablet from somewhere off to the side, and turning it on so the screen lit her face from below in a ghostly blue. "So, there's this Councilwoman named Guinevere—"

"We're not kidnapping a councilwoman, people will notice," Reboot cut in, her words sharp, but Sol was already leaning in closer, his feet taking him to stand in front of Reboot so he might get a look at whatever she had pulled up on the tablet. *Let people notice*, he thought. He wanted them to notice, to stop and think about what was going on, and ask the important question finally, the one that not even his live broadcast had gotten people to ask... *Why?*

"Of course not, don't be silly, honey. Besides, Guinevere is actually a halfway decent person. But she *is* being manipulated by an underling. An assistant named Cordelia Gareth, who supervises what information passes Guinevere's desk, and therefore—"

"What she signs off on, get to the point." Sol leaned over the workbench, careful of Pickle's gadgets to get a better look at the screen she was looking at. She was keeping it tilted close to her, likely to build suspense for her big reveal.

"Gareth is single. She's not in touch with her family. The only people who would even miss her are those at Guinevere's office."

"And if we send in a letter saying she's sick..." Reboot sounded like she was smiling.

"Exactly. They'll be none the wiser." Pickle was smiling,

the expression eating up her face so there was hardly an inch of pale skin untouched by it.

"Okay, but why this assistant? She doesn't have any real power. How do we know she even works with the other council members?" Sol wrinkled his nose, fingers tapping nervously on the metal workbench. "She just might be a shitty person."

"Except she lives in Heritage Heights." Pickle tilted her tablet so the display would turn, and Sol could *finally* get a good look at Gareth's file.

Sol whistled, shaking his head. "I don't even think council members can afford that place." He'd only ever ridden past Heritage Heights; it was the kind of place where the ultra-rich of Mythikos holed up away from the world. Its height disappeared into the clouds, and rumor had it that each floor had a single owner, and was outfitted with a swimming pool, a tennis court, and even a beach someone had managed to magic in. It was a haven. Certainly, no assistant should have been able to afford it.

Pickle nodded, her smile inching further up her cheeks, going a little manic round the edges.

"So where's the money coming from?" Reboot asked, her nails tapping on whatever desk she was sitting at. And *that*, that was the question he'd been taught to ask when he was just starting out. He remembered Reboot sitting him down in front of a tablet, leaning over his shoulder, and telling him to follow the money. That was the one rule of Mythikos: money talked.

"Same place Pendragon's was, when I looked at his accounts. And by the amounts she's receiving... she's higher up than Pendragon was." Pickle slid her finger over the screen to show Sol the bank records, and his brows show up.

"We can't be sure that she knows anything." Reboot sounded like she was frowning.

"No, we can't. But we can be reasonably certain that she at least knows the others under her in the organization who work within the council. They might not know who she is, but she'll know who they are." Sol tapped his chin in thought, his mind already running down all the paths this could take them. So many options. So many choices. So many possibilities! "If I were this person, I'd have someone invisible to keep an eye on all my people. Someone they wouldn't look twice at."

"Right. And who would think that someone pushing papers and getting coffee is the one who could actually turn them in to their boss?" Pickle's voice went up an octave in her excitement, leaning over the bench toward Sol.

"It's exactly what I would do." Sol nodded eagerly, Pickle's excitement infecting him, ratcheting up his nerves to an eleven.

Reboot sighed loud enough to make the speaker crackle with it. "Fine. So what's your plan?"

"Oh, that's easy." Sol grinned at the speaker, his fingers wiggling to take the tablet from Pickle where she sat back in her seat, her fingers drumming against the metal workbench with soft thumps. This was what he'd wanted, a way to stop playing whack-a-mole and start ripping the weeds out in clumps. Pickle had given him the opening, now he just had to run with it.

"I DON'T LIKE IT." J sniffed, scrunching up his nose. His bright green eyes narrowed on the table. Plans littered the available space with every detail Sol thought they might need. It hadn't taken him and Pickle long to settle on the details, not once he had brought his discontent with their current circumstances to her. The most arduous part had been in convincing Reboot to go along with it, but once he and Pickle got excited about something Reboot always had a hard time saying no. So really, that had been easy too.

"Yeah? What else is new?" Maz rolled her eyes. One would have thought that after a year of working together J and Maz would have gotten over whatever hurdles were in the way of them getting along. One would have been wrong. Sol desperately hoped for peace between his significant other, and his friend, if only to make missions less stressful, but thus far he'd had none of it. Both J and Maz seemed incapable of letting the inborn prejudices of werewolves and kitsune drop long enough to have a civil conversation. It was a pain in the ass. It was a headache. It was giving Sol *grey hair*.

"It is a little off brand for us." Rachel shifted nervously beside Dominic, her hands fidgeting in front of her. She was anything but new, having joined up just before the mission to pull Sol out of that hero transport a year ago, but she still acted like a rookie anytime they asked her to go out into the field. Like she was sure someone would look at her and realize that of course the wraith was up to something. Still, when they needed her, she was always there in a pinch.

"Exactly. We don't kidnap people." J nodded, running a hand through his blond hair to keep it back from his eyes that for the first time in weeks were free of any kind of makeup. More and more Sol watched his significant other hiding behind the shield of his other gender. Tucking himself behind kohl rimmed eyes, and red painted lips like they could protect him from everything that was out to get them in the world. Sol could understand it. He could understand the need to slip into a stronger, tougher, more confident self. Just how he did with Dusk.

"We'll put her back." Sol shrugged. His fingers tapped at his chin in thought. He didn't see where it mattered if one corrupt government official went missing, especially one who was essentially just a peon, or at least that's what he was telling himself. "Probably."

"See. It's the probably that worries me." J's shoulders slumped, his weight leaning more heavily on the hands he braced on the table, pressing himself forward into Sol's space. Sol met his green gaze, and almost immediately regretted it. The intensity there, it was... well, it was nothing new. But fuck if it didn't pin him in place all the same—prey caught in a predator's sights. "Eventide doesn't kill people. *Dusk* doesn't kill people. Not unless he has to."

"Well if she tells us what we want to know, then we won't have to." Sol tried to keep the tone as nonchalant as possible, but he knew that J would sense the anxiety tingle like a live wire over the bond between them. J knew, of course he knew, how the idea of this didn't sit right with Sol. But they had to do *something*. They couldn't just keep knocking down one threat at a time because it wasn't *doing* anything. Nothing was *changing*.

"If. And that's *if* she even knows anything to begin with. This is all speculation based on bank activity. You all don't have any actual proof. This is just guesswork. You don't *do* guesswork, Sol."

"I understand where you're coming from," Sol said, his arms crossing over his chest. "But we can't keep playing this game where we take one down and three more pop up. If we're going to make any real changes in Mythikos, we need to know the extent of their organization, and we need to start taking them down en masse. We need to show the people that this isn't a couple of bad apples, but a systemic issue that goes back for decades."

"And what happens when she tells everyone that she's been to the Eventide hideout? What happens when she says she's seen our faces and she has sketches done up? What happens when she leads them back to us?" J's eyes narrowed even further, his shoulders going stiff.

"She won't. Pickle and I have already set up a safe house far away from our usual places. When we're done with her, we'll just abandon it. There won't be anything for them to find afterwards. And we'll knock her out to get her there." Sol tilted his head, pointing to a paper on the table. "That's her schedule. She visits a tea house every evening on her way home from work. We've already gotten Rachel a position there."

J grunted, but didn't point out that Sol hadn't addressed the issue of Gareth knowing their faces. It didn't really matter to him if she did. In fact, he *wanted* them to know his face. To know who it was that would be coming for them when they did something to hurt the people of Mythikos.

"What if they don't let me make her tea during my probationary period?" Rachel's voice shook a little.

Sol's eyes narrowed, his mood morphed into something harder, more fierce. Dusk. The villain, coming to the surface and unwilling to take no for an answer, even from his own people. They didn't have time to go back and forth on this, and he was done talking about it. "Do none of you have faith in me and Pickle? Because if you want out, now is the time to do it. Walk right out that door and we'll never ask anything of you again. You can go back to your civilian lives. But don't come crying to me when the heroes pick you up and throw you into a cell on the Isle. I don't break out cowards."

The group as a whole made soft sounds of discomfiture, shifting on their feet as they avoided Sol's eyes. They had to know he meant it. He loved them all like family. He would do anything for each and every one of them. But he didn't have the time or resources to help people who weren't going to help him in turn. It was just a fact of life at Eventide.

J clicked his tongue in contempt, but he pushed off from

the table, and shifted his gaze back to the papers strewn about the table. "So Rachel will dose her. That gives us a window of a half hour or so to scoop her up off the pavement, and get her back to the safe house."

"Right."

"And once she's back there, who will she interact with?"

"Just you and me. No one that we use to interface with the public. I can't risk them being exposed when they still have to be out gathering intel."

"So you want *me* to scoop her ass up off the pavement." J grunted, his eyes narrowing again in annoyance, brows pinching together at the center. "And drag her for how many blocks to the safe house?"

"I'm sure you can handle one fairy, can't you, Lettie?" Sol smiled, his eyes squinting with the force of it. "You won't be going far. There's a hotel being refurbed a couple of streets over, construction has halted."

J raised a questioning brow.

"The funds for the project seem to have been... *misplaced*." Sol gave an innocent little shrug, tucking his hands into the pockets of his slacks. He wasn't fooling anyone, he knew that. Everyone in the room knew he was far from innocent, but it was nice sometimes, to lean back into the Dusk that J had known when this all had started.

"Of course they did. I hate you." J's eyes narrowed on him suspiciously.

"I love you too, Lettie!" Sol chirped, resisting the urge to lean into J like a flower seeking the sun. It would be all too easy to ignore the rest of the room and find comfort for his own rabbiting nerves in the sturdiness of J, but there was work to be done.

"I'll go with you, if you need a hand," Dominic offered, raising his hands a little as if in surrender. "I can wear one of Reboot's glamours."

"Fine, but just you. We shouldn't be wasting that shit. We don't know what else we'll need them for, and vampire blood isn't without its limits." J tugged at his shirt, straightening it further. "Come on, let's go check out the route."

Dominic nodded, and followed J to the door.

"No kiss goodbye?" Sol called after them.

J lifted one hand to flick Sol off right before the door closed behind them, and Sol sighed fondly. "Isn't he great?"

"Yeah... great," Maz muttered.

CHAPTER THREE

"Next time we have to kidnap someone, you're helping carry the body." J grunted under the weight of the limp figure of Cordelia Gareth slumped against her back.

"Calling them a body implies they're dead," Dominic offered from behind J, his own arms suspiciously void of unconscious assistant when Sol distinctly remembered he'd agreed to help. Not that Sol could really say anything about it, he'd have done the same. J was a werewolf, and werewolves were built with more muscle than the average fae. Why not put it to use?

"Shut *up*, Dominic." J moved over to the chair in the middle of the room, ducking so she could drop Gareth into it probably a little harder than was necessary. Gareth's head lolled back, her long blond hair falling loose from a tight bun to fall over the bright yellow pantsuit she'd worn to the office that day.

"Wow." Sol held up his hand as if to shield his eyes and smirked when J turned to check on him. "That outfit is *loud*."

J rolled her eyes, crouching to secure the iron restraints.

"I don't think that's the takeaway from this, Dusk," Rachel

called from the ladder in the corner of the empty room where she was hooking up a camera for Pickle to monitor the interaction, and keep a video record for later review.

"It's not." Sol shrugged, scuffing one polished loafer on the garishly patterned hotel carpet. Lightening the mood seemed the thing to do in situations like these—crime should be fun, after all—and since no one else was providing any levity, that left it to Sol, or at least that's what he'd decided. "But I mean... look at it. Is that more of a lemon or a banana, do you think?"

J let out a long breath of annoyance. "Who the fuck cares? When will she wake up?"

"I'm going with banana," Rachel supplied from the ladder, like a good sport. Sol had always liked her.

"Banana! Thank you, Rachel." Sol turned to grin at her over his shoulder. "How's the camera setup coming?"

"Almost done."

"Perfect." Sol leaned forward to better inspect Gareth's limp face. Her breathing was slow, and calm, her eyes jerking about beneath the lids in deep sleep. It wouldn't be long, and he'd finally get some answers. They were so close to... *something*. Sol wasn't sure what, but it was big, whatever it was. The very air changed with it, like a bonfire warping the way the very molecules moved. Soon.

"Is no one going to answer my question?" The chair creaked under J's ministrations to check on the restraints, but didn't budge from where it was bolted to the floor. She nodded, and moved back to stand next to Sol, her arms crossed over her chest.

"Well, it depends." Sol leaned his shoulder into J's, hoping the solidness of her would settle the humming in his veins. It helped a little.

"On?"

"On her metabolism, her exact weight, what specific kind

of fae she is, how much Rachel slipped her, her menstrual cycle." Sol ticked these off on his fingers like grocery items as he ran down the mental list of all the things in a body that could affect the chemicals they'd given her. "So the answer is..."

"Any minute now?"

"Any minute now!" Sol laughed, clapping his hands delighted. The excitement buzzed louder inside of him, and he half wondered if anyone else could hear it. "How's it looking folks?"

"We're all set on my end." Rachel folded the ladder back up and sat it in the corner where some very nice construction workers had left it behind.

"Dominic?"

"The feed's live, Dusk." Dominic held up the tablet he'd been working on to show Sol and J the screen which had a video of them with their backs to the camera, in front of a woman strapped to a chair in the middle of an empty room.

"Sound check, Pickle?"

"We're good to go on my end." Pickle's voice came over clearly through the comms in their ears. "Dominic and Rachel should make themselves scarce before she wakes up."

"Right. You heard the lady. Head over into the adjoining room." Sol moved to shoo them both through the door that stood between this room and the next, his gaze cutting back to the woman in the chair. She hadn't moved yet, but as he'd said, it was hard to tell when the drugs would wear off, and he wasn't willing to risk losing two of his public-facing agents. Not now that both he and J had to be more careful.

"Are you sure you don't need help?" Dominic frowned a little, his eyes flicking from Sol to the woman in the chair.

"Positive. And if we need anything, you'll be right next door, right?"

"Right."

"Good. Now, off you go." Sol shut the door between them with a decisive click and turned back to J, rubbing his hands together. It did nothing to help with the humming, which had begun to make his fingers twitch.

"So eager." J rolled her eyes at Dominic's retreating back.

"He just wants to be useful."

"He's like a puppy."

"Aww is my Lettie jealous?" Sol grinned; their mission momentarily forgotten as he focused instead on the delicious pink crawling over the tip of one of J's exposed ears. Merlin, if that wasn't the most distracting thing he'd ever seen...

J scowled, the flush spreading. "No. I just—"

"Ugh... what did that bitch put in my tea?" A high, hoarse voice asked. Sol jerked, regretfully ripped from their moment, and turned to see Gareth rolling her head from side to side, making a tangle of the fine hair which was already hopelessly knotted by J's rough treatment.

"Well. Rachel's been made." Dominic grumbled into the comms on Sol's hearing aids.

"We don't know that." Rachel huffed. "She may have not gotten a good look."

"Both of you, be quiet." Pickle hissed. "It's fine, Dusk. Just get her talking."

"And who the fuck are— Oh. You're Dusk." Gareth tilted her head, her watery blue eyes squinting up at Sol, a grimace curling her lips. "You're that fucker who keeps doing the cheeky billboards."

"Look, Lettie! I'm famous!" Sol signed, his hands moving excitedly over the words as he bounced on his toes.

"I'm getting too old for this shit." J huffed, her own words jerky and annoyed as her fingers danced with them, and she shifted her weight back on her heels.

"Oh stop, Lettie. You're not even thirty!" Sol laughed, his

fingers still moving instead of bothering to say the words out loud. "Do you think she understands sign?"

"Pickle, are we seeing any signs of comprehension?" J turned to make the pointed gestures to the camera in the corner, her fingers taking their time to move over the words so that Pickle would understand even in the low light of the room.

"No. Just annoyance. She looks super pissed, guys." Pickle laughed a little.

"Will you both shut the fuck up and tell me what you want already?" Gareth snapped, her hands clenching against the armrests that J had strapped her to.

"Still better be careful." J warned in small, quick movements that only someone who had been signing all their life could catch.

Sol nodded—a little annoyed because he had been doing this far longer than J and he did *not* need the warning—and clapped his hands again, before saying out loud, "Oh! We should probably do introductions. That's the polite thing to do, isn't it Lettie?"

"See if I care." J shrugged, moving to lean against the far wall where she could watch Sol work, her eyes a comforting prickle on the back of his neck.

"I'm Dusk, but you already knew that." Sol grinned, his eyes flicking over Gareth's face to read the emotions written there. There was no fear, just a weary irritation at having been trapped. Like she'd been expecting it but was no less annoyed at the forced interaction. Interesting. "And this is my delightful girlfriend, J. Isn't she beautiful?"

Gareth looked J over and gave a dismissive grunt before focusing on Sol again. "I've seen better."

Sol stumbled back as if struck, holding a hand to his heart and leaning into the part of Dusk—the ridiculous, overdramatic villain everyone wanted to see. "Wow. Rude! Did you hear what she said, Lettie?"

"Just get on with it already." Gareth snorted, rolling her eyes. "Cut the shit and tell me what you want."

"Congrats! You've just won bitchiest banana. Lettie, tell her what she's won!"

"No." J grunted. "Bite me. I'm not playing Vana."

"No fun! You're no fun!" Sol pouted, his lower lip poking out as he turned to follow J's progress across the room. The pouting, the dramatics, it was all part of the act. Part of the persona he'd built up years ago that people knew, and feared. It didn't seem to be bothering Gareth, not yet anyway, but she hadn't been left alone in a room with him.

"Whatever." J headed for the door, her boots loud in the empty room.

"Where are you going?"

"To bed! Call me when you're ready to stop dicking around and actually interrogate this piece of shit."

"Absolutely no fun!"

The only response was the slam of the door behind J.

"See, and now you've gone and offended my Lettie. You really shouldn't have done that. She's much nicer than I am." Sol whirled back to look at Gareth, his smile curling up his cheeks like a living thing. The mood chilled between them, Gareth's eyes opening a little wider in recognition of what she'd just done. It was less about being alone with Dusk and more about offending Dusk. Everyone knew that, and Gareth had managed to do both.

"You still haven't told me what the fuck you want." Gareth spat the words, her nose wrinkling in agitation, but Sol could see the forced bravado for what it was. She was nervous. Good. "Get on with it, already!"

"In such a rush." Sol strolled forward, his knees popping as he crouched before Gareth so that she had to tilt her head just so, to fix him with an unimpressed look. "Why is everyone always in such a rush?" He sighed, his elbow braced on his thigh, cheek squished against the closed fist. "You're going to tell me everything you know about whoever it is that's paying you. I want names. What they have planned. Where they're holed up at. Everything."

"Or?"

"There is no *or*." He laughed mirthlessly. It was almost cute how she thought this was a discussion, a debate. Almost. It was also annoying. "You're going to tell me." Sol shrugged, and rose brushing imaginary dirt from his pressed trousers, patience dwindling down quickly to nil. He didn't want to kill her, Dusk didn't take lives, like J had said, but he wouldn't hesitate. He couldn't. Not anymore. "I'll give you some time to think about that. Just give us a shout when you're ready to start talking." He hummed, his steps in time to the tune as he moved to the door between the rooms. Clicking his heels a little, he stepped through the doorway. "Lights off."

The lights turned off, washing the room in nothing but the light from the adjoining room.

"Good night. Sleep tight." Sol sing-songed, and then shut the door, leaving Gareth in the dark. "Pickle, keep track of her vitals. And start the track." A hum started, not loud enough for Sol to hear, but a soft buzz on his skin. Annoying, and threatening. Like the ticking of a clock counting down to zero. A sound perfected by Reboot to draw any fae to the point of crazed panic without tipping them over. *Gotta love vampire ingenuity*, he thought, *funny the things one can think up when they don't have to sleep.* "Wake me up when she starts to panic."

"Will do. Have a good rest, Dusk."

It didn't take as long for Gareth to freak out, as Sol would have thought it would, considering how high up in the organization Gareth seemed like she was. He would have thought one of the more trusted people, who was put in charge of controlling a council member, would have been tougher to crack. But it only took three hours for her heart rate to spike, and her breathing to start coming in ragged pants.

"You're good to go," Pickle said.

Sol grumbled, burying his face further in J's hair where she was curled up in front of him. He didn't want to wake up yet, three hours was not a long enough nap for as little sleep as he'd gotten over the last few days as he planned this whole thing out. But three hours was what he'd get, and he needed to get his answers before Gareth went completely batshit in there.

"She's been muttering to herself for the last half hour."

"Fuck." Sol yawned into the back of his wrist and rolled off the bed.

"Anything useful?" J asked, scrubbing at her face. She had lines on her cheek from where she'd been using Sol's jacket as a pillow. It was adorable.

"Hard to tell. I'll enhance the audio and we can play it back later. But you should get in there." Pickle's response was quick and perfunctory.

"On my way." Sol straightened his clothes, running his hands through his hair to try to look like he hadn't spent the last three hours snuggling his girlfriend and snoring so loudly J had tried putting a blanket over his face to muffle it. "How do I look?"

"The same as always." J grunted.

"So good, right?"

J snorted.

"Rude." Sol rolled his eyes. His gloved hand opened the door, and he headed through to the other room just as the lights flickered back to life, too bright for anyone who had been sitting in the dark for hours at a time. The hum of Reboot's spell stopped.

"I don't know names," Gareth said on a breath.

"You do. You can tell us all the council members who are in on this."

"Sure. But... but they're not who you really want to know about." Gareth's words stuttered. Her eyes flicked over Sol's face as if she might have been counting his freckles. "You want to know the head honcho. The underlings, they can just be replaced."

"The head honcho?" Sol tucked his hands into his pockets to keep from flexing his fingers eagerly. This was more than he could have hoped for. More than he ever thought he'd get. *This* might finally put a stop to this whole thing. And it'd been so easy. Why hadn't he been kidnapping people all along?

"Yeah. The big man. The one running everything. I don't know their name. I just know that they regularly run events to bring in new players."

"Players?"

"Influential people who they can pay to do what they want." Gareth shrugged, her head falling back against the chair back again. She was tired, he could see it. The spell had worked its magic, making her mind run on overdrive to try to figure out where it was coming from, what it could mean, and how to make it stop. There were dark circles under her eyes now. "They've been throwing more and more of those little parties lately. Someone keeps taking their players off the board. Not naming any names."

Sol cocked his head, a little grin tugging up to dimple his

cheek. It wouldn't do to look too cocky, he reminded himself, but then it was hard to stop sometimes. "Don't know who that could have been."

"Right." Gareth let out another long breath. "Anyway, I can give you locations, and access. I just... there's a card in my wallet. It's got a chip on it with all the data you need, and the key to get into it. It's... it's in the inside pocket of this stupid fucking blazer." She nodded towards her right side.

"I'll do it," J said from where she'd come to lean against the closed door. Her boots were loud in the emptiness. She kept her eyes firmly on Gareth, watching for any sudden movements as she pulled out the wallet. "Which one is it?"

"It's emerald green." Gareth kept herself carefully still as J flipped through the cards in her wallet. "That one. Right there."

J held it up for Sol to see, the surface shimmering in the dull light like a jewel, and dropped the tacky accessory that's leather coincidentally matched Gareth's outfit into her lap. J stepped back to Sol's side, and handed over the card. Sol turned it over between his fingers, hoping they wouldn't twitch and tremble as much as the rest of his muscles were, holding it up to the light to look at it more carefully. There was nothing on it, no words, no numbers, just a blank green card with an iridescent sheen.

"How do we know there isn't a tracker in this?" Sol tilted his head, eyes squinting at it. It was light, but just because there was no electronic tracker on it didn't mean there wasn't some kind of magic attached. He couldn't take any chances with something like that. Still, he knew that even if there were he might chance it. For the opportunity to take down the person who was running everything? Yeah... he'd chance it.

"They would have come for me by now if there were,

wouldn't they? To keep me from giving you anything." Gareth frowned.

"Maybe. Maybe not. Take it to the other room and have them run it through the system." Sol handed it back to J— even as his fingers tightened almost involuntarily, not wanting to hand it over—and waited until he heard the door creak behind her before turning back to Gareth.

"So what now? Are you going to drug me again and take me back?" Gareth's voice shook. Like she was sure Sol's answer would be that they were going to kill her and be done with the whole thing. Which was far more tempting than it might have been six months ago, but Sol wouldn't stoop to that. Not *yet*, anyway.

"No." Sol shook his head and had the distinct pleasure of watching her face distort further in fear. She seemed to understand that there were some things worse than death. Good. "We're going to leave you here. And then sometime in the future, an anonymous call will be made to the heroes with this location. They'll come and rescue you."

"That's it?"

"Well... I mean how *far* in the future that call is placed depends on how useful the information you've just given us is. It could be a couple hours." Sol shrugged, pulling back the sleeve of his dress shirt so he could look down at his watch. "It could be a couple of weeks. That's all up to you." He turned on his heel and headed back toward the adjoining room, then stopped right before the door, fixing Gareth with a smile, and giving her a small salute as he said, "It was a pleasure doing business with you Miss Gareth."

Gareth slumped forward in her seat, a soft whimper leaving her. Sol shut the door behind him, and turned back to where Dominic was running the card through Pickle's rigorous tests.

"That was too easy. She gave in to the tone too quick, and

didn't even make you physically torture her." J was standing against the door, shifting her weight anxiously from one foot to the other. "She just gave you what you wanted. Doesn't that seem weird to you?"

"It seems my reputation precedes me, Lettie. The name Dusk strikes fear into the hearts of—"

"Yeah. Maybe. Or maybe whoever is running this whole thing *wants* you to find them."

"Way to steal my thunder." Sol deflated.

"Let's start break-down. We've got what we wanted, and someone might start missing her soon. A doorman or something." Rachel had already started to pack up their gear, her hands seeming to need something to do now that the most nerve-wracking part was over.

"Yeah. Let's go." Sol grumbled, pacing about the room to gather their things.

CHAPTER FOUR

"Where are we going?" J asked for perhaps the fifth time since they had left the back room of a run-down 24/7 on the outskirts of Ilygroth that they had been calling home for the last month—the freezers were still working, and the previous owners had been kind enough to leave behind a microwave and a stock of frozen meals, so it seemed as good a hideout as any. Each time, J had grown steadily more annoyed. Not that Sol could blame him, he didn't like being in the dark either. But that was the thing about being the heir to the organization, Sol was never left in the dark. He knew everything about everything. Which only served to further frustrate poor J, much to Sol's amusement.

"My answer hasn't changed since the first time you asked me, an hour ago." Sol bit down on the inside of his cheek to keep from smiling as his fingers danced over the words, and J's irritation spiked through their bond. *Poor Lettie*. It was almost enough to make Sol reveal their destination. Emphasis on the *almost*.

"You're being a little shit on purpose." J's motions were jerky, and irritable, but Sol was grateful that they had switched to sign while they sat in the back of the self-driving cab. He and Pickle had come up with a way to hack the blasted things so they wouldn't track his movements when he used them, but better safe than sorry. Especially with how decked out in monitoring hardware every vehicle on the road of Mythikos was, to protect the people of Mythikos from malfunctioning self-driving vehicles, *of course*, not to spy on them. Not that there had been a report of a malfunctioning car in some two hundred years or so, but Sol supposed there was a first time for everything.

"How dare! I'd never!" Sol gasped, clutching at his chest in mock horror.

J raised one blond brow, his head tilting in question.

"No fun, Lettie. Absolutely no fun." Sol snickered, his fingers jittering over the words with a lightness that hummed through Sol like bottled sunshine. Happiness. It had been so long since he'd allowed himself to simply bask in it. Even when they'd been children, everything had been tinged by the competition between the pair of them. By the need to prove that he was better, faster, stronger, than J in spite of J's obvious advantages as a werewolf. For the first time in all the years they'd known one another, Sol knew, without a doubt, they were a team, and the joy that went along with that still hadn't faded a year later.

"Keep talking like that, and you can go back to doing this shit alone. I don't have to help you, you know." It was an empty threat, and they both knew it, but Sol poked out his bottom lip in a pout anyway.

"Don't say *that*," Sol whined, his fingers curling sulkily around the last word.

J clicked his tongue and rolled his eyes, but a fond smile ticked up at the corner of his lips. And that was enough to settle Sol back into silence. His eyes focused on the scenery passing them in a blur as the car took them to the center of

Mythikos. To a neighborhood with high walls, and wrought iron gates. The security was so tight it was a wonder they were able to slip through even in the inconspicuous taxicab.

"Riverswood?" J's voice had gone up several octaves as if he didn't know what to make of what he was seeing out the window. Like it couldn't possibly be real. Sol had to hide a smug grin in the collar of his coat to keep J from seeing it and swatting him for it. "Who do we know who lives in Riverswood?"

The walls blocking the estates on either side of the street stretched up to the sky, so high that there was no hope of seeing the sprawling manors on the other side. Sol had never much seen the point in them, not with the deflection magic that lingered in every square inch of the ground surrounding them. It was so thick that even looking at the walls hurt Sol's head, the urge to look away a throbbing ache building at the base of his skull.

"You'll see," Sol said, not taking his eyes off the house numbers in gilded letters on the outside of each compound.

"Say that again. See what happens." J grumbled, but there was no real heat behind it.

"We're almost... there!" Sol pointed to a house on the right side of the street. The wall the number was attached to didn't look any different from any others. But the magic that lingered in the air around this particular residence was a little thicker, Sol knew from experience, and a little more like home. The car parked on the side of the street, and Sol didn't waste any time hopping out.

"Shit. The spells here are—" J broke into a cough, and Sol steered him to one part of the wall that looked no different than the rest of it. Solid, and so thick that there was no hope of permeating it, even with his Voice. At least to those who didn't know any better, to those who the magic didn't consider family. Sol did know better, and he was well aware of the perks of being family to these particular magic users. J would be aware of it too, soon enough.

"Keep your breaths shallow. Sorry, I should have warned you." Sol patted his back, his keen eyes narrowing on the subtle difference where one piece of wall didn't quite match the rest. "This is going to be uncomfortable."

"What is?"

Sol didn't give J a moment to overthink it. He yanked J through the opening where two pieces of wall blended into a third that was further back than the rest, an optical illusion more so than actual magic. The warding magic slid over their skin, prickling like rose thorns and shimmering like mist, as Sol pulled them off to the right-hand side of the hidden alley, and through to the lush greenery of a forest on the other side.

J gasped, his body shuddering as he tried to shake off the lingering traces of the spells cast to keep people out. "The fuck was that?"

"A warding array. Pickle's magic. If I wasn't with you, those thorns would have eviscerated you." Sol shrugged, taking in a breath of the lingering scents of ozone, and rain-forest, and something like chamomile.

"Comforting thought." J looked back at the wall they'd just come through, his green eyes too wide in what might have been terror, or respect. It was hard to tell sometimes.

Sol gave his sweating hand a little squeeze, and pressed on through the trees. "Pickle and Reboot don't mess around with security."

"What happens if you go the other way?"

"You get lost in a labyrinth spell so complicated you could spend years traveling it and never see the same place twice. You'd starve before that happened, of course."

"Of course." J let out a long breath, clearly trying to shake the magic still lingering. "I thought Pickle was off-grid? I always imagined a cabin in the mountains or something. Somewhere you couldn't even get to without whatever teleporting magic she uses."

"This is the best place in Mythikos to go off-grid." Sol laughed a little at the ridiculousness of Pickle in the mountains somewhere with spotty wifi, and even worse cell coverage. She'd probably die within the week without someone to deliver her meals for her, or lose her mind with no systems to hack into but her own. "Everyone in Riverswood has so much money that the council and heroes are afraid to look too closely. So the best place to go off-grid, is really at the center of the grid. Kind of like the safety at the eye of a storm."

"Weird." J straightened his hoodie, peering through the wood around them as if he could see the house for the trees. He couldn't.

"Don't look at it too hard," Sol advised, tugging them to the right at a certain tree. He'd given himself a blinding migraine once glaring at the path through the trees trying to figure out how it all worked, and J got even more grumpy with a headache—no one needed that for the meeting they were about to have. "It's another labyrinth. This one was set up by Reboot. It's... nastier than the first one."

"How?"

"Reboot's magic has a tendency to make people insane if they look too closely at it. Byproduct of being a vampire, I guess. Or maybe it's the byproduct of having once been human, and being turned? I don't really know, vampires keep all that shit under lock."

"I thought you and Reboot were close."

Sol snorted at the word close. It was... rather an understatement he supposed, considering who Reboot was to him. But still, as apt as Sol would ever admit in front of people who didn't already know. He'd wanted to tell J months ago, but there was always a reason not to. This mission, or that intel gathering trip. Something to keep Reboot securely hidden behind this magical fence. "Reboot has only been a vampire for a short time. And her sire was... less than helpful. Pickle wound up staking him shortly after he turned Reboot. He was trying to force her to join his undead harem."

J blanched. "Gross."

Sol fell silent, concentrating on the signs of the path that he could sense through the air. A way created specifically for him, etched in blood, to lead him home. A subtle current on the air, a soft shift of the leaves. Nothing anyone else would notice, but something Reboot had trained him to home in on, like a tug on a fishing line.

"Ah. Here we are." Sol smiled as they stepped out of the forest and onto the expansive lawn of Reboot and Pickle's home. The grass was almost too green, and there was no sound of birds or bugs or even the cars from the street. It should be enough to make the hairs on someone's neck stand on end, but Sol always found himself relaxing into it. *Home*.

"You didn't tell me you were bringing Jericho," a voice said from the door off the side of the house they were closest to.

Sol turned, and offered Reboot a bright smile, his eyes crinkling. "I thought it was about time he get to—"

"MRS. TSUKI?!" Jericho shouted so loud the sound echoed off the house in front of them, and made Sol wince as his hearing aids crackled in his ears. Fuck. He'd forgotten just how loud J could be when he was pissed. "What in the actual fu—"

"No cursing on my property, Jericho." Adelia chided, shaking her head. "If you don't mind."

"I uh. Right. Uh of course." J stuttered, his hand tightening at his side in a fist, his mouth gaping like a fish. "But how are you...?"

"I believe that is a conversation best had inside. I'll prepare the good tea." Adelia turned back into the house, leading them into the big open kitchen, all gleaming marble counters, and white cabinetry. J was still gaping at her, his face oddly pale like he'd seen a ghost, which Sol supposed in a way he had. Adelia Tsuki was supposed to be dead, just like her son. Taken by cancer some years ago before Dusk was even invented. And Sol had been happy to let that fiction stand until they knew J was trustworthy, but enough was enough. J was family.

"Not the *good* tea, mama." Sol shook his head in disapproval, but he couldn't help the slow crawl of a warm smile climbing up his face. It was nice to have this out in the open now. Nice to know that he could have all of his favorite people in the same place again. Sol hadn't known how much he'd missed it until that very moment, and his whole body relaxed under the warmth of it. "Just the regular tea, please."

Adelia let out a sound of displeasure, but reached for a different cabinet. "If we must."

"Do I want to know what's wrong with the good tea?" J whispered, his hand grabbing Sol's and holding it tight enough that Sol worried for a moment he might crush the bone. He still hadn't taken his eyes off of Adelia, every little movement she made making J twitch in response.

"Hmmm probably not." Adelia laughed lightly, throwing J a fanged smile over her shoulder that looked far more threatening than Sol found comfortable.

Sol rolled his eyes. "Mama, we've been over this."

"Yes. Yes. You and Pickle have both been very adamant that Jericho has *changed*. But I suppose I'll just have to see that for myself, won't I? Head on through to the sitting room, Pickle's waiting." Adelia flicked her wrist, dismissing them.

"Can I trust you not to poison our guest?" Sol asked,

raising a dark brow at her, and not moving an inch under his mother's orders.

"You have my word, I won't poison Jericho tonight."

"Mama..."

She turned to look at him, her matching dark brows raised over the same brown eyes that she'd gifted her son. "I reserve the right to poison Jericho later if they prove to be a problem."

"Mama!"

"It's a mother's right, Soliel. Now go on, and see Ildri. I'm done arguing with you about this." Adelia turned back to the stove.

Sol let out a huff, and dragged J along through a short hall. He didn't stop staring at Adelia's turned back until she was out of view, and then he whirled around to fix Sol with an expression that seemed a cross between betrayal, annoyance, and confusion, which was ridiculously close to one Sol had called his constipated goldfish face not too long ago.

"Poison?" J hissed, his voice strained.

"Don't worry about mama, she just likes to threaten. You'll be fine. Probably."

The contemporary sitting room on the other side of the house was done in all white, apart from the dark, boxy, sectional. Ildri perched herself right in the middle of the couch. Her neon pink and blue hair was a beacon in the mostly monochrome space.

"Oh! You made it!" Ildri shouted, her voice slightly muffled as a wide smile stretched her face, and made her bright eyes crinkle. "I was worried about you when Adelia said she reworked the labyrinth. But you've always been such a smart boy, haven't you Soliel? Sit. Sit."

"Nice to see you too, Ildri." Sol laughed, tugging a slightly reluctant J toward the sofa.

"So Adelia is..." J started, his eyes flicking back to the hall they'd just come down.

"Alive, yes." Ildri nodded, her smile all teeth, an open threat for J to say something foolish.

"And when you said you had a crush on Adelia..." J said. He seemed to have quite a few questions, which Sol supposed was reasonable considering everything he had just found out. But *that* wouldn't have been the one Sol started with. Still, the lack of tact was very... J.

Ildri laughed, her eyes bright. "Oh, Adelia and I were already together at the time. We have been since before she was turned. About the time she and Sol fell off the grid. They needed someone to assist with the transition, and we knew each other from when Adelia was at university. I was one of her professors then."

"So the cancer?"

"Was very real," Adelia said, sitting the tea tray down on the big glass table in front of the couch. "But thankfully, Ildri knew a vampire with few qualms about turning terminally ill humans."

"Why didn't you tell me!" J rounded his ire on Sol, his green eyes narrowing to slits, the hand in Sol's going rigid, and too tight, making the knuckles grind against one another. "We've been working together for more than a year, and at no point did you think, 'oh hey, I should probably tell Lettie my mother is alive'?"

It was a fair accusation. But the thing was... Well the thing was that Sol had *wanted* to tell J, even that first day when he'd asked about Sol's mother in the interrogation room. He'd wanted nothing more than to spill his secrets at J's feet, and see what J would do with them. But he was under orders. It wouldn't be safe, they'd all decided that. Keeping Reboot, Adelia, hidden away in the shadows was the safest thing for her, and Sol, in the end, would do anything to protect his mother. It really was as simple as that. With his father long gone, she was the only family he had left.

"Reboot's identity is revealed on a need-to-know basis." Ildri's tone was soft, but firm, clearly hoping to alleviate some of the tension between J and Sol. "No one else in Eventide knows who she is. We can't risk the council finding out. You know what they do to unsanctioned sirings."

J swallowed, his hand tightening into a fist again, then he let the grip go and nodded. Although his eyes said that this discussion was far from over, and he'd be holding this over Sol's head for the foreseeable future, he said, "All right then."

"Wonderful." Adelia clapped in a gesture Sol saw himself using again and again when he wanted to close a conversation, and J seemed to relax even further into the couch. "Now, let's have our tea and then we can discuss this other matter."

"Why not discuss it now?"

"You'll spoil the tea." Sol shook his head, repeating the words Adelia had told him over and over again growing up. He knew J had heard them on more than one occasion, but he must have forgotten at some point. There were rules for tea drinking in the Tsuki household. "We only talk about nice things during tea. So just sip from your dainty little cup, and shut up."

"We don't say shut up either." Adelia's eyes turned hard.

"Sorry, mama."

CHAPTER FIVE

"It was too easy," J said, leaning forward on his elbows to glare down at the dregs of his teacup.

"I don't see where it was too easy. We had to kidnap her, and make her talk. That doesn't sound easy to me." Sol frowned, his nose scrunching up, so his freckles became a smear across his brown cheeks. Maybe it was too easy. No. He *knew* it had been. It had niggled at him since then, something about the whole situation had been... off, but he didn't want to admit it out loud. That would mean admitting that he'd misread the situation at the time, that he'd allowed the flush of victory to cloud his mind. He couldn't have that. "You just don't like undercover work."

"That's not it!" J growled, his brows pinching in the middle, green eyes turning that scowl on Sol. Not that it bothered Sol any, it never had. For all J's bluster, he was still a soft puppy dog on the inside. Nothing could change that.

"J's right," Ildri interrupted, her fingers steepled under her chin in a way that looked uncomfortable, and made Sol want to fidget. "It's almost like they wanted you to have this intel."

"To what end?" Sol countered, digging in his metaphorical

heels. "They have to know that I'm not going to let it lie. I'm coming for them."

"Maybe that's what they want." Adelia frowned, her too-pale fingers tight around her own empty teacup, dark brows drawn up in a sign of trouble that Sol didn't like. His mother should never look troubled like that. She was too good, too kind, for that.

"It could be a trap." Ildri nodded her agreement.

"You need to take protection." Adelia's dark eyes jerked from where she'd been staring off into the middle distance to settle on Sol with that unfamiliar intensity that reminded him over and over that she was not alive any longer. Not technically, at least.

"I don't need a guard dog, mama. This isn't baby's first mission. I can take care of myself." Sol huffed, crossing his arms over his chest. It could be a trap, maybe, but he could handle it. He always had before. He could take care of himself, and he dared anyone to tell him that he couldn't. "Besides, I'll have my Voice if I need it."

"There are so many things wrong with what you just said, I can't even count." J ran his hands through his blond hair, letting out a long, slow breath.

"Good thing I didn't ask you to." Sol snapped, irritation flaring in his chest. He'd been doing undercover work by himself since he was sixteen. He didn't need a babysitter. Not now. Not ever.

"To what?" J blinked, seeming taken aback by the tone.

"To count."

"I'm serious, Sol."

"So am I. I was doing undercover work while you were still training with your master in the apprentice program." Sol pointed at him, tone low, practically growling. "I've done this by myself before. I'll do it by myself again." If he were being honest with himself, which he didn't like to do when he could avoid it, Sol would say that the reason he was so against taking anyone else was that he knew how dangerous it would be. He knew that what lay ahead of them was something that they hadn't faced before. The gravity of it had him sagging under its weight. And J... well, J had almost died the last time he'd put himself to the task of protecting Sol. Sol could deal with a lot, but he didn't think he could lose J. Not now that he'd finally gotten him back.

J was snarling, his lip peeled back from his teeth, gums visible, green eyes practically glowing with the anger of the wolf curled up just below the surface. He was beautiful. And Sol would have had no problem telling him so if he didn't think he'd wind up with his nose bitten off for the trouble. But he wasn't frightening, like he hoped to be, because Sol was a fool for Colette Jericho, always had been. And even when he'd been at his lowest, when he'd been furious with J for the things he'd done and said, he'd never not loved J, he'd never been *afraid* of J. Likely never would be.

"What about a date?" Ildri asked, the suddenness of her too-bright voice making both of them blink, ending the stare-down.

"I'm sorry, what?" J tilted his head like a confused puppy dog, but didn't look away from Sol. His stare pinned Sol in place, like he was afraid if he looked away for too long, Sol would run off headlong into trouble all by himself. There may have been some truth to the worry, but Sol wasn't about to say so, and confirm J's suspicions.

"These rich types never go anywhere alone. Sol can't show up to an event by himself, he'll need arm candy of some kind. So we'll send J with you. That way even if you can't sneak in any weapons, you'll have his teeth and claws."

"That's not..." Sol swallowed around a lump forming in his throat. He wasn't going to cry. He couldn't cry. It would nullify any argument he could make and then he'd be stuck taking J into a dangerous situation. He tightened his fists in his lap, and sucked in a deep breath. "No."

"No? What do you mean *no*?" J sat up straighter, his chin lifting. "I'm the best we've got. And I've had your back on every other mission, haven't I?"

Sol opened his mouth to argue. To say that he didn't need J there. To say that he would be fine on his own. Or to plead with J to back down from this. To tell him to stay where it was safe.

Or maybe it was to explain the crawling sense of dread that was creeping up his spine like a premonition. But no words would come out. They all rushed for his mouth at the same time, and got caught somewhere in between.

"We're a team... aren't we?" J asked, but it sounded like he was asking something else. Like he wanted to make sure that Sol trusted him to have his back. "Aren't we?"

He couldn't let that stand, couldn't let J go on thinking that he didn't trust him, no matter what inner turmoil he was doing with. Sol swallowed the lump of words down his throat with a hard gulp, ignoring how they clung on the way down like sticky porridge, and forced his fingers to move. "We are."

J brightened instantly, smile showing off his pointed canines, and eyes going razor sharp with joy. All beautifully sharp edges on the outside, that was J. "Where do we start?"

"We start with this." Ildri held up the slim green card they had gotten off of Gareth as she stood. Her eyes bright with possibility.

"To the lab?" Adelia asked, a fond smile curling up the corners of her lips.

"To the lab!" Ildri crowed. Her strides long as she made her way out of the room, holding the card aloft as if it were some great discovery. Sol rose to follow her, he loved Ildri's lab, it was one of the few places in her and Adelia's home that was allowed to be messy. Everything else was neatly and orderly per Adelia's preferences. But Ildri's lab always looked like a tornado had dropped down out of the sky right into the center of it, caused a mess, and then dissipated a moment later.

"Not you, dear." Adelia shook her head at J, and J lowered himself back to his seat on the couch. "Or you." She eyed Sol, and he settled back again, giving her an aggrieved look.

"I can help, mama." And it would be better than stewing in the tension between Adelia and J who had been glaring at each other for half of the conversation, and pointedly *not* looking at one another for the other half.

"Not when she gets like this. It's better to just stay out of her way. You know that." Adelia clicked her tongue, setting her teacup down on the waiting tray.

"Fine." Sol tried not to sound petulant, but it was a near thing, and Adelia's smile softened in a way that said he may have missed the mark.

"Then what are we supposed to do while we wait?" J fidgeted in his seat. "I mean how long is this going to take?"

"Why don't I give you the tour?" Adelia rose, her face smiling, but her eyes pinched a little at the corners to show that she was actually annoyed at having to entertain J while they waited.

IT WAS SOME TIME LATER, an hour, maybe an hour and a half when they finally settled in Adelia's study. She looked distinctly uncomfortable having J in her space that way, but Sol had a hard time empathizing with her when she'd tried to poison his boyfriend.

"Who's that?" J asked, his finger outstretched to point at a picture frame on Adelia's bookshelf. It was positioned in a cluster of other family photos. Sol frowned, standing from where he'd perched himself on the settee in Adelia's office.

"Language." Adelia hissed, bearing her fangs.

Sol moved over to where J still had his hand outstretched to get a better look. It was a picture of Adelia, and a man who he had never seen before. The man was tall, and lean, and had Sol's nose full of freckles. But his smile looked pasted on. Like someone had clipped it out of a stock photo and placed it there, the expression not reaching his eyes.

"Sorry," J muttered. He turned a questioning look to Sol beside him, and Sol's stomach clenched sickeningly.

"I don't recognize him," Sol said, the world tilting, a little topsy turvy.

"That's Sol's father," Adelia said, standing from where she'd slumped into her chair so she could take the frame from the shelf and hold it between careful fingers. In spite of how gentle the grip was, it didn't look like she was holding something precious, but something poisonous. Like if she held it too tightly it might bite her.

Sol had to swallow past the rise of bile in the back of his throat at the words. His father. He'd walked past these pictures so many times, just glanced at them, seeing only what he wanted to see, the family Adelia had built for herself. The one he had added to with the introduction of every new member of Eventide. There was Ildri, of course, her mouth smashed against Adelia's cheek with Sol beside them, bent over and clutching his stomach through the laughter. But others too. Maz, and him, heads bent over a map as they sorted out where to strike next. Fizz, working alongside Ildri in the lab. Even pictures of their most recent additions Dominic, and Rachel. And so many more. People they'd lost in the scuffle, people who would never return. But he'd never so much as *noticed* this one. Because it wasn't important?

Because he didn't want to? Because he'd let his eyes skim over it like one might an irrelevant bit of code? All of those things could be true.

"I thought you got rid of all the pictures." Although Sol's lips moved, the words sounded strangely soft, distant, tight, hard to hear over the hammering of his heart in his ears. If he hadn't moved his hands along to them, he may not have realized he'd spoken at all.

"Most of them." Adelia gave a thoughtful hum. "I kept this one though. I just tucked it away, so you didn't have to look at it when you were growing up. But it's good to remember where I came from sometimes. Keeps me grounded."

"Where you *came* from? What does that mean?" Sol's eyes locked on Adelia, even as J shifted uncomfortably beside them, he couldn't look away from his mother. Not when she was saying something he didn't understand. Something that didn't make *sense*. None of this made sense, at all.

"Your father was..." Adelia drifted off, her fingers tightening enough on the frame that Sol would swear he heard it creak. She sat it back on the shelf gingerly, and let her fingers move with the words as if that made saying them easier. "He wasn't a good man."

"*What?*" Sol threw his hands out to his sides in question. His father wasn't a good man. It was the first time she'd said it out loud. Not that they talked much about him. Sol had never known him, dead long before the banshee was ever born, and it seemed too painful for Adelia to even try to bring it up. She'd never said why, but Sol had always thought it was because she'd loved his father so desperately, and he had loved her and their unborn child in return. He'd thought it was the longing...

Adelia's eyes met his, and she frowned, her lips pursed tight as if she were silencing herself. That was worse, Sol realized. Her forcing herself not to speak was worse than saying whatever horrible thing was going through her mind. Because he knew that if she couldn't say it...

"But you loved him." Or Sol had always thought so anyway. Although, now he wasn't sure. She had to have though, banshee were born from heartbreak. If she hadn't loved his father, then Sol would have been born human. And he'd needed to believe his parents loved each other while growing up the child of a single mother, and a banshee. He'd needed to believe that his father had wanted them.

"Yes." Adelia nodded, taking a deep breath, and forcing her fingers to move with the words when they came out too broken for Sol to understand. He hated how muffled people's words got when they were hurting. Like the pain alone put them behind glass. "But just because you love someone doesn't make them good. And it can't make them change when they don't want to, either."

The words landed like a blow. Causing Sol to stumble back a step or two, and into one of the wingback chairs on the other side of Adelia's desk. He wheezed, his lungs kicking up a fuss to regain the breath that had been knocked out of him. It... it made *sense*. It made so much sense. Why there had been no pictures left behind. Why his mother hadn't ever shared fond memories with him. He'd thought it had been because it was all too painful, and clearly, it was, but not for longing. No.

"Then why keep it?" J asked, putting voice to the words that Sol himself couldn't say. J had moved to stand beside Sol's chair, his hand resting heavily on Sol's shoulder to keep him grounded. To remind him that he wasn't alone. They were a team.

Adelia moved to sit in the chair beside him, turning so that she could take his hand and give it a firm squeeze. "Because I learned a lot from Soren, and I don't want to forget those lessons. I learned about passion. About having a cause. About the lengths people will go to for their cause. About what *I* was willing to give up for someone else's cause, and what I wasn't." Her grip tightened on Sol's hand to the point where it was nearly painful, her vampiric strength just barely contained.

"Why didn't you tell me?" The words scraped him raw as they crawled up his throat, causing more damage than the blade, than his voice, than anything else combined.

Adelia frowned, her fingers going white where they gripped Sol's, and if he were feeling anything at all he might have cried out for the pain, but he wasn't. Every inch of him had gone strangely numb and cold. If she weren't holding onto him, he might have run. Out of the office. Down the hall. Out into the chill night air. Through the labyrinth. Into the street. Away. Away. Away.

"Oh sweetie," she said, her voice kind, almost pitiable, and he hated that almost as much as the truth she said next. "Because you wanted a father so much."

"Mama I—"

"I've got it!" Ildri crowed, breaking into the room, her face flush with triumph.

Sol let out a breath, silently thanking whatever gods there were above for Ildri, for he didn't honestly know where he'd been going with that. What else was there to say? He couldn't deny her words, he had wanted a father so badly sometimes he had ached with it. The idea that his father hadn't left because he wanted to, but because he'd had no choice had been the only thing that made not having one easier sometimes. And now...

"Am I interrupting something?" Ildri frowned, her eyes darting about the room.

Adelia sighed, brows wrinkled. She took a moment to look over Sol, seeming to understand that he was happy enough to let the subject drop at least for the moment, and sat back in her chair again. "What did you find?"

"Well," Ildri started, tapping hard on her tablet, and nearly toppling it onto the ground. "It looks like it doesn't just have location information, it has dates too. Meeting times, I suspect. And there's one coming up, next month."

"Gareth said they held events." Sol nodded, sitting up straighter in his chair, his mind already jumping from talk of his father to the mission, relieved for the distraction. Now if he could not think about Soren Tsuki for the next few years or so, he'd be just as happy. Maybe he could forget about his absent father altogether, that'd be all right.

"Right."

"Great." J grinned viciously. "So we can go and kill—"

"We're not killing anyone." Sol rolled his eyes, but had to bite back a little bit of a grin. He knew what J was doing, taking on the overly dramatic role usually assigned to Sol in an attempt to alleviate whatever pressure remained from the previous conversation. It was sweet, really, if a little unnecessary and shoddily done.

"We should cut off the head of the snake. It might take a couple of days to stop wiggling but—"

"No. If we do that someone else will just fill their place. We have to destabilize the organization first. Then they won't have a leg to stand on when we come for them."

J clicked his tongue in approval, a little smile tugging up the corner of his lips, clearly pleased with his efforts to get Sol back into talks of strategy instead of something that was bringing him pain. Merlin, Sol forgot sometimes how perceptive, and downright *sweet* J could be.

"You have a month to plan an intel gathering op. Is that enough?" Adelia asked, standing to move from her chair and grab the tablet from Ildri.

"Should be." Sol shrugged. He'd done more with less, and

he wasn't afraid of a time crunch. If anything it would keep his mind too busy to think about... other things.

"They'll need cover IDs." Adelia tapped over the information that Ildri had found. "There's not much here. Not even a guest list. Just a date, time, location, and dress code."

"There's a dress code?" J curled his nose.

"Mhm. Black tie." Ildri grinned, her head bobbing with her excitement. "We're gonna get you all fancy!"

J groaned loudly, but Sol couldn't help the smile that crinkled up the corners of his lips. Maybe having a partner on a mission like this wouldn't be so bad after all, so long as that partner was J.

CHAPTER SIX

It itched. It shouldn't. It was just dye to cover the Banshee streak through his hair, a little makeup to cover his scars and freckles, and contacts to paint his eyes a dull, lifeless brown. It wasn't much, but it was enough for Sol to almost pass for... well maybe not normal, but *human*, surely. And it itched. Like he was wearing a woolen turtleneck. He wanted to claw at his skin until he'd peeled every layer away.

He'd spent the first few years of his life trying to fit into a role that didn't suit him, and covering up the markers of who and what he was now made his flesh crawl. Even if it was for a mission.

"I hate this." The hands of the reflection in the mirror twitched over the words. Sol forced himself to breathe, to look down at his hands, to remind himself that they belonged to him.

"It's only for a few hours," Fizz said, his voice just loud enough for Sol to hear over his shoulder without his aids. Sol didn't like that Fizz was there, not because it was Fizz, he loved Fizz, it was just that Fizz had more important things to do. He'd had to leave the soup kitchen in the hands of someone else to play gofer for Sol and J, picking up hair dye, and contacts, and the clothes that Pickle had picked out for them. It didn't sit right with Sol. None of this did, if he were being honest. He knew it was partly because of the crawling under his skin that every little change was a hair's breadth from setting him off. But knowing, and being able to stop something were two different things.

"And why can't I have my hearing aids?" Sol grumbled; the words strangely muffled in his own ears. He didn't like it. He didn't like any of it. It didn't feel right.

"Everyone knows that Dusk is a banshee, we need to hide any association you may have with the moniker." Fizz sighed. He didn't look comfortable with the idea either. "Just in case someone recognizes your face. We have to get rid of any identifying features."

"But there are plenty of deaf fae in Mythikos. It's not just banshee." He'd already had this argument three times with Reboot, and every time she'd said the exact same thing. They needed to make him look as unlike the face everyone had seen on the news as possible. That meant hiding anything that could make the two look too similar. She'd even wanted to put lifts in his shoes, to make him a little taller, but he'd drawn the line there. He couldn't run in lifts, and he wasn't playing a game of chicken over whether they'd get caught or not and not be able to escape. "I'm going in blind. I don't like it."

"I know. I'm sorry. But orders are orders." Fizz shrugged, holding up a pair of thick rimmed glasses for Sol to slide onto his ears. "You'll have J though, and she'll be able to tell you if anything is amiss."

"If we don't get separated." Sol rolled his eyes, tugging at the heavy cufflinks Pickle had dug out of somewhere, maybe from her own hoard of things she'd collected over the decades, who knew with her.

"Oh, I'm not letting you out of my sight all night," a low voice rumbled from behind him.

Sol whipped around, and his breath stuttered in his chest. Pickle had somehow wrangled J in a satin pantsuit with a long train trailing behind her. The off the shoulder neckline showed more skin than Sol thought he'd ever seen on J, while the fitted bodice left nothing at all to the imagination. Her long blond hair was pulled back into a fishtail braid that hung down her back, feathery strands framing her face like a halo.

"Holy shit," Sol rasped, his throat suddenly like cotton. "You look... um..."

J peeled her painted red lips back from her teeth in what some people might term a smile, but looked more like a victorious snarl to Sol, making her face all hard edges again. Her looks were a knife point Sol could, and would gladly cut himself on until he was ribbons.

"Can we just get this over with? These shoes are fucking pinching my toes." J grumbled, averting her eyes from where Sol was still trying to get his heart to stop pounding in his ears. Because he was a professional, and he could do this. Because he wasn't going to throw this whole thing out the fucking window just because his girlfriend looked unfairly attractive.

"Car's outside." Fizz announced, seeming to not care one lick for the crisis Sol currently found himself in. "You've got about forty-five minutes to get uptown."

"We don't want to draw too much attention." Sol fidgeted again with his suit jacket, like a little boy playing dress up in his daddy's suits next to J. When the fuck had she gotten so... so...

"Then you'll want to be a little late. Everyone else will be too. You'll just blend right into the crowd." Fizz shrugged. "But not too late. So you might want to get a move on."

"Right." Sol cleared his throat, forcing himself to turn toward the door. He heard the soft click of J's shoes behind him. Every step was a struggle not to turn around and catch another look at her. He wanted to sear what J looked like tonight into his brain, to hold it tight there were he'd never forget, because Merlin knew she'd never dress up like that if it weren't for a mission. But there wasn't time for such things, and J would hate being gawked at besides. "I hope they didn't put you in heels."

"Flats," J said, the word enunciated carefully enough that Sol could hear it clearly.

"Good. Good. They wanted to put me in lifts. I guess because I'm like..."

"Short?" J sounded like she was smiling, and when Sol looked back to shoot her a scowl, he could see her shoulders shaking with laughter.

"Don't be an asshole," Sol's fingers danced over the words, amusement making his nose wrinkle.

"You're one to talk." J's own long fingers moved slowly, and lazily over the words, a drawl that sent a shiver up Sol's spine.

"Are you two planning to flirt all night?" Fizz asked, his sharp teeth on full display as he laughed at them.

"Probably." J shrugged and moved to hold the door open for Sol.

They were out on the street and into the waiting car before the drizzling rain could ruin their clothes. The car pulled away from the curb, and silence reigned. It made Sol antsy, his fingers fidgeting with the heavy cufflinks weighing his sleeves down, and if he were to guess, it unsettled J too because she was shifting in her seat beside him.

"We've got this," Sol started, his tone forced into brightness to hide any of his own anxiety—he was the leader, he had to be confident in his plans. "Don't wor—" He stopped when J grabbed his wrist and pressed something into his palm. "What is this?"

"I can't have my partner at half capacity. You need to be able to hear to have my back," J's hands moved in sharp, precise motions, the words clipped and almost hard to make out for how fast they came in the darkness of the car, but Sol had years of experience making out J's words when she was embarrassed.

Sol looked up from the sleek black hearing aids J had just dropped into his palm, to the shadowed face of J herself. He'd never say as much—because he liked his nose unbroken, thank you very much—but she looked like she might be blushing. "Pickle said—"

"I don't give a fuck what Pickle said. You're no good to any of us, including yourself, if you can't hear for shit. I'm not pulling your ass out of trouble just because you couldn't hear what was going on around you. So put the fucking hearing aids in."

Sol settled the aids into his ears, adjusting them until they were tuned just right, and then he leaned over to press a kiss to J's cheek, and if the skin was warmer than usual, well… Sol would keep that to himself. "I love you, you know that?"

J clicked her tongue. "Of course you do. I'm the best."

"You really are." Sol let himself laugh, and enjoy the moment. Let it ease the tension that was gripping his insides. He wasn't alone in this. He had J, and they were a team. No matter what else happened, no matter how apathetic Mythikos may seem to her own suffering, Sol had J, and J had Sol, and right now, that was enough.

J huffed, her head jerking to look out the window as Mythikos passed them in a washed-out blur of lights and drizzle.

Sol let himself relax in the comforting silence of J, and the hum of the electric car on the road. But the closer they got to their destination, the more his hands began to fidget in his lap. The makeup on his neck and face was suffocating his pores. His leg jittered against the floor, knee bobbing up and down.

J reached over, without a word, and stilled the movement with her hand, giving his knee a firm squeeze. "We've got this," she said in a low whisper, and nothing else.

Sol let his breath out in a whistle but nodded. The car slowed, pulling up to an office building made of glass. Each window reflected the watery lights of the city around them, making it look like it was at the bottom of the ocean instead of sitting in the middle of Mythikos. "Is this the place?"

"The address is right." J squinted at the numbers on the building, her brow wrinkled. "It doesn't look like there's anyone inside. Do we go in through the main entrance?"

"No. Pickle said there's a side entrance down the alley. According to the invite on the card, there should be a bouncer there, waiting for us. He'll have a list." He forced his lungs to inhale another grounding breath, to sink into the cold, calculating character of Dusk. They couldn't afford any mistakes tonight, and it would make this whole thing easier if he checked Sol at the door.

"Are we on the list?"

"Not yet. But we will be, once I'm close enough." Sol shrugged. He tapped the phone in his pocket, and pushed the door open before grabbing an umbrella to shield them both from the rain. Once out into the street, he turned back to offer J his hand. "Ready?"

"Can I say no?" J placed her hand in Sol's, and let him help her from the car, even if she didn't need it, giving his hand a firm squeeze. He would have to keep them both safe.

"You can, but it won't change anything." The door to the car shut behind them, and J moved her arm to loop it through Sol's like they'd done this a hundred times before.

They hadn't. Sol and J had never been the sort for formal settings, even when they were younger. And now it felt strange to be in one. Like they were kids playing one of their games. All that was missing were Sol's light up sneakers, and J's crooked hair cut from where she'd gone at it one night with the safety scissors.

"Let's just get this shit show over with."

"Pull your train up a bit, I don't want it to get all grungy from the alley." It'd be a shame to spoil the vision that was J at the moment. All gleaming white in the dreary, blue half-light of a rainy Mythikos evening, more avenging angel than anything else. But those were thoughts best reserved for later.

"You're not the boss of me." J snorted, and rolled her eyes, but she reached back with her free hand to tug the train up so it wouldn't drag the ground.

Sol hummed, leading J down the alley toward a door deep in the shadows of the two buildings. A burly man stood outside of it, his wingspan taking up most of the space and adding at least another foot to his height.

"Name?" the man asked, his eyes glassy in the reflection of the tablet in front of him.

"Candra." Sol's fingers tapped nervously at the umbrella handle. He hoped it looked like impatience rather than what it really was. They had tested the software on the phone enough times to know that it should work with any device. It should pair automatically, and alter the list in front of the guard fast enough that he wouldn't notice the change. But there was always room for mistakes.

"Candra what?"

"Just Candra." Sol met the man's eyes, challenging him to argue, his tone all arrogance as he slipped further into Dusk. Dusk did this kind of thing on the regular. Dusk knew how to intimidate someone into not looking too closely at their list. Dusk would get he and J in and out without any trouble.

"I haven't seen you here before." The man narrowed his eyes in suspicion.

Sol raised a brow, hoping the short exchange was long enough for Pickle to work her magic. If not, they were royally fucked. Out of the bottom of his glasses, Sol saw the man's tablet blink, as if it had gone into hibernation and come back on right away.

J must have seen it too, because she whined, her voice high, and grating. "What's taking so *long*? It's cold."

"I know, baby." Sol shushed her lightly before turning back to the man. "Well? I hate to be kept waiting," Sol said, bordering closer to annoyance, a knife's edge most people didn't dare toy with in the face of someone clearly superior to them. Authority made people nervous, Sol had learned.

The man's jaw twitched like he wanted to say something, but he looked down at the screen, and scrolled through the list for a moment. When he came to the C's he cleared his throat, his eyes going wide. "Yes, there you are. I'm very sorry, sir."

"No worries. We all make mistakes." Sol smiled, false kindness and condescension dripping from every word. As they moved past him through the door, Sol patted the man's shoulder lightly, placing a tiny mic in the folds there. It would stick only as long as the man was at work, and then it would fall away somewhere on his way home, never to be seen, its job already done, and a list of names uploaded to the Eventide systems.

Beyond the door was a long, narrow staircase that led down, deep into the bowels of the building. Sol took a deep breath, taking his time to lower the umbrella so he could steady himself.

"Fucking asshole," J muttered under her breath as she waited.

"He was just doing his job." Sol couldn't fault anyone for that, even if it had slowed them down. Besides, the guard outside the door probably didn't even know what was going on behind it. He was just an underling. In an organization as big as the one they were dealing with there would be a lot of those. It wasn't like Eventide where everyone had a role to fulfill, and there were no small parts.

"The fuck he was."

"Do you need help down the stairs in that outfit?"

"No. I got it." J started down the steps, not waiting another moment for Sol. "Get a move on, we're already behind everyone."

"Right. Sorry." Sol laughed, hooking the umbrella over his arm, and then they started down in silence.

CHAPTER SEVEN

Sol and J descended the stairs to find a thick steel door waiting for them at the bottom. It slid into the wall beside it with a pressurized little whoosh when they got close enough, and Sol found himself holding his breath as they stepped through. J's nails dug into the soft skin of his forearm, and he reached over to pat the back of her hand lightly, hoping to provide some bit of comfort.

A moment later they were hit with a wall of sound. Soft jazz music, muttering, and glasses clinked on the other side. The whole place glittering and gilded. The door slammed shut behind them, another soft hiss of air, loud enough that Sol was sure everyone would turn to look their way, but no one did.

Sol squinted, the bright lights of the room burning his eyes that had long since adjusted to the dark of the outside and the stairs.

"Well... where do you think we should start?" Sol murmured the words more to himself than to J as his eyes scanned the room for any likely candidates. There were faces he recognized among the crowd—politicians, businessmen, public figures that everyone in Mythikos knew—and he made a mental note of those. But there were also plenty of people he didn't recognize. People who likely worked somewhere out of the public eye. That didn't make them any less dangerous, Sol knew that. They'd just have to be careful.

"Fuck if I know, I'm just the arm candy." J sneered, but she was looking too. Her gaze assessed anyone and anything within their line of sight, looking for the most likely suspects. It was moments like these that Sol remembered J had been a hero, trained by one of the best. She knew what she was doing even for all that he wanted to protect her. "You got anything to record with?"

"Just this." Sol tapped his temple, a cheeky little grin on his face.

"Fucking perfect." J rolled her eyes.

"Hey. I have a fantastic memory." He did, they both knew it. It was why he'd always tested so much better than J had in school. It had been the source of endless arguments growing up.

"Right." J's eyebrow twitched.

"Divide and conquer?"

"There's not a snowball's chance in hell that I'm letting you out of my sight," J growled, bearing her sharp incisors at him.

Sol laughed, his eyes squinting a little. It was cute how J thought she'd be the one doing the protecting in a situation like this. J may have been a hero, once upon a time, but these were Sol's people. Spiteful, deceitful, and every one of them out for themselves. He'd grown up amongst them, training for nights like this where he would disappear into the crowd and emerge hours later holding onto all of the threads that needed pulling. "We'll start at the bar. No one wants to talk to someone without a drink in their hand."

"Fine. But let's be quick about it. We're starting to attract attention."

Sol nodded, leading her through the crowd to the bar at one side of the room. He made a pointed effort to keep his steps casual, but certain, expecting people to move out of his way instead of the other way around.

"There's something off about these people," J said, her voice just loud enough for Sol to hear above the din of the room as she leaned in close enough that her breath was hot on his ear.

Sol made a soft questioning sound in the back of his throat, leaning his head closer to her. "What is it?"

"That man's shirt sleeves." J pulled Sol up in front of the bar, her eyes jerking to a man on the other side of Sol.

Sol looked out of the corner of his eyes at the man's cuffs, and frowned. They were frayed. One of the buttons a little loose as if he'd worn the shirt over and over to any fancy function he was invited to. As if he only had one nice shirt. That could only mean one thing, "It's not just money."

"They have to be offering them something else." J mumbled her agreement, leaning in to nuzzle at Sol's throat —a display that if Sol's body weren't buzzing on high alert with nerves would have been distracting, lighting up every nerve ending in any skin even close—her eyes open and sharp as she assessed their surroundings for threats. "Power maybe? Or maybe it's just their hatred."

Sol cleared his throat to pull his mind away from the sensation of J's lips brushing across the tender part of his neck. "For this many people? No... they're offering something—"

"What'll it be?" The bartender asked, her customer service smile wide, and voice forced what sounded like at least three octaves too high so she seemed polite, and approachable. It grated on Sol's ears enough that he almost winced out loud.

"Just champagne, I think. Right, sweetie?"

J rolled her eyes. He was probably going to pay for the pet names later, but that was future Sol's problem. Current Sol was getting a kick out of it. "Whatever you say, *baby*."

The bartender nodded, and turned to retrieve their drinks. J shot him a glare through lowered lashes, and Sol forced out a tight smile, and promised, "You can be mad at me later."

Sol turned to look around them again, lifting a hand to retune his aids so that he could hear some of the conversations around them. There was a couple to their left having an argument about what to do with their latest real estate acquisition, send a notice to the residences, or just call the police on them for squatting. And a group behind them having a chat about buying up some cheap property in Ilygroth to build a new summer home. But not just the ultra-rich surrounded them, the man with the worn shirt sleeves was mumbling something about 'unseelie trash' while scrolling through his phone.

"Incoming," J muttered, leaning her head onto Sol's shoulder.

A second later a woman slid up to the bar, her long manicured nails raking over the smooth sun-bleached wood before she slid her glass to the very edge. Close enough that if anyone were to jostle it, the glass would fall to the floor behind the bar and shatter.

"You two're new here, aren't you?" the woman asked, her form still slumped over the wood a little, nails tapping on it impatiently.

"What makes you say that?" Sol tilted his head curiously, a playful smile tugging up the corner of his lip. He kept his face impassive, but he was already drinking her in. Nails, professionally manicured. Fingers, laden in expensive rings. Dress, custom made, fairy silk if he were to take a guess. And if he were a betting man, which he supposed that he was, he'd gamble that she'd had someone do her hair and makeup for the night.

"Maggie served you right away." The woman's lips were painted a dark purple color, almost black, and when she pulled them back to snarl at the bartender, she revealed human teeth which did nothing to make her any less menacing. "Bitch only ever serves the newbies that quick."

"Maybe I just tip better." Sol shrugged, ignoring the way J's nails had started to dig into his arm again. Something about this woman was bothering her, and it wasn't just her attitude. But they'd have to wait till later to discuss that. It might have been something J could smell on her that Sol couldn't, he did envy J that ability.

The woman barked a laugh. "Tipping. That's cute. Gods, you really are green, aren't you?" She shook her head, her eyes narrowing back on Maggie who seemed to be struggling to pop the cork out of their bottle of champagne. "Should have known. Nobody tips here. Nobody pays either. It's all on the White Rabbit's tab."

White Rabbit. The name struck a chord in Sol, and his back stiffened with a jolt. J leaned in closer, to cover it, her body wrapping around him to tuck her chin over his shoulder so she could get a better look at their new "friend". "Who's the White Rabbit?"

Another barked laugh. The woman lolled against the bar further, her long locks of bright red hair flopping out behind her, standing out against the bleached bar and her dark brown skin. "He's our mysterious benefactor. He gives us everything we could ever want. Youth. Power. Wealth.... *Immortality*."

The word sounded strangely leading, like a siren's call. Which was odd because she was most definitely human. There wasn't an ounce of fae blood in her. But there was compulsion in her words. Magic laced around the syllables to coax people into doing what she wanted. Enough of it that Sol was sure if he were hearing it with his bare ears, and not through the electronics of his hearing aid, he'd probably have done anything she wanted.

J leaned in closer. "Immortality?"

"For the right price, of course."

"Of course." Sol nodded sagely.

The woman's eyes narrowed, her lips pursed as she watched them for a long moment, and Sol could practically see the calculations going on behind her eyes as she ran the numbers. As she figured out if they were worth the time and the effort. Whatever she came up with seemed to please her. She reached into the little purse tucked under her arm and pulled out a matte black card, pushing it across the bar to Sol. "Here. If you and your pet are really interested in the full package... you'll want to check this out."

"What is it?" Sol took the card, turning it over in his hands. It didn't shimmer as the emerald one that led them there had, but it was similar in other ways. Devoid of any words or numbers. Light enough to make it seem like there were no internal electronics. And the hum of magic didn't linger on its surface as something that had been spelled would have.

"The next level," the woman said as she stood, straightening out her dress. "Just don't forget to let the White Rabbit know that Reia sent you. You wouldn't want me to miss out on my commission, would you?"

"No. We wouldn't." Sol offered her a wide smile that he knew others found charming, but patently false on his face. "Thank you for this, Reia."

"Anytime, sweetheart." Reia waved just before she disappeared into the crush of people again.

As soon as she was out of view, J shuddered beside him,

shaking herself like a dog trying to dispel the water from its fur. Likely wiggling out from under the magic that Reia had tried to use on them both. "What the fuck was that?"

"That was us getting noticed by the head honcho." Sol twirled the card between his fingers for a moment, inspecting it. There was nothing. No writing. No sign of a chip. Nothing. But he knew that when there needed to be something, it would be there.

"She used compulsion on me." J snarled, irritated. "And she smelled funny."

"She tried to use it on both of us. It just didn't work on me." He didn't like it. It was bad manners to use compulsion on people at a party. It meant that you had some hidden agenda, and no one wanted to mix that with drinks. It was like talking politics, simply not done. Thank Merlin it had only been an auditory, and not a visual spell or they'd have both gone under, and one of them had to keep their wits about them. "Funny how?"

"Rude." J shrugged off the question, like maybe she didn't quite know the answer herself, and Sol sighed.

"Agreed. Come on, let's mingle.

"I fucking hate mingling."

"I know, Lettie. But that's what we came here to do." Sol tucked the card into his pocket, and turned back to Maggie just as she was handing them their glasses. With a quiet nod of thanks, he led J back into the crush of people, hoping that at the very least they would get some names out of the evening.

IT HAD likely been a mistake to abandon J under the guise of getting a refill. But Sol had hoped that maybe the group of people they'd been schmoozing with would grow complacent with just J there to listen. She'd been playing up the ditzy blond thing maybe a little too well, and people were always more likely to run off at the mouth when they thought the people around them were so vapid they weren't paying attention. Especially once they had a little alcohol in them.

But as Sol was making his way back, he saw one of them moving a little too close to J. Her jaw was clenched, shoulders forcibly relaxed as if she hadn't noticed. But Sol knew that if they took one step closer J was likely to snap and break their seeking hand. Which would absolutely ruin the whole fucking operation and then the list of names and faces, and the card burning a hole in Sol's pocket wouldn't mean shit. Because this whole group would pack up and go underground, looking over their shoulder for the foreseeable future. He couldn't have that, even if watching J break some creep's hand *would* be amusing.

"I wouldn't do that if I were you," Sol said, sweeping up to the person, his hand reaching out to bat their smaller one away from where they'd been making a grab at J. She let out a breath, only just loud enough for Sol to hear from where his shoulder brushed hers. "She can get a little bitey." He snapped his jaws for emphasis and had to swallow down a delighted giggle when the person took a not insubstantial step back.

The group, as a whole, laughed. The sound full bellied and friendly enough to let Sol know that his warning hadn't offended anyone, and if it had no one was going to mention it. Good. He didn't particularly need to be on anyone's shit list.

"What did we talk about Aero?" Chairwoman Erec asked, her head shaking, and tone scolding. "You can't just grab anything you want. We're awfully sorry about them."

"No harm done." Sol smiled sharply, his arm winding around J's waist, and pulling her in closer, a claim and a threat to anyone else who might thing to get too close. "But I think it might be time for us to start heading back. It's been a long night, and she didn't get her nap today, did you, snookums?"

J growled, ducking her face into Sol's neck to hide the sharp points of her teeth, but it didn't muffle the sound.

"See? I think that's enough for the night for both of us. It was wonderful speaking to all of you Councilman Lac, Chairwoman Erec, and Sergeant Aero. I guess we'll see you next time." Sol bowed his head politely.

"Of course. Of course." Chairwoman Erec said, waving her hand sloppily. "Don't forget to pick up your goodie bag on the way out."

"Goodie bag?"

"Yes, it's how the White— Oh you'll see. Just don't forget to grab the one with your name on it." She laughed, taking another sip from her drink.

"Will do." Sol gave a playful salute, and then turned himself and J toward the exit. The crowd had started to thin out, and he was relieved to realize they wouldn't be the first ones to leave. It would have looked suspicious. Along the wall beside the door was a long table, with another burly bouncer standing at one end, his face grumpy.

"Name." The man looked down at his list, his lips twisted in a bored expression.

"Candra."

The man grunted, grabbed a bag seemingly at random from the stacks, and shoved it into Sol's hands without a word. Sol and J headed back up the steps to the alley.

"Remind me again why you couldn't be the arm candy," J signed once the door had shut behind them.

Sol laughed a little, shaking his head. "We didn't want them looking at me, remember?" He leaned in to press a kiss to the corner of J's lips, silencing her grumbles. "Besides, you make a dazzling magician's assistant. Keeping their eyes exactly where I wanted them while I got everything we needed."

"Oi! What have we said about flattery?" J's voice was almost too loud for the quiet that surrounded them, making Sol wince a little.

"That it'll get me everywhere?" Sol's fingers moved slowly over the words, like a purr.

"I really hate you sometimes."

"Hmmm." Sol hummed. "No, you don't." And then they were back out in the alley. The rain had stopped, and the bouncer had been switched out for someone else. Sol smiled up at the man, giving him a playful wave, and led J back to the street where they flagged down a cab and made their way home.

CHAPTER EIGHT

Sol's eyes narrowed, the contents of the goodie bag from the party staring back at him from the surface of his makeshift desk in the old warehouse he and J were calling home this week. Well. Most of the contents. There had been a travel sized bottle of obnoxiously expensive brandy that Pickle had confiscated in the name of "science", but Sol was pretty sure she was just going to drink it. Not that he was one to judge, if he could get away with drinking on the job, he one hundred percent would. But J was watching him like a hawk, his green eyes narrowed.

"You should get some rest. It's been a long couple of days," Sol said, poking a pen at the money clip that had come in the bag. Everything had been scanned for spyware, but that didn't make the items any less nefarious in Sol's mind. Who still used money these days anyway? It was all bits and bites, and credits for most people. Sol hadn't even seen physical money before. Certainly, there couldn't be enough in existence for every person at that party to have needed a money clip.

"You need sleep." J's arms crossed over his chest, his tall frame leaning against the place where by all rights a door should have been. There had only been one door that closed in this warehouse when they'd taken it over. And naturally, J had demanded it be moved to the room they'd claimed as their bedroom. Sol hadn't argued with him on the matter, he rarely did on such things. J wasn't used to living rough like Sol was, making a home in storerooms, and abandoned quicky marts, but Sol had been doing this for years. He could sacrifice the privacy of a door on his office for J to feel that their "den" was a little better protected.

"I know. I'm just going to finish cataloging—"

J let out a long sigh, his shoulders hunching forward a little.

"If you're tired you should go to bed. I'll be in—"

"Do you even know what day it is?"

"What?" Sol looked up from where he'd been pushing the money clip around the desk with his pen, brown eyes wide.

"You've been staring at that shit for two days straight. It's *Saturday* morning." The word Saturday was said like it should have been significant, though Sol couldn't for the life of him think as to why at the moment.

"Okay?"

J rolled his eyes, but Sol saw the way his jaw tightened like Sol had just said something supremely offensive. "Have you even taken your aids out? You can't leave them in all the time like that, you know that."

"I'm fine." Sol shrugged, ducking back down to look at the sleek black card Reia had slipped him at the bar. He still didn't understand the significance of it. There were no chips, no wires, it was just paper. J hadn't been able to smell any magic on it either. It was so strange.

"Sol."

"Huh?" Sol didn't look up. His fingers traced the edges of the card, wondering if maybe it needed something. Maybe there was a missing piece to the puzzle. A splatter of blood, or to be laid out under moonlight or something. Magic had strange parameters sometimes.

"Sol," J repeated, his voice suddenly closer. Sol hadn't heard him cross the room. He must have been barefoot then, Sol thought absently.

"Yeah?"

"It's *Saturday*."

"I heard you the first time you said that, Lettie. But I don't really know—" Sol stopped, his hands pausing mid-thought. Saturday. The full moon. "Fuck. What time is it?"

"Still early. We've got till the sun goes down." J shrugged, and his posture seemed to relax as Sol realized what he was trying to tell him.

"Do we have everything you need?" Sol dropped his pen to the desk, and stood up, already going into preparation mode. J was right, the contents of that blasted goodie bag could wait, there were more important things to deal with at the moment. "Snacks? Protein? Your fuzzy blanket?"

"Fizz stocked us up while we were prepping for the party. He even made me a full moon kit." J scoffed.

"A full moon kit?" Sol stopped where he'd been well on his way to their makeshift bedroom to start pulling the extra blankets from the tub under the bed. J liked extra bits of fluff to curl up in when he was in his wolf form, and Sol had never been able to tell him no when he'd started rubbing a particularly soft blanket against his cheek in the store. He was a softy like that.

"Fucker bought me a squeaky toy."

Sol choked on a laugh, and made the valiant effort to swallow it down. "I'm sorry. That's not funny."

"It is kind of funny." J's lips curled up into a little smile. "But to answer your question, the only thing I *need* is for my boyfriend to stop dicking around with some shitty swag bag, and come pay attention to me for a little while."

"So needy." Sol teased, but he stepped away from the desk, and moved to wrap his arms around J's waist.

"You're the one who kept bitching the sedatives weren't healthy. Stop complaining and take some fucking responsibility." J growled, but he buried his face in Sol's scraggly dark hair and inhaled deeply, so Sol assumed he was already forgiven.

"Come on, let's get you some breakfast. I'll make you that really greasy extra crispy bacon you like." Sol tugged him away from the contents of the goodie bag, and out of the office, to the little break room that mercifully had been inside of the warehouse. It had probably been for the guards, but it had a little kitchenette attached. Not enough to cook a full three course meal or anything, but enough to make breakfast, which was J's favorite when he got like this. "We'll have Fizz bring by some takeout for dinner."

"Okay." J grumbled, his voice muffled by the hair in his face. "No more work?"

"No more work. Not for the next couple of days anyway. Everyone knows not to bother us during a full moon. Maybe we can watch that live action *The Shadow* movie that just came out. I've heard it's laughably horrible." Sol let go of J, and moved to start on his food. J followed behind, wrapping himself around Sol's back once he was stationed at the tiny stove, bacon sizzling in the pan.

"Are you going to pirate it?" J hooked his chin over Sol's shoulder to watch the bacon cook. Likely to make sure Sol didn't burn it, again.

"Of course I'm going to pirate it." Sol scoffed, but all he got for his efforts was a hard pinch to his side. "Ouch! What the fuck was that for?"

J growled softly, the sound vibrating up through Sol's back.

"Fine. I'll have Fizz rent it at the same time, so they make money off it even though I'm pirating it."

J growled again.

"You got a better solution? I'm all ears."

J grumbled, digging his hard chin into the bone of Sol's shoulder drawing out a hiss.

"Right. I didn't think so. Now stop being a bitch, and let me cook your breakfast."

"Don't burn the bacon this time."

"I'm not going to burn the bacon! Stop back seat cooking!" Sol kicked J's shin lightly with his heel, which earned him a hard snap of teeth to his shoulder. Huffing a laugh, Sol rolled his eyes. It was hard to focus on anything when J got like this, all surly, agitated, and adorable. "You're such a brat when you're like this."

J snarled, chewing on the sweatshirt in between his teeth. "Just finish my fucking breakfast."

Sol let out a long-suffering sigh, but returned his attention to the task at hand, dutifully ignoring the teeth gnawing away at the thick fabric.

IT WAS easy to fall into the softness of taking care of J during a full moon. Easy to put everything else aside, and focus on what J needed to get through the strain of his wolf running amok after having been locked up for so long. There was a blissful domesticity in snuggling, making food, and watching movies with J until late into the night.

It was so easy in fact, that Sol almost forgot about the goodie bag, and the glittering room, and the White Rabbit altogether. Until early Monday morning when he woke up to a very pissed off blond werewolf growling at the door to their warehouse hideout. The hulking wolf looked all the bigger with his hair standing at attention, and his tail sticking up in the air.

"What is it?" Sol asked, reaching for the stun gun that Pickle had practically forced into his hands about a year ago when he'd said that he and J were going off on their own. For protection, she'd said. And he appreciated her worry, but he didn't see much point when he had J to protect him.

J snarled, snapping his jaws, but not taking his narrowed green gaze off of the door.

"Is someone here?" Sol hoped J didn't hear how loudly his heart was beating in his ears at the thought of that.

J shook his head.

"*Was* someone here?" Was that better or worse? He wasn't sure.

J nodded.

"Did they leave something behind?"

J nodded again, his lips peeling back from his sharp teeth in warning.

"All right. You stay right there." Sol moved to the door, but stopped when J's teeth clamped down on the back of his shirt, and hold him in place. "Don't worry, I'll be careful. They aren't still around out there, are they? Can you smell them close?"

J stopped his snarling just long enough to sniff the air, his eyes closing as he focused. Then he shook his head.

"Then I'll just be careful. I won't pick whatever it is up until you've sniffed it. Is that okay?" Sol kept his voice soft, and gentle to keep from scaring J further. He knew that the wolf didn't really understand that the danger had probably passed. It had always been overprotective of Sol. Which was sweet, but wholly unnecessary in most situations. And someone stepping into their territory who wasn't supposed to be there, during a full moon no less, was enough to send J's instincts into a tailspin.

J let out a soft whine, like he wanted to argue further.

Sol settled his hand into the soft blond fur on the top of J's head, and rubbed at it gently. "I've got this."

J huffed, but he backed away, moving to stand a little bit from the door. He didn't sit, seeming too worried that Sol would need him, but he did give Sol the space to open the door.

"Thank you."

The door creaked on its hinges as Sol pulled it open, and on the other side was... nothing? Well, not a person, Sol amended when he looked down to see the small cardboard box resting on the pavement. It had a little tag on it that flapped lightly in the breeze. Sol crouched to get a better look, and wrinkled his nose at the scrawled handwriting that just said, 'open me'.

"Come give this a sniff for me, Lettie. Make sure it's not going to explode if I pick it up."

J huffed irritably, but Sol heard his nails tap lightly against the cement as he made his way over. A dark nose was pressed in close to the box, and J gave it a tentative sniff, before taking a much bigger one. When he had determined the parcel safe, he nodded.

"Thanks, Lettie. You're the best." Sol pressed a kiss between the wolf's ears, and scooped up the package, not missing how J's chest puffed out in pride as he followed behind Sol to the office.

The package was innocuous enough. A plain brown cardboard box devoid of logos or embellishments apart from the tag taped to the top. It looked about the right size to hold a coffee mug, and if hadn't appeared at their doorstep completely unprompted, Sol would have thought nothing of opening it right away. But no one apart from Fizz and Maz knew where J and Sol were. Not even Pickle or Reboot. It was just safer that way. And the warehouse had been abandoned so long the previous owners should not have been receiving packages there anymore.

J let out a soft, impatient chuff.

"I know, Lettie. I'm curious too. But we can't go rushing into things, can we?" Sol sat the box down, walking around the piece of plywood set across two file cabinets that comprised his desk. The tag was made out of similar stock as the tag on his goodie bag, the handwriting near identical. Sol tapped on his chin thoughtfully. "Ideally we'd want to have Pickle x-ray it."

J let out a soft noise like a sigh and a moment later he was standing beside Sol, glaring down at the box, completely devoid of fur. "It doesn't smell like magic or explosives."

"But it was sloshing around while I walked."

"Liquid then." J frowned, and before Sol could stop him, he'd reached over to grab the scissors and cut away the tape with a grunt. With the flaps peeled back, Sol moved onto his toes to peer inside.

In a nest of shredded paper was a crystal bottle with a cork stuck firmly into the top. The liquid inside was a blue grey color, and was glowing brightly enough to light up the entire inside of the box without any help from the dingy overhead lighting of the warehouse.

"There's another tag," Sol said, carefully removing it from the top of the bottle. He turned it over to see the same scrawled handwriting jotted across the crisp cardstock. "It just says 'drink me'."

"You've got to be fucking kidding me." J snorted.

CHAPTER NINE

"You're not just going to drink it, are you!" J asked in a shout that was almost too loud for Sol to even understand, the words crackled together into nothing more than white noise, even with his hearing aids in. Thankfully, he had enough good sense to sign along to the words.

"That's what it says to do." Sol shrugged, twirling the bottle in between his fingers, watching the way the light caught the crystal. Expensive stuff, if he were to hazard a guess. Probably made by one of those artisan sand nymphs who charged at least ten times the amount for whatever they made as it cost to produce it, too fancy just to poison someone, surely. The liquid inside moved this way and that, like bottled moonlight on the water, calling to Sol. Asking him to take just a sip, and see what all the fuss was about. If J hadn't been there when the bottle had been delivered, Sol probably would have done it by now, forgoing the rigorous tests J had insisted upon.

That had been why they'd called Pickle, for her to run some tests. Scanning the makeup through a little spell and the camera on Sol's phone.

"And you're just going to listen?" J growled, baring his teeth at Sol in a way that would have had most people cowing down to whatever the werewolf demanded. But just made Sol smirk a little.

"I don't see why not."

"Because it could be dangerous! It could be poisonous."

"It's not poisonous," Pickle said, her voice a little staticky from the speaker of the tablet that J had dropped one too many times.

"There? See? Nothing to worry about. It's not dangerous at all." Sol leaned back in his chair, his fingers fiddling with the cork on the bottle. J looked very much like he wanted to reach forward and snatch it from Sol's fingers if just to stop him toying with it, but Sol couldn't quite draw his eyes away from the glimmer of the potion inside.

"I didn't say that." Pickle sighed. She sounded like she was rubbing at the base of her skull where a headache had likely settled.

J gestured to the tablet as if to say 'see?!', his eyebrows moving up so far they almost disappeared into his hair.

"Well, there's really only one way to find out, isn't there?" Sol's grin dimpled his cheek, his eyes bright with curiosity. There was always only one way to find out in the end with these types of things. And it wouldn't be the first time that he'd used himself as a test subject to get to the bottom of some unknown substance, much to Pickle and Reboot's reproach. Though they wouldn't tell J that, he'd probably shit a hamster or something.

"You should let me try it."

"No." Sol's grin twitched, threatening to give way to a scowl at that idea. He couldn't let J risk that. J had already risked so much. "That's a non-option."

"What if it makes you sick?" Pickle's tone had gone scolding.

"Then I'll have Lettie to take care of me." He hoped that the charming smile, and the sing-song tone would have J caving, but he should have known better. J had never been the type to give into Sol when he was being like this.

"Be serious, Sol!"

"I am being serious." Sol's smile fell, his lips pressing into a hard line, and his eyes narrowed on the pacing werewolf. There were worse things, Sol supposed, than having a boyfriend who cared enough to try to stop him from doing something absolutely batshit, though at the moment he couldn't think of any. "Of the two of us, you're the most likely to be able to get help if something goes wrong. You can get me wherever we need to go if there's an issue. If you got sick and I needed to get you to a doctor, I wouldn't be able to get you there on my own, Lettie. And you could die while we wait for help. I'm not risking that."

J's shoulders hunched a little, his posture seeming to shrink in on itself at Sol's words.

"Let me do this, Lettie. Let me take this chance." He set the bottle on the table, his hands reaching out for J, hoping J would take the hint. J grumbled, and moved to him before slumping into his lap, and curling up there. Sol's arms looped tightly around him, brushing his fingers through J's long blond hair. "I promise I'll be careful."

"I don't have to like it."

"No. You don't have to like it," Sol agreed readily.

"I don't like it either," Pickle piped up, and Sol rolled his eyes. For some reason he'd thought maybe she had hung up. But it seemed she was just giving them space. Too much to hope for, he supposed. "But, from what the analysis shows, there's nothing harmful in it. My best guess is it's a reveal potion of some kind, meant to let the user see something they usually wouldn't."

"Your best guess is still just a guess." J's words rumbled softly against Sol's shoulder.

"*My* best guess is way better than the average person's." Pickle huffed, offended at J's lack of faith in her knowledge.

"Yeah but—"

"Lettie," Sol said patiently, because that's all he understood when he got like this. If Sol continued to be confrontational they'd just go round and round until they were both too tired to bother. "We need to know what the White Rabbit's doing. The only way we can do that is if we play along with their game."

"We don't even know how it *got* to us." The protest was weak, and they both knew it. They had already spoken to Pickle about the mysterious delivery of the package and how it didn't make sense. She'd had no good answer for it, but they had all agreed to pick up and move house as soon as they could. Which would be after Sol drank the damn potion, because he wasn't risking taking anything from the goodie bag with them to a new location lest that be what had tipped the White Rabbit off.

"You're just stalling now." Pickle sounded like she was rolling her eyes.

"So what if I am!" J bared his teeth at the tablet, the hair on the back of his neck standing on end in agitation.

"Enough you two." Sol sighed, rubbing at the bridge of his nose. He was tired, and there was still so much to do if he and J were going to move before sunrise. "Pickle, when we leave, I'm leaving all of this stuff behind. If you want to come and examine it, be my guest. Maybe you can find something I'm missing. But I'm not taking it along in case it's got some kind of tracking enchantment attached."

"Probably for the best. I'll have Dominic check it out. He's getting pretty good at that kind of thing."

"Perfect. I also want a list of everyone who knew of this

location. I was under the impression that it was just Maz and Fizz, but I'd like to double check. If we have a mole, I need to know about it." The words sat heavy on his tongue, made of lead and steel. Sol didn't like the idea that maybe someone in their organization was working for the White Rabbit, but he did want to rule it out. It would be better to know than to not, he reasoned. Even if it would hurt.

J was growling, the sound vibrating through his chest and into Sol's in a way that was oddly comforting, like a cat purring.

"Did J smell anything unusual on the box?" Sol could hear Pickle typing again. Likely sending out a message to Dominic about the contents of the goodie bag. Or maybe she was digging into whatever data she had on their team. There really was no way to know what all the pixie knew, and Sol had learned a long time ago it was better not to ask. She could be terrifying when she wanted to be.

"No. There was no lingering scent." J pressed his frown into Sol's shoulder, shifting around in his lap to try to get closer to Sol even though he was already plastered against his chest. It was utterly ridiculous, and Sol loved him so much it made his teeth ache.

"All right then, we'll just have to do a little digging." Pickle's typing picked up, her fingers working furiously against the keyboard. "Don't worry about it, Dusk. If we have a leak, I'll find it."

"What will you do to them?" J asked, a threatening edge to the question. Sol could only imagine what J would want to do to any potential moles within Eventide. It would probably involve leaving them alone with the wolf when it was hungry... Sol shook himself.

"Nothing." Sol shrugged, shifting in the chair where his legs had begun to fall asleep under J's weight. "At least not right away."

"Right. We'll want to watch them and see what they do first," Pickle agreed.

"So just... *surveillance?*" J tsked softly, and rolled his eyes. "You're not going to punish them?"

"Not if tracking their movements can provide us more intel on the White Rabbit's operations." Sol could practically hear Pickle's shrug on the other side of the phone. "If you're going to test that potion and get out of there before it's light out tomorrow, you better have a go at it now, Dusk. We don't know how long the effects will last, and I know you'd rather not be moving house in broad daylight."

"Right." Sol nodded, reaching for the bottle again.

"I'll stay on the line in case anything goes wrong."

"Aw, that's so sweet, Pickle! Thank you!"

J clicked his tongue, and snorted. "It's not sweet. It's self-preservation. Imagine what Adelia would do to her if something happened to you. She'd probably dig Ildri's grave with her bare hands."

"No comment." Pickle went back to typing, each keystroke more pointed than the last.

"Well, here goes nothing." Sol popped the cork and downed half of the glowing liquid in one go. It tasted like bright sunshine, burning a little on the back of his palette, but it went down smooth enough. He blinked for a moment, the world going hazy, and shimmery around the edges like looking through a rainbow prism, and nausea swelling at the back of his throat. Motion sickness, he realized, that's what this felt like. Then his vision cleared, and he let out a little breath.

"Are you all right?" J asked. He had pulled back so he could watch Sol's face carefully, and Sol could see the worry hidden beneath the scowl that J usually wore.

"I seem to be, for the time being. My vision went a little wonky there, but it's passed." Sol rubbed at his eyes, trying to clear away the film that had coated them in between one blink and the next. "Scoot over, let me get a look at the stuff on my desk." He nudged J carefully, and J took the hint to slide from his lap onto his feet again. But he didn't go far. He hovered over Sol's shoulder as if Sol would pass out at any moment, and he needed to be there to catch him.

"You're not going to be sick are you?" J's voice sounded strangely wobbly, like he was sure this had been a mistake from the beginning, and he was going to give Sol what for as soon as he was sure Sol wasn't going to die.

"No." Sol's chair made a loud screeching noise as he scooted it across the floor to get a better look at the contents of the goodie bag. He probably could have stood up, but he didn't want to chance whatever the potion had done to his vision throwing his balance off.

"Does he look green around the gills?" Pickle asked. She sounded worried, her voice obviously forced into something neutral.

"A little."

"I'm fine, both of you." Sol grunted, putting more weight onto his hands as he looked over the contents of the bag. He was a little wobbly, but nothing he couldn't handle. Overall, he was more annoyed at the nattering. If they'd just be quiet for a moment then maybe he could focus. "Stop worrying."

"Fat chance in hell." J huffed.

Sol didn't bother to roll his eyes, or shoot J the incredulous look he wanted to. It wouldn't change anything. J would still be J, and there was work to be done. He poked at the money clip, flipping it over when nothing happened. Then he moved on to the bottle of lotion and other assorted beauty products. Nothing, even when he smeared some on the back of his hand.

"Anything?" J was still hovering over Sol's shoulder, his hands opening and closing into fists in agitation.

"Nothing." Sol wrinkled his nose. "Everything is just—" He stopped, eyes catching on the black card Reia had given them that night. It glowed faintly like a flashlight that had been turned upside down on the table, the edges warm with color. "Hold on. This might be something."

Sol turned the card over. The light from it was too bright, and it was like he was seeing double, but a second later his eyes adjusted. On the crisp paper, which now looked to be white instead of black, there was a word scrawled in untidy handwriting, the *same* untidy handwriting as all the other cards, that just said 'photograph me'. And beneath it was a logo that seemed to read:

\/\/H1T3_R4BB1T

Sol stared at the logo, his mind working quickly to try to place where he'd seen the strange combination of letters, numbers and symbols before, and then he remembered.

"Well... that's probably not good."

"What is it?" J leaned in closer, his blond hair brushing the table as he hovered over the table.

"Pickle, remember that error code I told you to look up?"

"The one from the billboard? Yeah. Why?" Pickle sounded like she was leaning in closer to her phone. Like she could see what was going on without the camera on.

"That's his signature." Sol was glad for the support of the desk beneath him when his knees started to give a little. The White Rabbit had been watching him, even as far back as the billboard. Maybe before that. *Probably* before that. *Fuck*.

"Whose signature?" J's voice had gone tense. His hands gripping the table hard enough that Sol could hear the wood creaking beneath.

"The White Rabbit's."

"He's been watching us," Pickle said on a breath.

J snatched up the card, his fingers trembling. "What else does it say?"

"It just says 'photograph me'." Sol frowned, taking the card back from J and pulling out his phone to do just that before J could destroy it.

"Stop doing what that crazy fucker tells you to do!" J grabbed the card, his hands shaking. But it was too late, Sol had already done as it asked.

Sol frowned down at the picture. The handwriting and logo hadn't appeared on his screen, but in their place was smaller text. He zoomed in to get a better look, and found a date, location, and time, under the word 'auction' in big bold letters. "It looks like we have our next undercover op."

J was suddenly pressed against his back, head bent over his shoulder. "Auction? What the fuck kind of—"

"Pickle, I'm sending you the invitation. Get me anything and everything you can on this location." Sol rubbed at his eyes, the film finally dissipating from them as he forwarded the picture to Pickle. "Also, when Dominic comes by, have him take a sample of the paper everything is made on. Upscale stationary like that—"

"Might lead us somewhere. I got it. You two should finish getting packed up and head out if you're all right." Pickle was typing again, her fingers flying over the keyboard in faint clickety-clacks.

"I'm fine, Pickle, honestly. Just a little bit of a headache." Sol rubbed at his temples, ignoring the way J was still hunched over his back, a comforting weight.

"All right. I'll get on this. You get some rest." Pickle hung up without waiting for any reply.

"She said the White Rabbit could give someone immortality," J said on a breath.

"I remember."

"What does that even mean?"

"I don't know. But I'm sure we'll find out at that auction. Come help me finish packing."

J shifted his weight from side to side for a moment, his eyes still fixed on the black card that had been tossed onto the desk. Sol glanced down, and saw that in the glow of the potion beside it, the backside said, 'I'll be in touch' in that same creeping handwriting. He decided it was better not to mention that to J who would no doubt lose his proverbial shit over it.

CHAPTER TEN

Three days.

It had been three *days*.

The inaction was a physical itch. He had never before felt so utterly *useless* as he did in the exact moment that he realized all he could do was sit back and wait while his team did the legwork. He wanted to be out helping do the research. He wanted to be sitting outside of the address that the White Rabbit had given them, watching, and waiting for the man to slip up. But instead, he had been relegated to the loft space on the roof of an apartment building where he and J had holed up. The idea was that because the building's owner never did anything other than collect rent, no one would bother with a couple of people squatting in the one room efficiency on the roof that didn't even have proper air conditioning.

"I should be doing something," Sol said for the fifth time in the last hour. He'd taken to picking at the cuticle around one of his fingernails, and it was raw and red now, almost to the point of bleeding. If he didn't stop soon J was probably going to duct tape oven mitts to his hands. Not that she was much better. She was sitting on the opposite side of the futon couch, aggressively reading a book. Each page turn sounded like she might rip it from the spine if she applied just a bit more force.

"There's nothing for you to be doing." J grunted, turning another page.

"There is. Rachel and Maz are sitting outside the address today, looking to see the goings on. I could be there, helping."

"No, you couldn't."

"Yes, I could!" He *should*! He was the leader. He was *Dusk*, for Merlin's sake. He had spent most of his formative years doing *exactly* what Maz and Rachel were currently doing. Sol jumped to his feet abandoning all pretense of waiting patiently. "I should be helping them. If I can't help them, then... then... what's the *point*?"

J let the book drop to her lap, careless of if she'd lost her page or not, and let out a long sigh. "The point is, we know the Rabbit is interested in you. Interested enough to track you down and deliver that potion. And we know he's watching Eventide's movements. We can't have him connecting the two. If he realizes that you're *you*, then you and I can't go undercover to the auction."

"I hate it when you're sensible." Sol grumbled, lowering himself back down to the couch hard enough that the frame dug into his tail bone, and he winced, all the fight leaving him. "I just feel like I'm not doing anything. I feel..."

"Helpless," J supplied for him.

Sol grunted, annoyed.

J leaned over, taking his hand in her own, and giving it a firm squeeze. "I get it. Fuck, do I get it. It's hard to just sit around and wait. But we have the advantage here. We know something the rabbit doesn't, and we need to press that while we can. You're our trump card, and if we waste that then we haven't got much else. So just sit tight, all right? I promise you'll get to see some action soon."

Sol nodded, but J's words didn't ease the itching. Didn't alleviate the feeling that he wasn't doing *enough*. That by sitting around and waiting for answers, he didn't matter in the grand scheme of things. How was he better than the politicians? How was he better than the elite of Mythikos? If all he was doing was sitting around on his hands, waiting for someone else to do the work for him. He wasn't. He wasn't a hero. He was a—

His phone rang loudly, jerking Sol from his thoughts. He fumbled for a moment with the device, nearly dropping it before J snatched it and answered, her long fingers holding it up so they could both squeeze in and look at Pickle.

"Anything?" Sol asked, breathless. He ignored the little square in the bottom corner of the screen that showed his disheveled appearance—if he looked he knew what he'd see, dark circles under his eyes, unbrushed hair pushed back into a headband—smooshed in next to J's face. It would be better not to come face to face with how little sleep he'd gotten.

"There has been no activity at the address. But I checked the records for the warehouse. It looks like it's owned by one Bim Oakfur."

"Of fucking course it is." J clicked her tongue, shifting so that she could press her shoulder more firmly against Sol, nearly knocking him out of the frame.

"Who's Bim Oakfur? Why does that name sound familiar?" Sol scrunched up his nose in thought.

"He was the captain of my precinct at the hold."

"Ooooh right. That guy." Sol nodded. "We don't think Oakfur is the rabbit do we?"

"Not likely." J snorted, her jaw twitching in annoyance. "Oakfur is more the henchman sort. It's probably just in his name to keep the rabbit's name clean."

"Very likely," Pickle agreed. "I didn't think we'd get their name when I went looking anyway. But I knew we'd get someone we could talk to."

"You think Oakfur actually knows who the rabbit is?" Sol sat up a little straighter. *This*. This was something he could do. He could question a hero alliance captain. He could make Oakfur talk. That would be easy. So easy. And Oakfur already knew who he was so...

"Maybe. Maybe not." Pickle shrugged.

"I fucking doubt it." J clicked her tongue again.

"Only one way to find out, really." Sol grinned, leaning in closer to the camera in his excitement, his mind already working over all of the ways he could make someone like Oakfur talk. So many. So many ways. "Send me Oakfur's itinerary, and address."

"Why? What're you planning?" J turned to frown at him, her face so close that Sol could count her eyelashes if he wanted to. There wasn't time for that, not now, maybe later.

"We're just gonna have a little chat, Lettie. Don't you worry, your ex will come out of this in one piece." Sol leaned in to brush a quick kiss over J's mouth which left her green eyes widened and her lips parted just a little. He grinned to himself, wondering how many other ways he could leave the look of baffled awe on J's face. *Not now. Later*, he reminded himself. *Later*.

Then she sputtered, pulling back to scrub at her nose, hiding her pink cheeks behind her wrist as best she could. "Don't say it like that. It makes it sound like we dated, and that's gross."

"Sorry, Lettie." Sol laughed lightly and turned back to Pickle. "The address?"

"Already sent. Just be careful, you two. I don't want this showing up on the news, or the rabbit getting wind of it." Pickle wasn't looking at them anymore. Her eyes were focused on something just past the camera, likely her computer screen. "He can't know we're on to him."

"It hurts that you don't trust me, Pickle." Sol clutched his chest, poking his bottom lip out at her.

Pickle's blue eyes flicked back to the camera to fix him with an incredulous look. Her gaze narrowed on J, and she said, "If you have to kill that bastard to keep this quiet, I want you to do that."

"Yes ma'am." J gave a little salute. Sol gaped at them.

Pickle ended the connection before Sol could argue with her, and Sol frowned at his reflection in the darkened screen. "We aren't killing anyone."

"We'll do what we have to." J shrugged.

"Whatever." They wouldn't be killing Oakfur. Not so long as Sol was in charge, which he was, thank you very much. Although he wasn't going to deny J the joy of putting the man in a couple of casts if the need arose. "Come on, let's go get ready. I need to get out of this place before I crawl out of my fucking skin."

OAKFUR'S ROUTINE WAS... *boring*, to say the least. It mirrored how J's had been a year ago before Sol had fallen back into her life, and made a mess of everything. Oakfur had work, and he had home, and he had nothing in between. It wasn't really much of a life, if you asked Sol. But it did make what he had planned far easier.

"I don't see why we couldn't corner him at the hold," Sol said, his fingers pressing hard against the window as he worked to wiggle it open. It was on the second floor of a little row house in a neighborhood backed by one of the rivers in Mythikos. The backyard was full of enough trees to block any of Oakfur's neighbors from seeing where Sol and J were breaking in.

"Yeah. That would have gone over well." J grunted, her nails digging into the grip she had on Sol's calves. "Have you got it yet?"

"Almost. Just a little— Ah ha!" He grinned victoriously as the latch that hadn't been all the way locked finally gave under his gentle prying. "We're lucky he doesn't have those electric windows." Digging his fingers into the window frame, Sol heaved himself up through the little gap. "And that he's not paid up on his security subscription."

"Yeah, super lucky." J scoffed.

"Seriously though. You knock out the power, and those things are impossible to open. Trust me, I've tried."

"Do I even want to know about all your forays into breaking and entering?"

"Probably not." Sol turned to help J through the window, and once her feet were firmly on the ground, he shut it behind them. He brushed nonexistent dust off the slacks he'd insisted on wearing for this mission, and made a small turn about Oakfur's home office. You could tell a fair bit about a person based on their home office, and what he was seeing of Bim Oakfur did not impress Sol. "What do you think he's getting out of the rabbit? Because it's not money."

"No," J agreed nudging the little stack of books that Oakfur had used to prop up one leg of his very cheap pressboard desk. The desk gave a dangerous wobble like it wanted to cave in on itself but somehow managed to stay upright and mostly desk-shaped. "It can't be power either. He got his position because his father was the last captain."

"He's a leprechaun, right?"

J grunted her acknowledgement with a nod.

"So probably not immortality." Sol hummed, crossing his arms over his chest as he paced around the little room, taking everything in. The walls were lined with bookshelves, but the shelves themselves were mostly bare. Cobwebs hung from the corners taking up the space where books should have been. There were no pictures or mementos. By all rights it looked like Oakfur had thrown furniture into the room and never bothered with it again. He didn't even have a computer set up on the desk. "And Pickle said this, and the warehouse were the only properties with his name on them?"

"Yeah."

"Then what the hell is he getting out of this?"

"Don't know. But if we wait exactly fifteen minutes, we can ask him." J tucked her phone back into her pocket, shifting onto her heels. "Why don't we wait for him downstairs?"

"Ooooh yes! I've always wanted to sit in the dark and wait for someone to come home so I could scare them when they turned on the light!" Sol skipped over to the door, already halfway down the hall before he heard J following him. Maybe he had been cooped up in the loft a little too long if something like this was enough to excite him. He'd have to keep that in mind for the next time Pickle and Reboot decided to sideline him.

"You're so weird." J scoffed. "And he won't be able to turn on the light. No power, remember?"

"Point stands!"

"Weirdo," J said, but she sounded fond.

The pair settled into the living room, where the front door would open into when Oakfur finally got home. J had positioned herself in an armchair with its back to the kitchen, her eyes narrowed on the front door. Likely to stop Oakfur if he tried to reach for a weapon. Sol stretched across the couch; head propped up against one arm rest while his legs crossed at the ankles on the other. He wasn't overly concerned with Oakfur trying to shoot him, the leprechaun didn't seem the type from what Sol had seen of him. He'd want answers first, why Sol was in his house, how he'd gotten in, that sort of thing. Then he might reach for a weapon, but by that point it would be too late.

They didn't have long to wait. Oakfur was right on time, the lights of the cab he'd taken blazing through the curtains to burn at Sol's eyes in the twilight of the unlit house. The keypad on the other side of the door beeped, and Oakfur cursed, reaching for a key instead when the keypad refused to work. Then Oakfur was stepping through, toeing off his shoes, and reaching to flick on the light. The switch made a soft click as it was pushed upward, but nothing happened. Oakfur tried again, and still nothing.

"What the—"

"Bim Oakfur, right?" Sol asked, drawing the man's attention away from the malfunctioning light switch to where Sol was still stretched comfortably across his couch. Oakfur didn't look like much, in Sol's estimation, only furthering his suspicions that he was nothing more than a lackey. Maybe not even that. Maybe he didn't even know about the use of his name to lease a warehouse space used for nefarious purposes. Oakfur looked that level of hapless, which was a shame really. Sol didn't want to admit they'd come all the way out here for nothing in the end.

"It's you." Oakfur's eyes narrowed to see through the gloom of the room lit only by the streetlights outside. He didn't look like he was going to make a run for it. In fact, he took a step into the small living space, his hands at his sides. *Interesting.*

"It's me." Sol nodded, sitting up. He planted his feet on the floor in front of him, his elbows coming to rest on his knees. "Why don't you come have a seat? We have some questions."

"He said you'd come." Oakfur moved to the couch, his

socks scuffing softly against the thin carpet of the living room.

"Who said I'd come?" Sol could see J out of the corner of his eye. She had sat up straighter, her hands clenching the knees of her jeans as if she were readying herself for a fight, but he kept his own posture carefully lackadaisical. He was in no hurry to show Oakfur just how excited he was by those words.

"The White Rabbit." Oakfur sat beside Sol on the couch, settling his briefcase down onto the coffee table in front of him. He popped it open before pulling out a file folder that had been tucked into the pocket of the top. "He told me to give you this."

"What is this?" Sol took the folder, but didn't open it. He would have a hard time reading it in the low light anyway, and he wasn't willing to take his eyes off Oakfur, not when he didn't know where the Captain had stashed his gun. He was excitable, not stupid.

"Auction items." Oakfur's hands clenched together, his shoulders hunching forward a little more, trying to make himself smaller. "He said you'd find them interesting."

"I'm sure I will." Sol nodded. "But before we go, we have some questions for you."

"Right. Of course." Oakfur let a long breath out through his mouth, ruffling the red mustache above his lip. "Anything you want to know."

"Anything?" J asked, leaning forward more.

"Anything." Oakfur looked up at her, and met her eyes, resolute and wasn't that something? Sol perked up further, his own torso tilting toward Oakfur like a flower toward the sun. Information. He could do a lot with a little, and even if Oakfur only had a name... Well. Sol had been able to bring down entire companies with only a name. "I'll tell you absolutely anything I can about the White Rabbit."

"Why?" J's eyes narrowed in suspicion.

"Because I'm not actually working for—"

"The fuck you aren't!"

"Lettie, please." Sol soothed, shaking his head at J without looking at her, his eyes still fixed on the clench of Oakfur's jaw under his beard. "Let him explain himself."

J grunted her annoyance, but fell silent, her arms crossed over her chest.

"All right, Oakfur, explain. How aren't you working for the White Rabbit? Because this," Sol wiggled the folder so it made a soft clapping sound, "looks pretty damning."

"He's blackmailing me." Oakfur looked back down to his hands. They'd fallen limp in his lap, looking as defeated as the rest of him, all of the pride and pomp washed away with those words. "He found out I have umm... I have a daughter. She's about five. She's a... a goblin. He told me that if I didn't help, my daughter would wind up on one of those lists." Oakfur nodded to the folder still in Sol's hands.

"An auction list?" Sol blinked. "What does that mean?"

"Take a look, you'll understand once you read it." Oakfur cleared his throat. "Puck lives with her mother on one of the properties that the White Rabbit owns. I only get to see her once a month. Her mother and I don't get along. But Puck is... she's my *everything*." Oakfur's voice broke a little on the word, and Sol's heart gave a sickening lurch in sympathy. He didn't have children, but he did have someone who was his everything. "She's my little girl."

"Why are you telling us this?" J asked, her tone gruff, but Sol could hear the softness around the edges of it. Her heart was clenching in her chest just as Sol's was.

Oakfur looked up, his eyes glassy as they met Sol's. "Because someone has to stop him. What he's doing... it's horrible. You have to stop him, Dusk. You're probably the only one that can."

Sol swallowed around a lump that had formed in his throat, and nodded a little, not really sure what he was agreeing to. "All right."

Oakfur nodded, the tension in his shoulders leaving him in a rush before he lifted his chin. "I know we don't have the best history what with... what happened a year ago. But I want to help. If there's anything I can do, name it."

Sol scratched at the scar that ran down his throat nervously. His eyes flicked over to J who was frowning. He raised a brow at her, and got a subtle shrug in response before he turned back to Oakfur. "If there's anything we can think of, I'll let you know. But the information you've given us already will be helpful. Thank you."

"I can do other things too. I can get you—"

"That's quite all right." Sol held up his hands, the folder still clutched in one of them. If Oakfur was going to help them, it would be better not to use him up right away. Sol knew Reboot and Pickle would agree. Having an inside man hinged on keeping that inside man hidden, and Oakfur going hog wild helping right off the bat would only draw attention to himself. "This is enough for now. But we'll uh... Someone will reach out to you to get any more information you have that might be useful."

"If you insist." Oakfur grumbled a little, his shoulders sagging.

"Trust me, Bim, this is enough for now." Sol reached over and patted the man's shoulder lightly, hoping to comfort him. "You've done enough."

Oakfur nodded, and Sol and J took that as their cue to rise and prepare to leave.

"We'll be in touch," Sol said from the door.

"That's what he told me, too." Oakfur's voice was quiet, almost lost in the sound of the breeze outside.

"What?" J stilled, she and Sol turning to look at Oakfur

again. The man hadn't moved. But he seemed to be holding his breath, his shoulders rigid where they'd risen up close to his ears. The air was thick with tension, the pin waiting to drop, the gun waiting to discharge.

"The Rabbit said he'd told you that he'd be in touch. That I should tell you this is him... getting in touch."

The words made Sol's hands sweat, the hair on the back of his neck prickling a little.

"We should go. He might be watching us right now." J's voice was low in Sol's ears. And Sol let her drag him out the door and into the night.

CHAPTER ELEVEN

Sol opened the file folder Oakfur had given them as soon as he entered his and J's newest hideout, unable to wait to see the information they'd been provided. At the front there was a handwritten letter in the same messy scrawl as the other notes. But that wasn't what made his heart stutter in his chest. No. It was the name at the top of the letter. The person who it had been addressed to.

Not Candra.

Not Dusk.

Soliel.

The room spun, and Sol wasn't sure when it had happened but somehow the hard ground of their shared room was suddenly digging into his knees. The folder, along with the rest of the papers were scattered out around him, the letter clutched so hard in his grip that it was wrinkling under the pressure. Sol pressed his other hand to his chest trying to calm the too loud beating of his heart, but it didn't help. Nothing helped.

No one should have known that name. That name was

dead. *Erased*, according to Pickle. It was just Sol now, or Dusk.

"What is it?" J asked, but she sounded like she was in another room, more muffled bass than actual words. "What's —" J cut herself off with a sharp hiss as she snatched the letter from Sol's hands. He hadn't even gotten the chance to read the rest of it—it was a rather lengthy letter—just his name, written in that careless hand. Right there at the top. "Fuck."

Fuck is right.

"We need to call Pickle and Reboot." J's fingers shook around the letter, already reaching for her phone.

"No!" Sol swatted the device out of her hand, sending it skittering across the hard floor, and likely cracking the screen. "You can't tell them. They'll pull me. They'll lock me up in their manor and I won't be able to—" Sol swallowed around something sharp in the back of his throat. *To protect you*, is what he wanted to say, but he knew what J's reaction to that would be. No. It was better to keep such thoughts to himself. "I have to do this."

"You don't."

"I do!" Couldn't J see? Couldn't she understand? That this was something Sol didn't have the luxury of a choice in. That, in order to be the hero he'd wanted to be since he was little, and playing heroes and villains on the playground, this was something he *had* to do. That he would have to put himself in danger. "I do," he repeated more quietly before reaching for the papers that had fallen from the folder. His hands shook when he got a look at the first sheet. It was what looked like a medical file for a little boy. A wraith. He couldn't have been more than five or six. "Look at this, Lettie."

"What is it?" J leaned in closer to peer at the paper in Sol's hand. She kept the letter in her other hand, far out of Sol's reach.

"Auction items... That's what Oakfur said... but these are..." He picked up another. A teenage kelpie with black eyes, and a small but soft smile. "These are files on *people*!"

"What does that mean... Years of life," J read off the paper, her voice slow as if she were sounding out the words.

"Immortality." Sol sat back on his heels, his weight slumping backwards against the wall behind him, like a puppet cut from its strings. He should have known. There were only two ways for a mortal to attain immortality: be turned into a vampire, or steal it from someone else.

"What?"

"He's auctioning off their years."

"Their years?"

"Like the witches did back before the war, when they'd take children to make themselves young again." Sol let the paper slip from his grip as one hand lifted to clutch at his chest again. His heart was clenching so hard he wasn't sure how it hadn't stopped yet. How long had this been going on? How many children had lost their lives because the elite of Mythikos couldn't stand the idea of growing old? Why hadn't someone stopped this *sooner*?

"You don't have to do this," J said again, her hand reaching for Sol's to draw it away from his chest. They were warm, pressing heat into the chill of his half numb fingertips. It should have brought comfort. It should have maybe drawn him away from the cliff he felt like he was standing on the edge of. Made him step back from the precipice. It did none of those things. Because that letter was still there, glaring at Sol from J's other hand, the paper almost blindingly white in the yellowed lights of their room.

"I do." Sol swallowed again, less sharp than before, softened by his resolve it would seem, and he lifted his head to meet J's eyes. "I do have to do this."

J frowned, her mouth opening like she wanted to disagree again, but then she stopped and let a short breath out through her nose. "All right, but we're calling Pickle and Reboot so we can fill them in on... all of this."

"Except the letter."

"Sol, I really think we should—"

"Except. The. Letter." Sol narrowed his eyes, his voice low, and firm. This was an order. Not a discussion. "If they know about the letter, they'll pull me off this, and we'll lose the advantage."

"What advantage?"

"He showed his hand."

J's face contorted into thought, chewing on her lip for a moment. She didn't like it, Sol could see that easily enough, but she had to admit, he was right. "For now, we'll keep the letter between us," J conceded with a long sigh. "But if it becomes a problem—"

"Fine. Fine. But that's up to my discretion."

J's frown tugged further down her face, but she nodded and pulled away to go and retrieve her phone.

THE LETTER. It was all coming down to the letter. Sol had read, and reread it so many times over the last couple of days that it was starting to show signs of wear around the edges. But still, there were parts of it that didn't make sense to him.

Sol's eyes burned a little, and he scrubbed at them, focusing on the scrawling handwriting again in the dim yellow light of their small living room. J had gone to bed long ago, saying that it was time they got some rest. They'd probably thought that Sol would follow behind them dutifully, and Sol knew he should have. The dark eye bags sagging against his cheeks were a physical sensation.

But...

But there was something *there*. Something hidden away amongst the simple words that the White Rabbit had left behind. Something he needed to sort out before he slept.

SOLIEL,

You didn't think I'd know that name did you, dear boy? It was hidden away so deep, behind firewalls, under misinformation, tucked away somewhere that no one would be able to find it. But I didn't need to find it, did I? No. No I did not.

So, I'll forgo your faux monikers. Dusk. Candra. The White Fox. The New Moon. All those names you've worn over the years, trying them on like normal people try on shoes or coats. We'll leave them at the door. Move forward without them. And I'll say simply this:

Hello, Soliel.

It's good to be called by your name, isn't it? Although, I'm sure your little friend calls you by your name, don't they? Colette Jericho. The werewolf. The ex-hero. Your childhood best friend. Yes, I know about them too.

But I digress, that's not really the point of this letter.

The point of this letter is to say hello and to welcome you through the mirror, to wonderland. You're a clever boy, you'd have to be with who your parents are. You know what I'm doing here, don't you? You see what I'm giving the people of Mythikos. Whether or not you agree with my methods, you must agree that I've certainly given the people of Mythikos something they wanted. I know what you're thinking, that I've turned them against each other. That I've given the people an enemy. And yes, I suppose I've done that too. Not that they didn't want me to, mind, but I've also given them something else. Hope. It's a dangerous thing.

Who am I? How do I know your name? What's my end game? Well... that's for me to know, and you to find out, dear boy. Meet me at the Copper Diner on the corner of Blossom and Shadow at first dusk (haha, get it?) in exactly one week, and I'll give you another clue.

XOXO,
W.R.

He'd gotten the letter seven days ago, and it had haunted him since. J had threatened to burn it more times than Sol could count, and he couldn't really blame J at this point. He was bordering on obsessive, and he knew it. But he couldn't seem to stop it.

Sol had gone back and forth on what to do about it. To go. Not to go. Still, as he tugged on the overcoat with the moon and sun brooches pinned firmly to the lapels, he supposed there had never really been an option. He was going to go. The White Rabbit had likely known that. He had known that Sol would want answers, and maybe even a chance to face his enemy before the auction. He didn't think this would be enough to put a stop to the auction itself, he wasn't delusional enough for that. But—

"You're going, aren't you?" J asked from where they stood with their arms crossed, leaning against the door frame of the bedroom. The bed was messy behind them, like they'd been tossing and turning all day when they were supposed to be resting.

"Yes." What was the point in denying it? He was putting on his overcoat. He was slipping on his shoes. He had the letter folded up in his pocket. Of course he was going. "You stay here. I shouldn't be too long."

"There you go again," J snorted, pushing off from the door and heading to grab their own coat, "making decisions for other people without asking what they want."

There was no bite to the words, but they stung all the same. J was right, Sol had done that. He had selfishly decided to leave J behind while he faced the consequences of their actions a year ago. He had wanted to keep J safe, and in doing so, he had hurt them both more than he ever could have imagined. But that didn't change the facts, and the facts were that the White Rabbit hadn't invited J. And already knew too much about J, in Sol's opinion. It would be better to keep them as far from someone like the White Rabbit as possible.

"I'm going with you this time."

"It could be a trap." Sol knew better than anyone that that wasn't going to stop J from going along—if anything it would just encourage them to stick closer to Sol—but he had to say it anyway. He didn't really believe it though. Yes, it could be a trap, but it probably wasn't one. The White Rabbit was having *fun* with all of this, he wasn't going to cut their game so short now that Sol knew they were actually playing.

J grunted their agreement as they slipped into their shoes without bothering to change out of the sweatpants and hoodie they'd worn to bed. "More reason for me to go."

"He doesn't want you. He wants me."

"Sucks to be him."

"It's probably not even going to be that dangerous. He set the meet at a reasonable time, in a public place."

J met Sol's eyes as they turned up the collar of their coat. They looked pissed. Which... was completely fair. "Are you trying to talk me out of it because it's not dangerous enough or because it's too dangerous?" J raised one blond brow.

"I don't... I don't know." Sol fidgeted with the buttons on his coat, his shoes squeaking a little as he shifted his weight. "I just don't want you to get hurt."

"I swear to fucking Merlin," J mumbled, the words almost too soft for Sol to pick up even with his aids in. "I'm going with you, and that's that. So just shut the fuck up, and let's go. The sun's already starting to set."

"We can be fashionably late."

"No we can't." J rolled their eyes, pushing past Sol to head out the door and down the overgrown garden path onto the sidewalk.

"I don't even think he'll show up." Sol shrugged, his hands tucked deep into the pockets of his overcoat. He wanted to reach out and hold J's hand. To let J ground him as they so often did. But he didn't deserve that, not now. Not when doing that could drag J down with him. Because... because the White Rabbit knew about J too.

"You think it's a test?"

"Or another information drop. But he'll be watching." Of that Sol was sure. He didn't know how the White Rabbit would be watching, he just knew that he would be. And it was that more than anything that made him want to leave J behind. He didn't want the White Rabbit watching J. He wanted to shield J from the White Rabbit's hungry gaze for as long as he could. It was likely already too late for that though, wasn't it? "He wants to see how desperate I am."

"What would that achieve?"

"I don't know yet. But I'm sure I'll figure it out. I just... I need to give it a little more thought." Sol rubbed a thumb over his gloved fingertips, focusing on the soft leather against his skin.

J was quiet for a long minute as they walked toward the train platform that would take them to Blossom and Shadow. But that didn't fool Sol, the discussion wasn't over. He knew that. Because he knew J.

"I still think we should tell your moms," J said finally, their voice soft in the early evening air. "They might have some more—"

"No." Sol shook his head, pushing his hair back from his face when it moved to cover his eyes. "We aren't telling them. They'll just— They'll just get nervous over the fact that he's singled me out. They'll think it's too dangerous."

"They're not wrong." J scoffed.

"No more dangerous than anything else I've done." Sol let out a soft laugh, hoping to make light of the situation even as the heft of it weighed down his shoulders. Because Oakfur had said, 'you're probably the only one who can.' And those words had stuck with Sol for days now. A ball chained to his ankle. What if Oakfur was right? What if he was the only one who could stop the White Rabbit? Then it was his duty to—

"That doesn't change the fact that his interest in you is creepy." J plopped down as the train started moving, rattling along the tracks. They let out a hard huff of breath.

"Oh Lettie, what's there to worry about? I have you to protect me!" Sol leaned heavily into J's side, nuzzling at their neck where the bond mark rested.

He got a soft grumble of acknowledgment for his troubles. But a peaceful and pleased smugness settled into the bond between them. Good. He didn't need J on edge. One of them had to be calm for this, while his own anxiety sat like too much carbonation in his stomach. What if this was a trap? What if they got there and the White Rabbit was waiting? What if he wasn't? No. He needed to calm down. To relax.

"What pronouns?" Sol asked, his breath warm against J's neck. He couldn't smell things like J could, but he took comfort in their closeness. Took comfort in the routine of asking J for their pronouns before making assumptions. An old ritual, well-worn, and soft. Not quite enough to dissipate the bubbles in his stomach, but enough to ignore them for the moment.

"He."

"Okay." Sol hummed happily, turning his head to rest his cheek against J's shoulder. "My big scary boyfriend."

J snorted, but didn't say anything, he just relaxed against Sol.

CHAPTER TWELVE

THE COPPER DINER SHONE LIKE A BEACON IN THE DARKNESS. The rest of the neighborhood had either rolled its sidewalks up well before dusk or had closed down entirely. One could never really tell in Mythikos. But either way, the warm lights of the diner reflected against the polished metal of the outside like a mirror, making the whole building seem to glow like a lighthouse in a storm.

"I don't like how quiet it is around here," J grumbled under his breath. He had taken Sol's hand when they got off the train, and not let go. Sol gave it a squeeze, focusing on the warmth through the soft leather of his gloves.

"It'll be okay."

"It could be a trap."

"Yes, I know." Sol let out a breath that ruffled his hair. He thought to remind J that they had talked about that before they'd even left the house a half an hour ago. But that would only make J grumpier, and Sol didn't need a grumpy J. He needed an alert J. A J who was going to spot or smell any signs of trouble. "We'll be careful," he said instead.

J nodded and grabbed the door to hold it open for Sol. The inside of the diner, while well-lit and comfortable looking, was unsettlingly silent. There were no soft murmurs of conversation. No sizzling of bacon fat on the griddle. Not even the squeak of the waitress's patent leather shoes. Nothing. Just the stillness of a tomb.

The hostess looked up from where her head had been ducked behind the little podium, her pale gold eyes flat and almost lifeless. "Two?"

"Excuse me?" Sol frowned, his head tilted to one side.

"A table for two?" The hostess asked like adding the extra three words to the sentence had been a struggle, and she hated him for making her do it.

"Yes. Thank you." Sol pasted on a wide smile, hoping it would get her to relax a little. It didn't. She grunted, grabbed two menus from the podium and turned to stride into the restaurant without a sound. "I guess we follow her."

"Yeah." J put his hand on Sol's lower back, and stayed close at his side as they followed the girl through the rows of empty booths. Sol didn't have to look at him to know that J's eyes were swiveling this way and that, taking in the whole of the open space in a careful sweep, looking for threats. It put Sol a little more at ease, his posture relaxing back into the warmth of J's steady presence at his side.

The girl slapped their menus down on the table, the sound too loud in the otherwise quiet restaurant, and then strode away without another word.

"Well, I don't think he picked this place for the service," Sol joked. He slid into the side of the booth with his back to the room and the door, letting J take the one with a view of the entire restaurant. He knew well enough how J felt about having his back to a room. He also knew that out of the two of them, J was more likely to pick up on a threat than he was.

"Probably not for the food either." J's lips twitched up a little at the corners with his own joke, as he took one of the menus to look it over. Sol took the other, opening it to reveal a little piece of folded paper that fluttered onto the table with a soft sound that seemed a million times louder than it should. J stiffened, his green eyes narrowing as they looked around the room again. "What's he want now?"

Sol carefully set aside the menu, ignoring the way his hands shook as he picked up the piece of paper, and carefully unfolded it. There were words on the inside, that same untidy scrawl as everything else, and his stomach clenched at the sight of them. "He just says to order the earl grey, and that our tea party is on him."

"Our tea party—He knew I'd come with you." J's fingers tightened on his menu so hard that Sol could see where his nails were leaving marks in the thick plastic sheath they'd used to protect the cardstock.

"It's a fair assumption that you'd come with me. It doesn't mean he's watching us." Sol shrugged, trying to sound reasonable in the face of the fear that was crawling up his spine. He couldn't shake the prickle of eyes on him. It tickled at the back of his neck like someone brushing their fingers over the baby fine hairs there, making him almost shudder. He forced his shoulders to remain still. He didn't want J to see how uncomfortable he actually was. It would just make J pull them both out of there, and then he'd get nothing. Discomfort was a small price to pay for answers.

"He could be back in the kitchen right now, planning to poison us both." J hunched forward over his hands to hide the quick motions of his signing.

Sol supposed that was true but... "This seems an awful lot of trouble to go through just to poison us."

J lifted his hands to respond, likely to rip Sol a new one

for being stupidly naive, but was cut off by the loud sigh of an approaching disinterested-looking waitress.

"What'll it be?" She pulled a pad from the apron around her waist, not even bothering to meet either of their eyes, just staring out the window into the dark night.

"I'll have the—"

"He'll have a pot of the earl gray and the chocolate French toast. I'll have the hungry man's breakfast. Eggs over easy. Bacon, not sausage. An English muffin instead of toast. Just water to drink." J cut in, his hands clutching the menu a little too hard again. He ignored the head tilt Sol shot his way, and handed their menus back to the waitress before she disappeared. "What? I'm hungry."

"I see that. But I thought you were worried about him poisoning us."

"On the off chance that he's not," J shrugged, "may as well get a free meal out of it."

"Hm. Fair point." Sol picked up the paper again, turning it round and round in his fingers as he tried to find some other meaning behind the words. But there were none. Just the simple instructions to order the tea, and that the White Rabbit would pay for whatever it was Sol and J wanted to eat. Under different circumstances, it might have seemed that the White Rabbit was trying to look after them, in his own strange way. But these were not different circumstances, and Sol wasn't nearly as foolish as he liked to pretend he was.

J's fingers drummed against the table, filling the silence that stretched between them, but Sol didn't speak nor move to break it himself. Both too deep in their own thoughts to bother with conversation. By the time their food came, Sol had read and reread the little note at least a dozen times, memorizing it word for word, and tracing his fingers over the looping handwriting of the White Rabbit's signature, and J had gotten severely twitchy, jumping at any small sound. Including the sound of their plates being settled onto the table between them.

"Thank you." Sol offered the waitress a bright smile. Which she just scoffed at, and turned to disappear into the back again. Sol reached for his plate, picking up his fork, but J yanked it across the table before he could dig in. "What the fuck, Lettie?"

"Gotta make sure it's not poison." J leaned in closer to the plate, giving it a deep sniff.

"So, what? Are you my poison tester now?" It sounded ridiculous, but Sol really wouldn't put it past him. J had done a number of stupider things to protect Sol from getting hurt, including taking a knife to the gut and nearly dying. Sol hated that protective instinct as much as he loved it.

"If I have to be," J said as simply as breathing, and cut off a little corner of Sol's food to stuff into his mouth before Sol could say anything to stop him. He chewed for a moment; his nose scrunched up in distaste.

"What is it? What's wrong with it?"

"I just don't know how you can eat that shit. I just had one bite and already I can feel the cavities forming." J shoved the plate back across the way to him.

"Want to check the tea too?" Sol started to pour some into the little teacup the waitress had brought him, and stopped almost immediately, leaning forward to eye the softly glowing liquid just barely covering the bottom of the cup. "It's that potion again."

J had leaned forward too to give the cup a delicate sniff. "It is. There must be more to the note that you can't read without it."

Sol nodded, pouring more of the potion into the teacup.

He lifted it to his lips, taking a little smell of it himself. It certainly smelled the same, and it glowed the same. There could be no mistaking what this meant. J was watching him, his green eyes narrowed in thought, but he didn't stop Sol as he took a long, slow sip. The potion was warm this time, giving it a pleasant tingling sensation as he swallowed it down. And then he squeezed his eyes shut against the strange sensation of the world made of rainbows, breathing through the dizziness.

J reached out, taking his free hand to give it a grounding squeeze, and Sol thanked Merlin for J, and for him always knowing what Sol needed.

It seemed to go by faster this time, the adjustment period. Sol opened his eyes, letting out the breath that had lodged itself in his chest in one long whoosh, and looked down at the note again. Underneath the words in black there were words in blue that said, 'I hope you brought that letter.'

"Fucking bastard," Sol said on a laugh.

"What?" J reached over to take the note from Sol's hands, and turn it over between his own fingers even though he couldn't see what Sol could. Sol slid the teacup to him, but didn't wait for J to take a sip before pulling out the letter, and carefully smoothing it out onto the table between them. He let his fingers flex against the paper for a minute, and then looked down to rake his gaze over the scrawling handwriting, looking for anything new.

But there didn't seem to be—

No.

No. That couldn't be.

That didn't make sense.

"What is it?" J snatched the letter from Sol's hands and looked down at it himself.

There, underneath the letters, WB, was a signature, sloppy, and hard to read. The only letters that could be made out clearly were a S and a T at the beginning of both names. But the White Rabbit had very kindly written the name in all capitals below that.

Soren Tsuki
    P.S. Hello, son.

CHAPTER THIRTEEN

Sol wasn't sure how they got home from the diner. He didn't remember finishing their food; they may not have. He didn't remember buttoning up his overcoat, and heading back out into the damp night air. Or climbing aboard the train back to the little run-down neighborhood where he and J had holed themselves up. It was like one moment he had read those words, 'Hello, son', and the next he was sinking down into lumpy couch cushions, J's hands on his shoulders.

Something of his mental state must have shown on his face because J had squatted down in front of him, and was pushing hair back from his face with gentle fingers.

"Are you back with me now?" The words sounded raspy, and almost broken, but he didn't stop stroking his fingers through Sol's hair. Sol leaned into the touch on instinct, and J didn't pull away from the contact as he might have a year ago.

Sol shook his head. He wasn't back with J. He was still floating somewhere in the dark. Far away from everything else. Nothing felt real. And everything that might have been real was soft like snow around the edges.

"I'm going to go and make you something to eat. Can you focus on your breathing for me?" J gave Sol's hair a soft tug, grounding him.

Sol inhaled deeply through his nose, let it out through his lips, and nodded.

"That's it, just focus on your breathing. I'll be right back. Are eggs okay?" J hadn't moved from where he'd squatted down in front of Sol, and it was easy then to meet his eyes and focus on his words. Were eggs okay?

Sol shook his head, no. No. They weren't.

"Toast then." J nodded to himself, his fingers flexing in Sol's hair.

Sol thought about this too, and when words failed him, he gave a nod of assent.

"Are you going to be all right in here by yourself? Or do I need to let you koala me while I make it?"

Sol considered that. J was the only thing anchoring him to reality, but he didn't want J to have to work around him to make whatever he was going to make. That usually ended up with something getting burnt, or J cussing up a storm. Besides, he didn't think he could move his legs at present.

"I need a yes or a no to the koala thing, Sol." J prompted again.

Sol shrugged.

"You do realize that's not an answer, don't you?" J sounded exasperated, but also so soft and fond that Sol couldn't help but smile a little. "All right then, I'll be quick."

"Okay," Sol managed to sign, the word somehow not getting stuck between his mind and his fingers. Maybe he was coming back around. Maybe toast would be good for him.

"That's it," J encouraged softly, and gave Sol's scalp a little scratch before standing and heading off somewhere. Likely to the kitchen. But Sol couldn't see anything beyond the narrow focus of his hands in his lap, and the floor below his feet.

He focused on his breathing, listening to the way the air moved in and out of his lungs too loudly, the sound grating on his nerves. And then suddenly the letter was back in his hands, and he was staring at the place where the White Rabbit's name had been revealed. The potion had worn off, so he couldn't see the signature anymore, but it was burned into his mind. Along with the smug tone that accompanied the words, 'Hello, son'. Sol didn't know what his father sounded like, but he imagined the man's voice was very similar to his own. Maybe a little deeper. Maybe a little more confident. But similar enough that Sol could practically hear it in his head.

"It's a taunt," J said when he returned, making Sol jerk out of his reverie. He tried to ignore the voice of Soren Tsuki playing on loop in his mind, threatening to muffle J's voice. J passed Sol the plate of toast and waited for him to take a careful nibble. It took too long for his mind to clear, but J was patient, and Sol appreciated that. When he finally met J's eyes, J repeated, "It's a taunt. Your father is dead, Sol."

Sol swallowed the toast, ignoring the way it made his mouth a little too dry. It didn't matter, it was nice to have something in his stomach. Maybe he hadn't eaten at the diner after all... Maybe J had rushed him out of there after they'd read Soren's name on the letter.

Hello, son.

"What if he's not?" Sol asked, his fingers tightening around the edges of the toast enough to make it fold in half. He ducked his head to frown at the slowly softening bread. There was butter pooled in the middle where J had slathered on enough to offend anyone else's tastebuds, but Sol appreciated it. The savory flavor brought him back to himself. He took another bite, chewing slowly as he thought over his next words.

J looked like he wanted to say something else, but he didn't interrupt Sol's thoughts. He just let him work through them, slowly, but surely.

"What if the White Rabbit *is* my father?" Sol said around a cheek full of toast.

J shouted something, but the words got lost somewhere between J's lips and Sol's ears. The sound went muffled and garbled like Sol was hearing it underwater. When there was no recognition of what he'd said on Sol's face, J let out a long, shaky breath, and ran a hand through his long blond hair.

"What if he's the White Rabbit?" Sol asked again, his voice small in the space between them.

"He's not." J remembered to sign along to the words this time. Sol was grateful for it. It was hard enough to focus without J's volume making things difficult to hear. "This is just to get you to that auction. He's just trying to make sure you let yourself out in the open where he can get to you. It's a trap."

"No." Sol sat the toast down on the chipped plate that J had perched on his legs so he could sign the next words. "No. If he knows half as much about me as he seems to, he'd know he doesn't need to dangle my father's name in my face to get me there. He'd know that the file of innocent children he intends to auction off would be enough."

"We need to call Reboot about this." J rocked back on his heels, his hands moving slower, almost hesitantly, as if he expected an argument.

"Yes. Let's call my mother." Sol set the plate on the couch beside him, and reached for the phone in his pocket. "I believe she has some things to answer for."

J gaped a little, watching with wide eyes as Sol dialed

Reboot's direct line. He reached out to still Sol's fingers before he could hit the send button. "Aren't you afraid she'll pull you off this operation once she knows who's the head of it? I mean... the White Rabbit is dangerous. And he's clearly done his research on you."

"I'd like to see her try." Sol hit the send button, turned on the video feature, and held the phone away from his as it rang through to his mother's line. Reboot answered a total of four rings later, her dark hair pulled away from her ashen face in a loose bun. Before she could open her mouth to say anything, Sol's sharp voice cut her off, "The White Rabbit is my father, but you said my father was dead."

Adelia let out a breath through her nose, her eyes pinching shut in something like pain. "That is not what I said."

"That is what you led me to believe." Sol narrowed his gaze on the look of stress that lined his mother's face. She may have been immortal from the vampire bite, but that hadn't gotten rid of the years of wrinkles being human had left her with. And right at that moment, all she looked was tired. So very tired. But he wasn't going to let her off that easily. Because he needed answers.

"He was gone." Adelia gave a helpless little shrug. "He was gone, and he broke my heart."

"What did he *do*, exactly?" She'd said before that Soren wasn't a good man, but she hadn't explained, and right now he needed to know. If the White Rabbit actually was Soren, Sol had to be prepared for all of what that meant.

Adelia opened her mouth to speak, then seemed to think better of it and pressed her lips together again, her jaw working as she seemed to chew on her words. "He was a part of an anti-fae movement. They wanted to go back to the old days. The days before we all intermingled like we do now. When magic was kept in the dark."

This wasn't as surprising as Adelia likely thought it was, Sol realized. The White Rabbit had made it perfectly clear that he was willing to suck Unseelie dry in order for others to be immortal, or more youthful, or whatever it was people thought they wanted. But it wasn't just that. Was it? "It's humans. He's selling them to humans," Sol breathed.

"I expect so." Adelia frowned, her eyes glancing off to the side of the camera as if looking at something beyond her phone. "When we broke it off, it was because of Ildri. He found out that Ildri and I were friends, and he just... he lost it, Soliel. I've never seen him so angry. That's when he started scaring me. I decided to run."

"But that wasn't the last you heard from him," Sol said. He wasn't sure how he knew, but this was where her story was leading. That there was something more to it than all this.

"No, it wasn't." Adelia took another deep breath, letting it out so slowly that her shoulders seem to sag with the action.

"You have to tell him," Ildri's voice floated through the speaker from somewhere off screen. "He needs to know all the facts. It's time."

Adelia nodded, her gaze drifting, expression almost vacant. "It was when you were very small. Maybe not much more than a few months." She bit at her bottom lip, seeming to weigh the events in her mind as she thought. "He found us, I don't know how, but he did. And he knew what you were. He knew that he'd sired a banshee."

Sol knew they had moved a couple of times before he had met J on the playground when he was little. He knew that his mother had talked about moving again, but had been talked out of it when Sol said he'd made a friend, and didn't want to leave J behind. But he didn't know why. She'd never explained her decisions to him, and he'd never asked her to. He always assumed she'd had a reason for how overprotective she was. For how all of his devices were so hard to get into. For the strange smell of magic that lingered in the air in the apartment. But he'd never asked. Children usually didn't.

"Did he come to the house?" Sol asked, his throat a little dry.

"He did."

J growled softly, his hands tightening where they had come to rest on Sol's knees at some point.

"I got in touch with Ildri again after that." Adelia shrugged. "She helped me hide. I couldn't— I didn't know— I couldn't have known what he planned to do with you. But now—if he's the White Rabbit—seeing what he's doing with the others, I can only assume he meant to auction you off. Banshees are immortal, after all."

That sunk into him. *Banshees are immortal.* Some saw it as a gift from the gods that they should lose their fathers and then be granted immortal life from their mother's heartbreak. Others saw it as a punishment. Sol had never really thought about it because he'd always assumed he wouldn't make it, something would kill him, long before it became a problem. Sol was left to his thoughts as J filled Ildri and Adelia in on what had happened so far, with the letter, the diner, and the signature. Everything that had threatened to bring Sol's very world down around his ears.

"We're going to send an extraction team to pull you both," Ildri was saying, her words only just filtering in through the chatter of Sol's inner thoughts. "If this is really Soren, we can't let Sol put himself out there like that. Soren will be gunning for—"

"No." Sol lifted his head, frowning, he didn't realize he had even lowered his gaze to watch the subtle shift of J's expressions.

"Sol. You can't go up against your father. He knows what you are. And obviously, he's been watching you all this—"

"No. I told J before that the White Rabbit showed his

hand by revealing his interest in me. We know he knows who I am. And we know he wants me for some reason. I'm the only one who might be able to get close enough to him when his guard is lowered." Sol's hand tightened around the phone, and it took everything in him to keep it from shaking. He had to do this. He *had* to. If only for the chance to finally know the man who had sired him, for better or worse.

"Fine." Ildri let out a breath, and Adelia, who looked very much like she wanted to argue further, stayed silent. He couldn't see it, but he imagined Adelia was clutching hard onto Ildri's arm, her nails digging in the way J's sometimes did when he was particularly stressed.

"I'll be careful," Sol assured. "And Lettie will be there with me! He'll keep me out of trouble."

"You had better, or mark my words, child." Ildri shook a finger at him from where she'd pushed herself into the frame next to Adelia. Her face was pinched in an expression the likes of which he'd only ever seen once before, when he'd first told Ildri of his plan to save J a year ago. She'd been pissed then, and she was pissed now. She'd been infuriated at the idea of the young man she'd helped to raise putting his life on the line for someone who didn't seem like they deserved it. But she'd understood then, just like she did now. Ildri always did. She seemed to see that there were some things Sol just had to do, whether they were safe or not. He was so lucky to have her.

"Yes ma'am." Sol gave a little salute, and then he hung up, slumping back into the lumpy couch cushions again, suddenly too much in this world, and not enough floating off to the aether as he had been before. Everything was too loud, too bright, too sharp. There were too many strings tying him down to the earth—Ildri, Adelia, J, Maz, Fizz, Eventide—and he couldn't bear to cut any of them.

"You don't have to do this," J said for what might have

been the millionth time since all of this had started not more than a few weeks ago. "You don't— You don't have to use yourself as— as *bait*."

"I don't see where there's much choice. I have to see how far down it goes." Sol yawned, brushing his hair back before he ran his hand down over his face to scrub at his eyes. He was exhausted all of a sudden from the weight of those strings.

"How far down *what* goes?"

"The rabbit hole."

"Gross. You're starting to sound like him."

"Well, what's that saying?" Sol cocked his head thoughtfully, his nose scrunched up. The words sprang to his lips like they'd been placed there by someone else. "The one about knowing thy enemy?"

"Don't know. Don't care." J grumped. "I'm still. . . I'm just —I'm worried about you, Sol."

"Oh, Lettie. I know you are. But you really have no reason to be. I'm going to be fine. We're all going to be fine." Sol leaned forward to brush a soft kiss over the crease between J's brows. He was sure they *would* be fine. He could outwit the White Rabbit, Soren, he was sure of it. Especially with the help of Eventide. There was nothing to worry about. Not a single thing. "Come on, we should get some rest. In the morning I need to start planning. Now that we know who the White Rabbit is, and what he's after, we can start researching him. Follow the money, as Ildri likes to say."

J huffed, but stood, stretching out his legs. Then he reached down to take Sol's hand and tug him along. "Promise me you're not going to hole yourself up in your office again, and not get any sleep."

"I don't make promises I can't keep."

J clicked his tongue and rolled his eyes, but his lips twitched a little at the corners.

CHAPTER FOURTEEN

SO MUCH COULD GO WRONG. SO MUCH *WOULD* PROBABLY GO wrong. There were too many variables. Too many unknowns.

It was terrifying.

It was exhilarating!

And Sol had lost himself days ago to the push and pull of planning their next big op. He wasn't even sure what day it was anymore, or what time, because he'd been locked away in his office for so long. It must have been at least a few days, because his hair had gone decidedly greasy at the roots, making it slick back when he ran his fingers through it.

"You look gross." J's tone was blunt as he loomed over Sol where he was seated in the middle of the empty floor.

A desk probably would have been better for his back, but the floor just had so much room for activities! There were blueprints for the warehouse somewhere under profiles of all of the people he remembered from the club. He just needed to dig a little—

"Hey! What are you doing?" Sol wriggled trying to get out

of J's grip where the other man had latched onto his collar and started to tug him to his feet.

"Repaying a debt." J grunted, hooking his arms under Sol's so he could drag him bodily to the door.

"What does that even mean!" Sol dug his heels into the thick, dusty carpet, trying to keep J from continuing to drag him along, but it was no use. J had at least a head of height on him, and years of hero training had built up enough muscle that if he really wanted to he could probably lift Sol over his head. Sol was no slouch, but there was just no fighting werewolf genetics combined with the hero workout regimen.

"It means you're taking a fucking shower."

"I don't have time for that, Lettie! I've got to finish up the planning. The mission is in..." He wrinkled his nose trying to think. What day was it again? He couldn't remember. He didn't even know the last time he'd eaten, much less slept.

"Two days. The mission is in two days." *Two* days! J's voice was strained, but Sol knew it wasn't from the weight of all but carrying him to the bathroom as J kicked the door open, and turned the light on with his elbow. It was something else. Something like worry, and concern, and panic all rolled into one. It made Sol want to soothe him, but there wasn't time for that either.

"Then I really don't have time to—"

"You do. And you *will*." J growled, kicking the door shut behind himself, and moving to block it. "You haven't taken your aids out in days. I don't even want to think about how long you've been in that binder. It's not safe, Sol. You know that!"

Sol stopped, finally standing on his own feet, his back to the shower as he looked at J, *really* looked at him for perhaps the first time in a week. The full moon had come and gone, and J hadn't bothered Sol as he dove headfirst into researching his father. In fact, J hadn't asked for much of anything since they'd heard about Soren Tsuki. It wasn't like him....

"Lettie, what's wrong?"

J looked up from where he'd been glaring at the tips of his boots like they'd kicked his dog. The expression did nothing to hide the tired lines of his face or the way his eyes were a little bloodshot. Had he been crying? Sol couldn't be sure, but it looked like it. Something in his chest squeezed at the thought. J shouldn't ever have reason to cry, and now he was crying because of Sol? Unforgivable.

"Lettie, talk to me," Sol said, his voice soft. Now that he was paying attention, J was right. His ears ached from keeping his aids in for far too long. And the fabric of his binder had started to cut into him, probably bruising, and definitely chafing the tender skin along his ribs. He didn't even think he wanted to look at the damage he'd managed to do to himself.

"I'm worried about you." The words came out like someone had to rip them from J's throat.

"Oh, Lettie." Sol sighed, his shoulders slumping forward. He closed the distance between them until he could rest his forehead against J's shoulder, letting J absorb some of his weight. "You don't need to be worried about me. I'm fine."

"You're not—You're not *fine*," J bit out, the words sounding sharp on his tongue.

"I am. Look at me," Sol stepped back, holding his arms out to gesture to himself, "all in one piece. Totally fine."

J narrowed his eyes like he wanted to argue about that statement, but he didn't. Instead, he said, "Get in the fucking shower. Now."

"So bossy." Sol huffed. He turned to start shuffling out of the button up shirt he was still wearing from their excursion across the city to clean out a data bank. Sol had been hoping for something about Soren, but there hadn't been anything. In fact, there hadn't been anything about Soren anywhere. Not in that data bank, or the next one, or in the back records, or property records. The White Rabbit kept a low profile. Which, Sol should have seen coming, but he hadn't. He did respect it though. It also made the... desire to know more about the man all that much stronger.

"What are you waiting for?" J grunted, grabbing the collar of Sol's shirt to tug it off his arms where Sol had drifted off into his own head and forgotten about it.

"Sorry. I was just thinking." Sol shrugged out of the shirt, and winced a little when the red, agitated skin at the edges of his binder caught his eye.

"I'm going to go get the ointment." J sighed. "Do you need me to help you get it off?"

"No," Sol said, perhaps a little too quickly. It wasn't that J hadn't seen him without it before. It wasn't even that J hadn't helped him out of it before. But the redness, and the bruised feeling that had settled just above his ribs, told Sol that he didn't want J to see what was beneath it. Not yet. Not until he'd investigated it himself.

J's brows raised, but he didn't question it. He just nodded, and turned to leave the bathroom so he could retrieve the ointment.

Sol took his time with the binder. Working it slowly out of the deep crevices it had cut into him with a hiss, as he braced against the sink at the lightheadedness of suddenly too much air in his lungs. He tried not to look closely at the skin underneath, knowing what he'd see, and instead, once he'd taken out his aids, he climbed into the shower. The water was only lukewarm, the little abandoned house they were inhabiting didn't have a modern water heater, but it was heavenly.

Sol lost track of things again. The white noise static of the water hitting the ceramic tub, and the soft throb of his ribs finally free, he let his mind wander.

He had a name. That was pretty much it. Soren Tsuki. But otherwise, there was nothing. It was like the man had never existed at all. Or if he had existed, he had erased every trace of himself. Even Ildri hadn't been able to find anything about him. No birth records. No death records. No marriage records. No records of employment. No records, at all. Which was... disturbing. Because even when Ildri had gone through and erased every mention of Soliel and Adelia, there were still traces. But with Soren, there weren't even any traces. Nothing for—

"Hey," J's hand poked Sol between the eyes to draw his attention. The hesitant draw of his fingers looked worried, like he'd maybe repeated himself a few times before Sol had finally noticed. He moved both hands around Sol's head to sign, "You've been mumbling to yourself for the last five minutes. Where's your head at?"

"I'm sorry." Sol let out a breath at the obvious disapproval in J's tone, ducking his head as J almost violently dried his hair with the towel. No amount of J chiding him was going to stop the rabbit quick pounding of his pulse, or the way his mind jumped about excitedly. He hadn't been challenged, really challenged, in such a long time. And here was a puzzle he could solve. One that would keep him busy for the foreseeable future, and at the same time might finally bring an end to the troubles of Mythikos. It couldn't be that simple, he knew that, but it seemed like it was right then. "I just— It doesn't make sense that we haven't been able to find out anything about the White Rabbit. There should be something."

"Does it scare you?"

"No. It doesn't." Sol laughed, a little manic grin creeping

up at the edges of his lips. Maybe it would be better if it did scare him. Maybe being frightened was the appropriate response, but he wasn't afraid. No, exhilaration hummed through his veins so loudly, he thought he might crawl out of his skin. The lightheadedness of his binder coming loose had nothing on this heady buzz. "It's fascinating."

J pulled back, the towel still draped over his hands to squint at him in the mirror, and say, "Don't do anything stupid" in a slow, careful way, ensuring Sol read every word on his lips.

"Depends on what you classify as stupid." Sol shrugged.

"Soliel."

"It'll be fine, Lettie." Sol grabbed the towel to finish drying his hair. "Probably."

THERE WAS A CALL, quick, and perfunctory. Just an update on what J and Sol had learned, and then Pickle and Reboot had gone back to whatever they'd been doing, and Sol was left in charge of the undercover part of the op. Now that they had information on what the White Rabbit was auctioning off, and some of the potential buyers, they needed to get to work.

"So it's just another sting." Rachel shifted on her feet, her hands fidgeting in front of her. She'd been unnerved by the news that they'd stumbled upon some kind of fae trafficking ring. The whole team had been. And Sol couldn't blame them for that, but he had other things to think of.

"Yes, and no." Sol sighed, pinching the bridge of his nose. He wished people would stop using old police terms for shit like this. This was not a fucking buddy cop movie. "It's still intel gathering. We need to know where he's keeping everyone if he's not holding them hostage at the warehouse. We'll still get buyer names, and faces, we'll expose all of them if we can. But our primary target is the White Rabbit. I want to know how he works, and I want to bring him down."

J grumbled something under his breath, his blond brows pinched together. He'd been unusually quiet since their phone call with Reboot and Pickle, likely still upset by the fact that Sol had decided not to tell the rest of the crew about Soren, or the fact that he'd called Sol out by name. It was on a need-to-know basis, in Sol's opinion, but they'd be fighting about that later, Sol was sure.

"What is it?" Maz leaned in to elbow J in the arm. "That time of the month? I thought the full moon was—"

"Say that again, see what happens," J snapped, his hands clenched into fists at his sides. He seemed unreasonably angry with the whole crew, and Sol couldn't really put his finger on why. Nor did he have the mental bandwidth to try.

"Is it—"

"Maz." Sol growled, his own patience wearing thin. He just wanted to get back to the house and finish their prep work. "Do us all a favor and shut the fuck up."

Maz grumbled, crossing her arms over her chest as she leaned against the wall behind her. The conference room fell silent around them apart from the sound of the radio one of the construction workers on the top floor had left on. It was a nice space. Big table. Lots of windows. A projector built into the ceiling. Arguably perfect for this kind of thing. But the openness of the floor plan left Sol exposed. More so than he'd already been, which was quite a lot once he realized how much Soren Tsuki knew about him...

"All right. Any questions?" Sol tucked his hands into the pockets of his jeans, hoping he came across as relaxed when he was anything but. Tension buzzed through his body, making his clothes feel too tight. He needed to get the fuck out of that room. He needed to tuck himself away in the windowless office space back at their hideout and go over the blueprints *at least* three more times before the op the following evening. He needed—

"You don't have to raise your hand, Dominic." Sol sighed, lifting his own hand to try to rub away the pressure building behind his eyes.

"Sorry. I just—Anyway." Dominic laughed nervously, lowering his arm. "What happens if someone notices the extra surveillance on the outside?"

"There's a plan in place for that," Sol said, cutting off J's long-winded lecture before it had even properly began. He saw J shut his mouth out of the corner of his eye, looking even grumpier. Wonderful. Because that's what he needed right now.

"No there isn't!" Maz sputtered.

"Sure there is. It's called, 'everybody dies'." Sol shrugged, unbothered.

Maz's face turned a truly intriguing shade of pale, and Sol wondered how long before her head exploded, or her skin became the same color as her silver hair. One one thousand. Two one thousand. Three one—

"You're not helping, Sol." J tugged on his sleeve lightly.

"Right. Sorry," Sol said, not really meaning it. If they couldn't take a joke. . . that was a *them* problem. But he looked around the room, and realized J was right, he wasn't helping. All his little joke had done was make everyone in the room look even more nervous. "There's an extraction plan on the tenth page of your packets. Please review it and let me know if you have any questions. Maz is in charge of getting everyone out with their heads still attached to their—" He bit his tongue, and forced himself to not finish that sentence. "If there are no other questions, we should split. We've got work to do."

They parted ways, and Sol was left to run everything he knew about the White Rabbit—which was precious little, but a man could hope that this time something would click—through his head for the nth time, the rest of the world fading away as his mind raced.

J seemed to be doing the same thing because a few minutes into their quiet trudge back to their current hideout he said, "He knows who you are."

"I am aware of that fact." Sol rolled his eyes. He didn't know why J needed to state the obvious. He'd been doing an awful lot of it lately, and to be quite frank, Sol as getting tired of it. If J couldn't provide any new facts then he should leave Sol alone to think.

"He's going to know you're coming."

"Very likely."

"You know what that means, don't you?"

"I do." Sol nodded. He did. He probably knew better than J what that meant. It meant that Soren would want to capture him the first chance he got. It meant that putting himself within his father's reach could very well be the last thing he did. He also didn't really care.

"You could send someone else. Any one of the team would be good enough. You don't have to sacrifice yourself like some—some *chess* piece just to draw him out." J's voice was low, but that didn't hide the heat there. He was furious at Sol for the decision he'd made. Angry that Sol would be willing to sacrifice himself for something like this. Which was... strange. Because Sol had thought that out of all of them, J would have been the one to understand. They'd wanted to be heroes together, after all, and heroes made sacrifices.

"I do have to." There was a certain amount of peace to

saying those words out loud now. Acceptance of the lengths he would go to for his cause. "This isn't up for discussion, Jericho. You can either fall in line, or you can leave. Your choice."

"And let you go in there alone? Not likely." J crossed his arms over his chest, his chin tilting back a little with a determined set to his jaw that Sol found himself wanting to kiss until it softened. He wouldn't. Not while they were having an argument. That was one of their rules. They had to let each other feel how they felt, they couldn't use physical intimacy as a way to negate those feelings, even if they didn't agree with them.

"I wouldn't be alone," Sol reasoned. Just because he couldn't kiss it away, didn't mean he couldn't try to make light of the situation. He *needed* to make light of the situation. Because otherwise this conversation would feel more like a death knell than anything else, and as much as he knew what he was risking, he didn't think he was ready for that. "I'm sure I could get *someone* to go with me. Maz maybe. She looks pretty good when we dress her up."

"You see how that's worse, right?" J turned to scowl down at him, the bright purple light from a neon sign painting him in shades of soft lavender that made his green eyes seem that much darker. Merlin, he was beautiful.

Sol shrugged. "A villain's gotta do, what a villain's gotta do."

J snorted, but he was smiling, and his tone came out fond. "Some villain you are. Putting your neck on the line to save a bunch of kids."

"Well if I don't make a very good villain then you must be saying that I'm a—"

"Don't even say it." J gave him a friendly shove, making him stumble across the darkened sidewalk.

"Awww, but Lettie. You think I'm a *hero*!"

J clicked his tongue, but didn't say anything to the contrary. And Sol, for once in his life, decided not to push his teasing any further, for fear of disrupting the warmth in his chest.

If he was a hero, then he really couldn't back out. Not now. Not ever. Mythikos needed him.

CHAPTER FIFTEEN

THE ACHE ALONG SOL'S RIBS WAS A COMFORT—A FORCE THAT kept him in the moment and in his own body as he dyed his hair, and covered his freckles, in preparation for the auction. His skin was still too tight, like he was wearing a layer over top of himself that was itchy, and that he'd like nothing more than to scratch away. But the dull throb helped. It reminded him of who he was under everything else. He was grateful for it.

J handed Sol his glasses, and Sol slid them onto his nose with a soft sigh. "I don't see why I need to disguise myself."

J cut him a look in the mirror that looked like she wanted to say, 'because I said so'.

"Because he's not the only one who will be there and we don't want to spook the other buyers," Pickle said, her voice sharp and echoing in the tiled bathroom of their hideout. She sounded like she was on edge. They all did. Well, everyone who knew about Soren did. Reboot had opted to not even participate in the call if she wasn't needed, and Sol hadn't pushed her even if his mother bowing out did sting a little.

"Fine." Sol slid the glasses further up his nose till the

bottom of the frames brushed against his cheeks. His fingers flexed as they lowered to his sides, and he drew in a slow, calming breath. "How does the location look?"

"No one has arrived yet. I'll connect you to Maz, she's getting our people set up there." Pickle's fingers made soft clacking noises against the keyboard, but her voice sounded far away. Not like he couldn't hear it, he'd won the battle, finally, over his hearing aids but like she wasn't paying attention. Like she was distracted by something.

"Aww. Don't want to talk to me anymore, Pickle? I'm hurt!" He clutched at the fabric of the black suit they'd put him in, just above his heart, even though he knew she couldn't see him. He'd lean into the overly dramatic nature of Dusk if it would get everyone off his back for a few minutes.

Pickle snorted, short, and dismissive. "Get out of this thing without getting your ass caught, and we'll talk."

J had left the bathroom, her footsteps silent as she headed to the main room to finish getting ready. Leaving him alone to face Pickle, and whatever wrath she thought he deserved. *Typical.*

Sol's fingers fell to grip the chipped ceramic sink in the too-small bathroom. The lights flickered, a warning that their time there was almost up. They'd have to move soon. Find another hideout. Stay one step ahead of everyone who was chasing them. Merlin, he was so tired of not having a home to call his own. How many years had it been?

He leaned over the sink a little more, pressing his face in closer to his phone where Pickle still waited for some kind of response. She could have hung up. She could have switched him over to Maz. But she'd waited. He was oddly thankful for that.

"I'm going to be all right. You know that, don't you?" Sol asked, his voice soft in the pause that rested between their voices. He understood Pickle's worry. He understood J's protectiveness. He understood Reboot's concern. But they had to know that he'd be fine. He always was. No matter what Mythikos threw at him, he always came out on top. Why should this be any different?

"Do I know that?" Pickle's voice still had that sharp edge to it. Like she was seconds away from telling him off in no uncertain terms, and pulling the plug on the entire mission.

Sol chewed on his cheek, forcing himself not to tell her that he *always was*. It would be a flippant response, and she didn't deserve a flippant response. She'd been there for him too much to be given that when she was sincerely worried.

"I was okay last year, with the issue regarding the Hero Alliance," he said instead, hoping it would soothe whatever nerves she had. Pickle liked data, and statistics, and Sol's track record was pretty good as far as missions went, all things considered. He'd never been caught when he wasn't meaning to.

"That's different, Sol." Pickle sounded like she was rubbing at her face, her words muffled through her wrist as she scrubbed at her eyes. "I was there. And we knew J."

"We didn't. I knew the old, Lettie. I didn't know the—"

"The car's here," J said, her shoulder pressing into the door frame where she waited for him. Tonight, Pickle had put her in a pair of wide legged forest green pants that came up to her waist, and a lace short sleeved shirt to match. Dangling earrings drew attention to her long neck, which looked oddly bare with the bonding mark covered in makeup.

Pickle made a noise that sounded like she was put out by J's interruption. "I'll patch you over to Maz. She can get you filled in on your way there. Make sure you leave your phone behind. We'll only be talking via—"

"The coms on my hearing aids. I got it, Pickle." Sol pressed a button on his phone, letting the communication pass to the device in his ear. "That means J will be out of the loop."

"I'll just have to stick close to you." J shrugged, turning to head down four floors to the lobby, and out the front door to the car that was waiting on the curb. Sol followed behind her, his eyes adjusting slowly to the growing darkness as he climbed in beside her. "Probably better I don't have that fucking fox in my ear anyway."

Sol choked on a soft snort. "Lettie, leave Maz alone."

"What's that dog saying now?" Maz grumbled into his ear. Sol heard a soft breeze move across the mic on her end. She must have already been set up outside of the warehouse.

"Nothing."

J raised an eyebrow, her head tilting to one side so the strand of hair that had fallen loose from the twist on the back of her head fell across her neck. Sol reached over to brush it back behind her ear, giving in to the urge for closeness that sat like an itch in his palms.

Sol shook his head, silencing any further questions. "What's the warehouse look like?"

"Like a warehouse," Maz grunted.

"Maz." Sol sighed, leaning in to knock his head lightly against J's shoulder. She brushed her fingers through the short hairs at the back of his neck to soothe away any lingering nerves. It was nice. Sol had forgotten how nice it could be doing things with J. How they had been a team all those years ago. He was so happy to have her back by his side, where she belonged.

"People are starting to show up. I've clocked a couple of the ones on your list from that party. But it's much more... low key than that."

"Low key how?"

"You might be a little overdressed." Maz sounded like she was shifting uncomfortably where she sat.

"Well. That's no matter. We want attention."

"Yeah, but... what *kind* of attention?"

Sol smiled to himself, all teeth. "Any kind."

Maz huffed a breath that said she was unhappy with his response, but didn't say anything else, and Sol tumbled back down into his head as the car moved almost silently through the streets of Mythikos. The lights unfocused as they went by in a blur.

He'd get answers tonight. He'd form a plan tonight. He'd find a way to put a stop to the White Rabbit, and hopefully bring peace to this city again. He had to. He likely wouldn't get many more chances, and if he didn't seize the ones available to him they'd pass by without so much as a nod.

"We're here," J said, pulling Sol from his wandering thoughts as she nudged him toward the door.

"Maz, how many people have already gone in?" Sol reached for the door, pushing it open before he turned back around to help J out of the car.

"You won't stick out like a sore thumb, don't worry. I mean aside from being overdressed; I don't think this thing is going to draw as large of a crowd as the last function anyway. And everyone is going to be a little distracted." Maz made a noise in the back of her throat, her eyes on them as they headed toward the door. "We never got an invite list for it. In case you were going to ask."

"Hmm." Sol hummed, noncommittally. That *had* been the next thing he planned to ask. He was glad she was able to understand him without words. It made this whole thing so much easier.

"We also weren't here when they brought their captives in. I don't know if that means they're being kept here, or if there is a portal, or if we just missed the delivery." She sounded like she was frowning now, her clothes shifting with some kind of nervous movement. He wanted to tell her not to worry about it. That they'd figure it out once they were in there. But J had tugged him up to the door, and there was a large bouncer staring down at them.

"Name?" The woman grunted, her dark eyes narrowing.

Sol saw J shift out of the corner of his eye. Her posture going a little straighter as stress lined her face. They hadn't talked about this. About what name Sol would give when they got to the door. But Sol had thought about it. And he knew what he wanted to do. He also knew that his team would not approve, that's why he hadn't brought it up to them. Not that it would matter if he told the truth or not, no one in Mythikos knew his real name, they just knew the monikers.

Sol titled his head to one side, his lips quirking up at the corner. "Soliel."

"What the actual *fuck*, Dusk?" Maz hissed in his comm, the sound loud enough to make his aids crackle. Sol reached up, to turn the volume down on the comm, if just for the moment. Maz's string of cussing, and the panicked chatter of the rest of his team, faded into the background as he focused on the tense moment between himself and the bouncer.

J didn't say anything. She didn't jerk her head to look at him. But he sensed her gaze out of the corner of her eyes. Her arm curled tightly in his, the muscle twitching. Fury flashed sharp, and hot through the bond, letting him know just what J thought about him giving his real name. But... it was done now, wasn't it?

The bouncer didn't even look down at her list. She swept her eyes over Sol, assessing. As if she'd heard the name before, had been told to look out for him, and somehow the person in front of her wasn't matching up with what she'd imagined in her head. "You're Soliel Tsuki?"

"I am."

"I don't suppose you have any... identification on you, do you?"

Sol barked a laugh, shaking his head. "No. I don't. I'm dead, remember?"

"Right." The bouncer's jaw ticked.

"You can check with the White Rabbit if you like. I'm sure he'd *love* to come out here and see what all the holdup is about. I can't imagine he'll be starting the auction without the person he invited... *personally*." Sol pulled the letter out of his pocket, flashing it just fast enough for the bouncer to see the White Rabbit's signature down the bottom, and his name on the top. But not slow enough for the woman to read it if she should try.

She shifted, her lip between her teeth as her eyes flicked back down to the list, and then up to Sol.

"What do you think, darling? Will he enjoy being questioned when he's preparing for an auction?" Sol turned to raise a brow at J. J pursed her lips, annoyed at being drawn into this little scheme. He could tell all she wanted to do was to dismiss the conversation and go back to being the silent arm candy.

"Doubtful." J flashed the bouncer a quick smile, all teeth, and elongated canines.

"From the mouths of beauties," Sol cooed, making J huff and avert her gaze. She might have been blushing, but Sol couldn't take his eyes off the bouncer long enough to check. Pity.

The bouncer shifted on her feet a moment more before letting out a long breath. "Fine. But if you're not him..." Her eyes narrowed on Sol in a threat, and Sol wondered what she honestly thought she could do to him that the White Rabbit wouldn't do himself.

"Guess that'll be my problem, not yours. Won't it?"

"Yeah. It sure as shit will be." The bouncer muttered under her breath.

Sol reached up to pat her shoulder, before they headed inside. J's fingernails were digging into the meat of his forearm through his jacket, but the buzz of conversation, the room full of people, and the sound of his team still losing their collective shit was enough of a distraction from it that Sol turned his focus to finding them seats amongst the rows of chairs.

Back to the mission.

Back to what was ahead of him.

Back to the White Rabbit.

CHAPTER SIXTEEN

On the far side of the room, just past the rows upon rows of chairs, was a raised platform. Spotlights, bright enough to burn, cast circles across the dark wood, leaving nothing to the imagination. There was no place to hide on that stage, no way to escape. It was just the pale cement wall, a narrow set of stairs, and the exposure that came from being on display in front of a crowd of strangers. Sol shifted, sweat trickling down his back at the very thought of being exposed like that. J gave his arm a little squeeze, but he hardly noticed, too intent on the stage, and the heat coming from those lights.

A young man stepped out onto it, and Sol's focus narrowed to the point where everything else in the room fell away. The man's clothes were neatly pressed and expensive. His hair coifed in a way to make him look boyish and charming. But that wasn't what drew Sol's attention. No. It was the freckles along the man's nose and cheeks. It was the smile that dimpled just to the right of his lips. It was the nose. . . that was shaped very much like his own. Those features, they were Sol's. And they were set into a face that was so much. . .

younger than Sol had been expecting. Younger than Soren had been in the picture with his mother in her study.

The man on stage, who *had* to be Soren Tsuki—because who else could he be?—didn't look older than twenty at most. But... but there Sol stood, his twenty-six year old son.

Sol's stomach soured at the realization that Soren had used whatever magic he intended to sell at the auction on himself. He'd made himself younger than he should have been. He'd kept himself that way. Soren was human, that shouldn't have been possible. But there he was, only just more than a teenager. Merlin, Sol was going to be sick.

Soren rolled back onto his heels, his hands in his pockets as he surveyed the small crowd he'd drawn. They hadn't noticed him yet, the crowd still milling about, and murmuring to themselves. Soren's eyes swept over them, seemingly searching. Then it seemed like he locked eyes with Sol, and Soren's smile twitched up just a fraction. Still not quite enough to reach his eyes which were the same shape as Sol's, but had a lifeless quality to them that made Sol shudder.

"Friends," Soren called, clapping his hands together in an overly excited gesture that reminded Sol a little too much of himself, and made him cringe. The room fell still, all eyes locked on the man on the little stage as Soren paced toward the edge, his toes almost hanging over it. "Compatriots... Family." Soren shot a wink that Sol knew was directed at him, but the whole room gave a little titter of laughter. "Welcome! I hope you've all gotten a refreshment from the bar along the back."

Another little mumble of laughter, and agreement as several of those around them held up full glasses.

"We should have gotten drinks," J mumbled under her breath.

"No need." Sol shook his head. No one was going to be

looking at them, not so long as Soren was on stage. It seemed that his showmanship was commonplace at these things from the looks of excitement Sol saw around him.

"Good. Good." Soren was making his way back towards the center of the stage, walking backwards, his eyes still firmly planted on Sol. Or they felt like they were, anyway. There was really no way to tell with at least sixty people crowded in around him. "Well, if everyone is comfortable?"

People murmured their agreement, the whole crowd seeming to settle back into their seats. One person down the row in front of Sol even went as far as to lean back in their metal chair until it was on two legs. Sol very much wanted to reach over and kick the back leg so that they tumbled out of it. But just as he was about to, J cut him a dirty look, a silent reprimand.

Sol huffed, turning his attention back to Soren.

Soren nodded his approval to the room at large. "Then without further ado, let's get this party started!"

Music started from somewhere in the back. It was soft enough that Sol couldn't tell what it was, but the bass vibrated in the depths of his ears. It made him twitch a little in irritation. His grip tightened around J's arm. He didn't know when they'd switched roles so that he was the one clutching onto her, but his nails were leaving red indents on her uncovered forearms. She didn't seem to care. She reached down and patted his hand lightly.

Sol let out a breath, forcing himself to relax, and refocus his attention on the stage at the front where two burly guards were pulling a child onto the stage. A little girl wraith. Her hair was streaked all over in red, her head bobbing a little under the weight of it. Sol started to rise before he even knew what he was doing, but J's hand tightened on his, keeping him where he was.

"Not yet. Let's get a look at the process first." J signed in tiny motions, almost too quick for Sol to read.

"She's a child," Sol said, his joints aching with the weight of those words. He couldn't believe he even had to explain to J why they needed to stop this. Why he needed to rise from his chair right that moment, and save that child.

There was noise around them, but Sol could hardly hear it over the hammering in his ears. He saw movement out of the corner of his eye, and watched as a hand went up to bid, accompanied by some sound that didn't quite reach his ears.

"She's a child," Sol repeated, his fingers twitching.

"I know." J let out a breath, but her eyes were focused on the little girl where she listed to one side into one of the big adults. "We'll get her out."

"Maz," Sol murmured softly, the word just loud enough for her to hear through his mic.

"What?" Maz grunted.

"I want to burn this place to the fucking ground." The person beside Sol turned to look at him with wide eyes, but Sol didn't bother to spare them a glance. If he ignored them they'd likely think they had misheard him.

"That can be arranged," Fizz said, with a note of glee.

J pinched Sol's arm hard enough to draw him away from thoughts of dancing flames, and the screams of people with more money than empathy to look up at her. "What?"

"You saw where they came in from, right?" J asked, her fingers working fast over the words.

Sol shook his head. He'd been too focused on Soren, and the stage, and the easy air of entertainment that had spread through the crowd around them. It was appalling, and Sol's throat itched with the need to use his Voice. To decimate everyone around him until they were a puddle of brainless lumps on the floor.

"That door." J nodded in the direction, and when Sol

looked over, he saw the white painted door. It was the same color as the wall, almost indistinguishable from the rest of the room. But if J had seen it then it must have happened.

"Maz, it looks like they're bringing them in from a door off the southwest corner of the building. What do you see?" Sol asked, ducking his head into J's neck so no one would overhear him.

"No doors. No windows. If that's the way they're bringing them in, they must be using some kind of portal magic."

"Fuck." Sol hissed, his nose pressing into the space below J's ear.

J made a sound of concern.

"Next up on our list is this lovely little spot of sunshine," Soren said, his voice burning into Sol's ears, and making it hard for Sol to focus on anything but. Sol lifted his head just enough so he could watch as the two burly figures brought out a stumbling black-haired child. Their hair hung over their face, dripping distractingly with what looked to be black water. *A kelpie in distress, then.*

"Sol," J murmured, bringing Sol back to the moment. Back to his plan. Merlin, if he had fire magic, this place would already be in flames. Sol shook himself.

"No doors. No windows."

"Shit." J leaned in to *thunk* his forehead lightly against Sol's, and took a breath in the space between them. Everyone else was too busy with the auction, listening to people call out bids, and trying to outbid each other to notice them. It was nice. Or it would have been if they weren't in the middle of a warehouse where Sol's fucking father was auctioning off children so the elite of Mythikos didn't have to grow old.

"Can we get any readings on what kind of spells they're using?" Sol tucked himself back into J's neck, hoping to hide the burning in his eyes. There wasn't time to cry. Crying could come later.

The kelpie was gone, replaced with a redcap. Not immortal, but with strength and speed that no human could ever hope to possess. The teenager looked sullen, and like he wanted to fight, not drugged like the others had been. Like maybe they were keeping him there by some other means, and that twisted Sol's insides up into more knots as he remembered what Oakfur had said. That the White Rabbit wasn't averse to using people to keep others in line. Was it a younger sibling, or a parent? Sol hoped to never find out. He hoped to get the boy out of there before he did.

"No. The building's got some kind of blocking array on it. We can't get a read on any magical signature." Maz sounded more irritated than usual, her words going a little disjointed toward the end. Broken. Choppy.

"You're breaking up, Maz." Sol frowned, his hand reaching up to adjust his hearing aid, but it didn't really seem to help as static cut in through whatever Maz was trying to say in reply.

"What's going on?" J's tone had gone worried, heavy. Sol stiffened against her side, holding onto her more tightly. They'd lost contact with the outside. They were on their *own* in there.

"I just lost connection with Maz."

"That's not supposed to happen."

"No. It's not."

"I'm going to go check out what's on the other side of that door. You stay here." J nudged Sol to sit up with her shoulder, and then pressed a kiss to his cheek. "I'll be right back, baby," she said for anyone that was listening. "Don't make any purchases without me."

"I'll come with—" Sol was already half out of his seat, but J put her hand on his shoulder and shoved him back down.

She leaned over him, brushing a kiss to his jaw. "Stay

here. Watch the crowd. I won't be long." She pulled back to check that he'd heard and understood.

Sol nodded, though his fingers flexed against his knees. He didn't like them separating. Not when they were cut off from the team like they were. Not when J didn't have any way to communicate with him if she needed him. He watched her make her excuses to the couple who was sitting beside them, and step out of the row. Then he turned to see if Soren would notice, but he didn't seem to. Soren looked like he was too busy making note of the highest bidder and moving on. Good. That was good.

And then Sol waited.

And he waited.

And he waited.

Five more auctions came and went. The crowd began to grow softly restless. But J never came back. The door remained closed tight but for the comings and goings of Soren's people, and every second that passed his heart sunk a little lower.

"And that's it, folks." Soren clapped his hands together, looking pleased with himself as his brown eyes pinned Sol to his chair. Sol was frozen with. . . something. Not quite fear. Every hair on his body stood on end. "That concludes our auction for the day. But as always, you're welcome to hang out, mingle, get to know your fellow bidders. . ."

The room erupted in soft chatter. Chairs scraping as people stood from their seats. But Sol couldn't move. He tried. The muscles in his legs tightened with the urge to stand, and run. To make his way to the door where J had disappeared and never returned. But he couldn't.

". . . And Soliel." Soren called over the noise of the crowd.

Sol's heart stopped altogether. It had been pounding away in his chest, but at the sound of his name from Soren, the man's gaze, so eerily similar and definitely locked with his, it stopped.

"A word?"

Sol swallowed thickly, but nodded.

"Good. Follow me."

Sol rose from his chair, movements robotic as he made his way past faces flush with drink and their own victory. It didn't matter that there was a clear exit. It didn't matter that his team was waiting on the outside to extract him. He wasn't leaving without J. This was it. This was the end. Soren led him to the door, and Sol followed him through.

CHAPTER SEVENTEEN

He couldn't feel J, he realized perhaps too little, too late.

In all of Sol's hyper focus on Soren and the counting of victims and the panic of J not coming back, he hadn't noticed when the gentle thrum of her reassurance that sat in his chest like a second heartbeat, had just stopped. Gone silent and dormant. Not completely gone, no. The weight of J's heart still sat there along side his, but it wasn't moving anymore. The steady beat that he'd grown so used to, wasn't there. So... she wasn't dead. Sol tried to take whatever solace he could in that fact, but it was very little, if he were being honest, as he rubbed at his chest where a dull ache had started up in place of the beating.

"If you hurt her," Sol growled, his fists clenching at his side.

Soren chuckled lightly. "Come now, son. No empty threats between us. We're family."

"It's not empty."

The crowd around them continued to murmur softly, and every step toward that door felt like it lasted hours. Like Sol would never get to see J again because it would take him forever to even get to the door.

"Of course it's empty." Soren continued, unbothered. "You can't contact your team, our jammers made sure of that. You have no weapons, according to the scans we have on the doors. All that's left to you is your Voice. And you won't use that unless you absolutely have to, because you've already been warned that if you do, it might render you mute." Soren shrugged. "See? Empty."

"There are other ways to hurt someone outside of a weapon or my Voice." Sol's bitten down nails dug into his palms, making the knuckles and joints ache under the strain.

"Oh of course there are." Soren pushed the door open and led Sol down a long, narrow hallway that had not been on the blueprints. In fact, now that he was thinking about it, there had been no door on the blueprints at all. This warehouse had been one big open room, nothing more. Sol's footsteps echoed off the walls in a strange way, the sound distorted by whatever magic was holding the structure together. And it *was* magic, because there was no other way to explain a hallway that was not really a hallway in a building that was a single room. "But you won't use any of those either."

"Won't I?" He was seriously considering it by that point, if only to get Soren to stop looking at him with that knowing expression. *Smug bastard*.

"Oh. I'm sure you'd like to. But you won't." Soren shook his head, a fond sort of smile tugging up the corner of his lips, which didn't seem to crinkle any part of his face as if it didn't dare give him the appearance of wrinkles. "No. I know what Colette means to you."

"Don't call her that."

"Her name?" Soren stopped in the middle of the hall to tilt his head in question. The bright white walls were starting to give Sol a headache, but he breathed through it to level Soren with a glare.

"No one calls her that. And you know it."

Soren's smile spread into something malicious and cold. Unlike the soft, excited smiles he'd been wearing so far, it was more a curl of the lips than a smile. It showed no teeth, and the only other place it showed on his face was in the razor-sharp glint in his eyes. Like the light brown color had hardened over, and turned into something... *dead*. "Do I?"

Sol stared at him, meeting his gaze head on. What else was there to do? He knew a challenge from a feral animal when he saw one. He'd seen the same expression on enough faces throughout his years in Mythikos' underground to know that if he let his eyes drift now, it would be seen as a sign of weakness. "You do."

Soren tilted his head, his gaze never moving from where it was locked with Sol's, an interested carnivore, trying to figure out a new challenge. "I suppose I do." Then he blinked, and turned his head back to the hall that seemed to stretch on forever. "This way."

Sol followed behind him, letting the silence stretch between them for an eternity that was not more than a couple of breaths before he said, "You use it on yourself, don't you?"

Soren made a sound of interest in the back of his throat.

"What you're peddling. The magic to give them youth, and years. You use it on yourself, don't you?"

"I had to make sure it worked."

That didn't sound right. It didn't fit with the picture Sol's mind was painting of Soren. He didn't think that his father would use himself as a test subject. Not until he was reasonably sure that it would work. No. There had been others. There had been mistakes. The question was, how many? Where were they? What had happened to them? Had they died in the effort? Or had they been caught in some horrendous loop? Sol would have to find out. He'd have to go hunting. He couldn't leave them unnamed, and unrecognized. Besides, the people of Mythikos needed to know. They needed all the facts. And the only way to expose Soren and his corruption was to expose all of him.

"How long?" Sol asked. That would be the first step, knowing how far back he had to dig. Pickle could find anything, so long as she had a date range. And so long as the records existed, that is. Sol would just have to hope that they did.

"Ah. Here we are," Soren said. He turned to press his hand against a piece of the wall that looked just like any other, and waited as a light scanned over his palm. With a soft hiss, and a tinkling of bells, the wall disappeared, leaving an empty doorway that led into what looked to be a study. The walls were covered floor to ceiling in stuffed bookshelves, and two sturdy leather sofas sat on a thick rug, facing each other. "Take a seat. They'll be with us in a moment."

"They?" Sol didn't sit. He wanted to be able to run if the need arose. Not that he knew where he'd go. The doorway they had come through had disappeared, leaving only a solid wall lined in books. And even if he had been able to find his way back to the hallway who was to say he'd ever be able to get out of it again? Maybe it would just go on for miles, as it had seemed to. Sol did a careful turn in place, to take in the room, and found no other exits. Four walls. All solid. Bookshelves covering each and every one, except in the small space where there was a crackling hearth. "This is cozy."

"What? Did you think I spent most of my time in some cold, sterile lab?" Soren snorted softly, rolling his eyes. He flopped himself onto one of the sofas, the leather creaking under his weight, as he kicked his feet up on one of the arms to make himself comfortable. "Sit. Sit. Make yourself at home."

"I'll stand. Thank you." Sol leaned against the arm of the other couch, his arms crossed over his chest, eyes fixed on Soren.

"Suit yourself." Soren shrugged, his torso sinking further into the couch until his head was pillowed against the arm, hands resting on his stomach. He closed his eyes, letting out a long breath as if he were settling in. Then there was that sound of hissing air, and tinkling bells again, and two big men came in, J a dead weight between them.

Sol twitched, but held himself where he was. He wanted nothing more than to run to her and check on her. To get a good look at the bruise that was half hidden under her tangled blond hair. But he wouldn't. He wouldn't give Soren the satisfaction of seeing the weakness that J was to him. Even if Soren already knew, he didn't have to *see* it.

"You can put her down in the chair over there. They aren't going anywhere." Soren lifted his hand, gesturing carelessly to a wingback chair in the corner, where the two men dropped J, unceremoniously. "Good. Now. Leave, the both of you."

"But—" One started to object.

"I said go! Soliel and I have some matters to discuss. In private."

The two men looked at one another, and then shrugged, before disappearing through the doorway again. Sol watched it closer this time, making note of how the magic shimmered in the air. He wasn't sure what kind of spell it was, but he would figure it out. He would find a way out. And he would be taking J with him. Soren's eyes were on him, heavy, and amused, but he didn't do anything, just let Sol examine the process. When Sol returned his gaze to Soren's, the man was smiling, faintly, a shadow of what he maybe would have looked like if he were really Sol's father. As if he had been there throughout Sol's life, to help raise him, to help guide him, and he was *proud*. It made something strange twinge in Sol's chest. Something like... hope? Maybe. He wasn't sure. And he didn't think he wanted to be.

"You won't get out of here without me. You need my palm print," Soren said by way of explanation.

"What do you want from us?" Sol asked, not letting the tremor of emotion show in his voice. It wouldn't do him or J any good if Soren realized how he was affecting Sol.

"My dear boy," Soren sat up, his feet planting on the floor as he turned to face Sol fully, "I want you to join me."

"Join you?" Sol snorted, incredulous. J was shifting a little where she sat, seeming to wake up from whatever they'd done to her. Good. If Sol could just keep Soren's eyes on him, maybe they had a chance. That shouldn't be too hard, J was a prop to Soren, nothing more than a reminder of what he held over Sol. More threat than person. Sol tore his eyes away to look at Soren again.

" Join my organization, and we'll make Mythikos into something better, together." Soren spread his hands out in front of him, palms up, like he was offering Sol a platter with the world on it. It was oddly... *tempting*. The chance at having a father. The chance to really make a *difference*. "I'll give you all the resources you could ever want to make the changes that you see fit."

"I have resources."

"Not like what I could give you, my dear boy, trust me."

"Stop calling him that!" J roared, her body already in motion to throw Soren to the ground. "He's not *yours!*"

Soren laughed, putting up very little fight as J pinned his arms. J's knee pressed into Soren's back to hold him down. "Ah. Would you look at that. Your pet hero didn't need rescuing after all, my dear boy."

"I said stop *calling* him that!" J dug her knee into his back hard enough to make Soren wince. "How do we get back?"

"Get back where?" Soren's voice had a teasing edge to it. Like he was playing with them. Like he wasn't aware of the fact that J could snap his spine right then and there if she so chose. But he had to be. He had to know. He was arrogant, not stupid.

"Back to the warehouse!" J snarled, her nails sharp points, leaving trails of ripped suit, and blood on the floor.

"He said we need his prints. When we came in, he put his hand to the wall." Sol moved to J, reaching down to grab Soren's wrist, and give it a sharp tug. "Help me get him over there."

"Where do you think you'll go?" Soren asked as they hauled him to the spot on the wall where the door had disappeared, Soren didn't fight them, but he wasn't making things easier either, he'd gone completely limp. Sol held his wrist up to the spot where he'd seen him do it in the hall. On this side the spot was a book, the intricate gilded cover facing out. "I own all of Mythikos."

"You let us worry about that." Sol shook his head, and smiled a little, giddy with relief when the doorway opened again, and the cool air from the hall hit his face. "J, knock him out."

"Can't I just kill him now?" J grumbled, clocking Soren hard enough that it sent him sprawling to the floor in an unconscious heap.

"No. We talked about this." Sol led her out into the hall, turning to the left, and heading back the way they'd come. It would have solved a lot of their problems to kill Soren while they had him at their mercy, Sol knew that. But it might also create other problems for them. He hadn't been lying when he'd cautioned about a power vacuum in the organization. This had to be handled correctly if they were going to dismantle the White Rabbit's entire operation, and save everyone under his thumb. Sol wasn't taking any chances.

"We've talked about this," J mimicked, her tone nasally.

"What did you find while you were. . . wherever you were?" Sol gestured vaguely, hoping that—

An alarm blared, the sound so high and shrill that Sol almost couldn't hear it at all. But he also definitely couldn't hear anything over top of it, not even the crackle of his aids as he normally could.

"I'll tell you when we get out of here," J signed, then grabbed his hand, and started to run. There were no more words, or if there were, Sol couldn't make them out, so he didn't bother with them. J's grip was so hard around Sol's fingers that the bones in his knuckles ground together. But he wasn't going to let go. He was never letting—

The door. The one to the warehouse. It had come up so much quicker in their haste, that Sol had almost missed it. It was shut, maybe locked.

"Get out of the way. I might have to force it." J dropped his hand, and then she was shouldering the door open hard enough that someone let out a soft scream on the other side.

Sol went through first, and turned back to grab J, but. . . but. . . but she was gone. Everything was *gone*. No sterile, white hallway that seemed to never end. No J. *Nothing*. The door J had forced, opened onto a bare stretch of crab grass just outside of the warehouse, and nothing more.

Someone was screaming.

Screaming so loud Sol thought their heart might break. And his throat was burning from the sound.

Oh. It was *him*.

He was screaming. His knees cold, and aching where he'd fallen to them on the hard cement of the warehouse floor. Sol's fingers grabbed at the crab grass where the hall had been but a moment before, ripping it out of the ground in clumps.

Whatever magic Soren had used to keep the hall in place, had collapsed, and taken J with it. Back to Soren's hideout. Or into some kind of pocket dimension where she'd be lost. Or *something*. The point was she wasn't there anymore. Sol had stepped through the door, dropped her hand for a second, and by the time he was on the other side of the threshold everything behind him had disappeared, leaving behind only the vacant lot beside the warehouse.

"Dusk. Dusk. What is it? What happened? Where's Jericho?" Someone asked, their hands tight on his shoulders trying to pull him away from the empty doorframe. But he couldn't tell who it was, and he didn't care. He didn't think he'd ever care about anything again. He clung to the frame, not wanting to walk away, not yet. Because maybe she'd come back. Maybe whatever magic Soren had used would malfunction and J would be right there on the other side just as she'd been a moment ago.

"Soliel. Soliel!" Someone else shouted, a masculine voice.

"We've got to get him out of here. Someone called the heroes. They're already en route."

"Fuck.

"Dusk! Stand up!"

"He's not moving."

"I can't even get him to talk. It's like he's gone catatonic."

"I just wish he'd stop fucking screaming."

Someone wrangled him to his feet, and then he was being hustled out into the cold night air.

"Pickle, we need a route."

Sol lost focus after that. It was a struggle just to stumble along with the not so gentle pushing and pulling of the people around him. He couldn't be bothered to think of anything other than the tripping of his feet, the ripping of his heart, and the absence that had taken up residence in that place in his chest where his bond usually hummed. It gaped like a hole. Like someone had reached into his chest and ripped it out. It. . . it felt like dying, and not being able to, all at once.

"We'll get Jericho back," someone promised. But the words lacked conviction. Like they didn't know how they'd do it, even if they wanted to.

"We will," another voice said, and Sol thought he saw them nod out of the corner of his eye.

CHAPTER EIGHTEEN

They had been running for what felt like hours. Long enough that the cold, damp air scraped his scarred esophagus. Long enough that he didn't really know where they were anymore. Long enough that he'd almost forgotten what they were running from.

Almost.

"I'll come in with you," Dominic said, his hands fluttering around him like he could catch Sol if Sol decided to drop to the ground again. He probably could, but Sol wasn't about to fall into another fit of panic. Not where anyone could *see* anyway. He was a good kid, younger than Sol and smart, and he'd done a lot to help Eventide. But Sol couldn't let any of them see him like that again. He was supposed to be their leader for fuck's sake.

"I'm good." Sol's palms itched from where he'd been smacking them against the cement floor for Merlin knew how long. Maz said they had found him there long after everyone else had cleared out of the warehouse. Sol didn't know how many minutes or hours that had been after the portal had closed, taking J with it. It didn't seem to matter. Maz said he'd still been screaming.

Dominic's dark brows disappeared into his dark hair. "You sure? I mean you—"

"I said I'm good!" Sol snapped. The dilapidated apartment building loomed, casting its shadow over both of them. It wasn't uninhabited, not like most of the places where Sol and J had holed up over the last year. But the people of this building didn't care about the comings and goings of their neighbors. It was infested with nixies and gremlins, and half the time it smelled like cat pee, but it was closer to home than Sol thought he'd been in a very long time. Their apartment was "vacant" according to the landlord, but Sol paid him under the table to give them any runoff electricity the building could spare, and keep things quiet. He'd have to move soon, on his own, without J there to grumble about the lack of hot water, and the cramped space—they'd already been there too long.

Dominic was still standing beside him, rocking on his heels, caught between motions. Should he stay or should he go?

"Dominic."

Dominic turned to look at Sol, his movement stilling, dark eyes wide in his brown face.

"Get the fuck out of here. I want to be left alone," Sol said. And had he said that to anyone else on his team, Fizz, Maz, certainly J, they'd have heard it for a cry for help. But not Dominic. He hadn't been around long enough. He wasn't comfortable enough to insert himself into his leader's life and not let go. Sol should probably have felt bad about that, but he didn't. Not if it would get him out of spending the evening with someone hovering around him waiting for him to do something stupid.

"Maz said that I—"

"Look at me." Sol waited until Dominic's eyes met his, and he raised a dark brow. "Do I look like I give a fuck what Maz said?"

"No, but—"

"Maz isn't the leader here. I am. And if I say to leave, you leave. You have shit to do. There's footage to go over, and I'm sure Rachel has some soil for you to examine or something back at the lab. I'll be fine on my own."

Dominic hesitated still, bouncing a little on his toes, caught mid-run from the fury in his leader's gaze, and the fear of Maz ripping him a new one.

Sol let out a breath, his shoulders sagging. He loathed how everyone on his team seemed to care so fucking much. They shouldn't have to be worried about him. They shouldn't be hovering over him like vultures waiting for him to keel over. Not when J was in that man's clutches. Not when they hadn't managed to save *anyone*. Not when they still didn't know where the White Rabbit was keeping his victims. "I'll call you in the morning."

"And if you need something," Dominic insisted.

"And if I need something."

Dominic watched him for a moment, before seeming to decide to take Sol at his word, then nodded. "All right. I'll see you tomorrow."

Then Dominic turned on his heel and headed down the street toward the old subway station not even a half a block away that made this location so undesirable to normal people, and so acceptable to people like Sol and J. Sol waited until Dominic had made his way up the steps, then headed through the steel gate that was meant to act as a deterrent to criminals, but was never ever locked. J had tried once, last week, to lock it. The people behind them had just pushed on through as if J hadn't bothered, so clearly it was broken.

Sol flicked the light switch next to the door when he'd finally made it to apartment 507. Nothing happened. Light switches had seemed so novel to him when he'd first gone underground. The lack of automatic motion sensors, or even voice commanded homes seemed a world away from what he was used to. But they'd quickly lost their charm when he realized that meant he had to either buy a lamp, or walk across the bedroom in the dark, trying to avoid stubbing his toe on any of the splintering furniture, when he was getting ready to go to bed.

The bulbs didn't even come on in that dim way that said they were heating up, or running on lower power than usual. No. They stayed stubbornly silent, cold, and dark. Fuck.

"Well, someone didn't pay their bill this month," a smooth voice said from around the corner where the bed was tucked against the singular window in the tiny one room efficiency.

Sol didn't give his father the satisfaction of whipping his head around as if he were surprised that Soren had somehow found where Sol and J were living. He shouldn't have been. Soren had been watching them, or *him* specifically, for years it seemed. And as unsettling as that thought was, Sol was also, regrettably, a little flattered. His father had taken an interest in him, and his work, in some way or another. Whether it was to single Sol out as an enemy or something else, he didn't know. It didn't matter. All that mattered was that *someone* had noticed him, and what he was doing.

"Why are you here, Soren?" Sol asked, moving to sit on the low coffee table that sat across from the end of his and J's bed, all while forcing his breath stay steady and even, which was a challenge given how his heart rabbited in his chest. The one room apartment had just enough space for a kitchenette, a couch, the coffee table, and a bed big enough that J could starfish out on it whenever she so chose. Which was almost every night. It was arguably adorable, but Sol wasn't about to tell her that on pain of death. He set his hands on his knees as he lowered, to rub the sweat from his palms along his slacks.

"Your little friend didn't let me finish back there." Soren huffed out a breath of displeasure as he leaned back onto his hands on the unmade bed. It was weird seeing him there. It set something twitchy and raw off in the center of Sol's chest. He didn't like thinking of Soren in this space. Of his scent lingering on the covers. Sol couldn't smell him, not like J would be able to. But she'd be pissed if she found out that he'd had his dirty ass on her bed.

"Sounded like we were done to me." Sol shrugged disinterestedly. He wasn't sure what Soren thought he'd achieve with all of this, but it didn't matter. Sol had a team. He had an organization that was helping people. He didn't need Soren's... whatever Soren thought he could give him. Still, sweat trickled between his shoulder blades, soaking into his binder as he tried to keep himself in check. The vice grip he had on his control was slipping, but he had to maintain it. He couldn't let Soren see him without it. "Where's J?"

"Oh, don't play coy with me, I invented that act." Soren clicked his tongue and sat up, bracing his elbows on his knees so his face was pressed mere inches from Sol's. "You didn't let me lay out my terms."

"Your terms." Sol barked a laugh, shaking his head as he leaned back a little, stretching his hands up over his head. Nonchalant. That's what Soren had to believe he was, and Sol had always been good at pretending. "I have to say, I'm not interested in your terms, old man. How old are you, anyway? A hundred? Two hundred? Were you around when the war happened?" Sol shot him a cheeky grin, but Soren didn't rise to the bait. Pity.

"Cute." Soren's eye twitched, the only sign that he was

genuinely irritated by Sol's words. "You probably get that snark from me."

"I don't think snark is a trait that's inherited genetically. I think it's a learned behavior."

"A learned behavior of a clever mind," Soren shot back, his eyes lighting up a little with the back and forth. His interest was clearly peaked by the way Sol refused to be cowed by him.

"Mama is arguably very clever. And besides, I'm not sure cleverness is inherited either. IQ maybe, but IQ doesn't always equate to intelligence." Sol tilted his head in thought, before shrugging it off. "Fine. You came to tell me your terms. What are they?"

"You join me, or your little friend is next on the auction block."

Sol's eyes narrowed, his fingers gripping his forearms where he'd folded them behind his head. He had known that was what Soren would say. J was the only bargaining chip he really had. The only thing that could be held against Sol like a blade. Well, maybe not the only thing. But certainly, the only thing Soren could get his hands on. "And you think that's enough to force me to join you?"

"No. No, I don't." Soren laughed a little, shaking his head until his dark hair fell into his eyes the way Sol's so often did when it needed a trim. "But here's the thing, son. Those people out there in the city? They don't give one single fuck about you, and what you're doing. If there was a bounty placed on your head tomorrow, you wouldn't have to wait more than a day for someone to scoop you up and cart you off to the Alliance. They don't care about what you're trying to do for them." Soren stretched his feet out in front of him, crossing them at the ankles. The toes of his very shiny shoes tapped against Sol's own more worn pair. "And it doesn't matter how much they need your help. What it comes down to is that they don't *want* it."

"This isn't about what they want," Sol said, the words false even in his own mouth. Because Soren was right, and Sol knew it. He'd noticed how so much of Mythikos just didn't care. They didn't want to be saved. And who was he to force that on them?

"You're running yourself and your people ragged for a city that just doesn't care." The words landed like a slap to the face, but Sol didn't flinch. He'd known that from the beginning, after all. Or if he hadn't known, he'd realized it quickly enough. "But with me?" Soren smiled a little, holding his hand to his chest. "Things would be different."

"Different how?"

"Well, for one, you wouldn't have to worry about the heroes. I've got them covered. And for two, you could get the recognition you really deserve. I mean, you've done so much for them, Soliel. Given your life for them. Isn't it time they paid you back?"

"Recognition?" Something giddy and bubbly simmered low in Sol's gut. Like when a person drank too much fizzy wine and then tried to do a cartwheel.

"Yes. I think you'd look quite nice on people's screens. The voice of a movement, a real one, not one planned in the dark. What do you think of that?" Soren continued as if Sol hadn't spoken at all.

"What would it cost me?" Sol's toes flexed against the worn-down soles of his shoes. There was always a cost, but if it was low enough...

A smile lit like a spark at one corner of Soren's mouth, and spread like wildfire across his mouth, dimpling both cheeks, but not crinkling his eyes. Like a predator that had just found its prey's favorite hiding spot. "Not much. I'd just want you to keep your nose out of my little... side business."

"So you'd want me to let you continue to harvest Unseelie children like cattle."

"Oh *tut tut*. Harvest. Cattle. These are such ugly words."

"Would you prefer sacrifice and victim?" Sol said the words through his teeth to keep from shouting them with the anger that cut through the champagne bubbles in his stomach.

"Would it make it better for you if it weren't just Unseelie?"

"No it would not!"

"I see." Soren frowned, rising to his feet. "Well, I've been more than generous."

"Have you?"

"Yes. I have." Soren stretched a little, his joints crackling with the movement, as if he were much older than he looked. "You have eight hours to give me your answer. And in the meantime, here." He reached into his pocket and pulled out a phone.

"What is this?"

"I thought you'd like to talk to your little friend. To make sure we haven't done anything... deplorable to Jericho while they've been under our care."

Sol snatched the phone away from him as if it were a lifeline.

"Remember, dear boy. You have eight hours. If I haven't heard from you in that time... Well. It won't be good for you, or Jericho. My number's in there. It's under Pops. I wish you'd call me that." Soren titled his head, his teeth glinting in the yellowed light coming through the windows.

"I'm not going to," Sol said, swallowing around some emotion he didn't quite understand. It wasn't loathing, like it probably should have been. It was something *else*. Something more... twisted.

"You might change your mind." Soren gave a little gesture

as if to say, what're you going to do, then headed for the door. "I'll be seeing you," he called over his shoulder almost like an afterthought. Then he shut the door behind himself, leaving Sol to the emptiness, and the silence, and the soft ticking of his time slipping away. He had eight hours to save J. There was work to be done.

CHAPTER NINETEEN

Eight hours seemed like a lot of time. But it wasn't near enough to orchestrate a successful rescue mission, and Soren had to know that. He had to know that he was giving Sol just enough time to hope, not enough time to plan. Still, Sol wasn't going to let that stop him. He'd gotten by with less.

His fingers twitched over the phone that Soren had given him, his connection to J. To check in, to make sure J was all right. To prove Soren was keeping his word, and had not harmed J. It would have been easy to make the call, and just sit on the phone with J until their eight hours were up. To listen, and make sure that J would still be there when Sol decided whatever he was going to decide. But it also would have been unproductive. And as comforting as J's voice would have been in that moment, Sol didn't have time for it, as he was reminded by the time on the Home Screen of the phone, slowly counting down from eight hours.

7 hrs 50 mins

"Fuck." He'd spent ten minutes staring at the phone trying to make up his mind. To call or not to call. Imagining what J might say...

Sol shook himself. "Now isn't the time."

He slipped the phone into his suit jacket, and went to grab his own from where he'd left it charging on the night stand a few hours, and a world away. When he'd still thought he was in control of this situation. When J had still been at his side. When it seemed like Soren was only two steps ahead of them instead of ten. His thumbs moved quick across the screen, tracking through all the backdoor precautions that Pickle insisted were absolutely necessary, but just seemed like a hindrance when Sol could hear the clock ticking down like it was audible in his ears.

"Whatever you're calling for, no. Just no," Pickle said brusquely. She sounded like she hadn't slept in days, even though she'd sounded just fine earlier. Like she was tired, and needed coffee, and didn't want to talk to anyone else because she'd spent the last 72 hours fielding calls by idiots.

Oh good, she's already heard about the fuck up at the warehouse.

"Soren was here. At my apartment." Sol braced for impact. Because that's all he could really do when delivering the news that their current nemesis knew where he was living, and had given him eight hours to make an impossible choice. Things had gone from bad to worse in such a short amount of time, he was just holding on for the ride.

Pickle's typing stopped, her very breath stilled. That silence on the other side of the line stretched on long enough that Sol wondered if she just wouldn't answer at all. A car buzzed down the street, lights moving across the dark wall in Sol's empty room. "When?"

"When I got back. He just left oh... fifteen minutes ago? I'd say."

Pickle made a noise that sounded like she was breathing out through her teeth, and maybe scrubbing at her face. Never a good sign. "What did he say?"

"He said I have eight hours to make a decision on if I want to join him or not." Sol swallowed around something tight in his throat that made it hard to talk. It would have been easier to sign this conversation. But then Pickle would have also seen whatever his face was doing, which he was sure would have been distressing for both of them.

"And if you don't?"

"It doesn't matter. We're going to get J out before I have to respond. So what do you have for me by way of information?"

"Dusk, what if—"

"I'm not considering any other possibility outside of us finding this son of a bitch, and bringing J home." Sol's words were soft, but firm. He didn't have space in himself to think about any other options. To think about what might happen to J if he didn't agree, and didn't get to her in time. It would only slow him down. "So tell me what you've got on Soren Tsuki."

"We shouldn't rush into—"

"Ildri, with all due respect," Sol said without much respect in his tone at all, "I'm not asking for your advice. I'm asking for information. If I can't get a team together in the next six and a half hours, then I'm going in alone. So you either help me, or you get the fuck out of my way."

"Adelia isn't going to like this," Pickle muttered, but he could hear her typing already. Hopefully pulling up something useful that would lead him to where Soren was keeping J.

"Then don't fucking tell her!"

"Sol," Pickle said, her voice almost pained, and Sol sucked in a breath through his clenched teeth, realizing exactly what he'd just done. He shouldn't have snapped at her. He'd never snapped at her. She didn't deserve that.

"I'm sorry. I'm so sorry, Ildri. I just... I can't—"

"We're going to get J back, Sol." The sound of her fingers flying over her keyboard hadn't ceased, and something about it soothed him. Pickle had always liked things a little more old school, and he was sure the keyboard she used now was a holdover from centuries ago when they were big, clunky things prone to sticking, and losing keycaps. But it was hers. And he'd grown so used to the sound over the years. The reassuring knowledge that so long as Pickle was there, and she had her keyboard, she could make everything okay again.

"Okay." He let out a breath, his shoulders sagging as he dropped onto his bed. "Yeah. Okay."

"I've compiled a list of known locations, and reached out to everyone who isn't working on something. We don't have a lot of people available right now. I'm sending a portion of this list to all of them, and asking them to report back to me with their findings. I'll let you know if anything comes up."

"How many addresses are there to check?" Sol's leg jittered, making the springs in the bed creak unhappily. It was becoming increasingly difficult to sit still. He needed to be doing something. He needed to be *out there*, trying to find J, and bringing her home.

"A lot. But with everyone free working on this, we should be able to check on all of them and mobilize in six hours. Your part of the list is already on its way."

Sol's leg stilled, a surprised noise sticking in the back of his throat.

"Didn't think I'd make you sit this one out, did I?"

"Actually, I did." Sol laughed, standing up so he could put her on speakerphone and get changed. If he was going out looking for J, he needed to be comfortable, and stay hidden. He gravitated toward one of J's sensible black hoodies, tugging it down over his still dyed hair.

"As if me not sending you the addresses would manage to stop you." Pickle snorted. "But Sol, if you find anything, you let me know. You don't go running headlong into trouble. Do you hear me?"

"I will."

Pickle let out a soft, self-deprecating laugh. "Don't lie to me."

"Fine. I'll think about it." Sol huffed, blowing dark hair out of his eyes. "Can I go now?"

"Yeah. You can go. Just be careful, and seriously, call me if anything comes up." Then she hung up without another word, and Sol tucked the phone into his other pocket. It felt weird having two phones on him. They were heavy, making his pants slip like they might slide off his waist if it weren't for the belt.

7 hrs 40 mins

Instead of heading out of the apartment and taking the stairs down, he went up toward the roof. He didn't know if Soren had anyone to watch the place outside, but he had to assume that he did. It was always better to be paranoid than to find out too late that you were being watched. The wind coming in from the forest a few blocks down the road battered against him, but Sol made his way across the roof, and looked down at the dark street.

It was late enough that the world seemed to be sleeping around him. All of Mythikos holding its breath to see what would happen next. But even in the darkness of the hour, there were a couple of people below, making their way through the streets as if they owned them. As if they weren't afraid of the night.

Sol turned to the building next to his, and grabbed the ladder that would lead up to the next roof top. And on. And on. Until he was able to drop down onto the platform of the train station where he'd last seen Dominic. He was panting by then, breath fogging in the chill, late night air, but there was no one to see him. No one to wonder about the man who had dropped out of the sky, not bothering to go through the turnstiles and pay for his passage. Just the electric hum of a train on its way.

He pulled out his phone to check the first address, and nodded to himself. It would be a long few hours, but he was going to find Soren, and he was going to get J back. The train pulled up, mostly empty but for a few half-asleep passengers, and Sol set off to the first address.

3 HRS 43 mins

He'd been to ten addresses, and it felt like he was just playing hunt the McGuffin across all of Mythikos. Like someone was sending him on a wild goose chase to waste his fucking time while the hours ticked away much too quickly. Sol was on edge, and losing it. The sun was shining too brightly, like he was under a spotlight, sweat trickling down the back of his neck from the heat of it. And he didn't know how much more of this he could take. How much longer he could follow his father's trail across the city without any answers, or any sign of J.

There had been no word from Pickle, and Sol got the sinking feeling that no news was bad news in this particular instance. What if they didn't find J in time? What if Soren decided J was more trouble than she was worth? What if—

His phone buzzed in his pocket, and he pulled it out, not even glancing at the screen before answering with a curt, "What?"

"I can't finish my list. I just got called in for a shift at the cafe, and one of us needs to keep some semblance of a normal life." Maz's voice was calm, and direct. Like she was ordering at the deli. Not like she was passing off information on an enemy that could potentially get them all killed, or arrested, or worse. "I'm sending you the files now; you'll have to finish it up yourself. I think I've got five, maybe six addresses left. You think you can do that?"

Sol's jaw ticked a little. "I don't have much choice, do I?"

"Not really." Sol could hear her shrugging on the other side of the line, her jacket making a soft shushing sound. "Look. I know you're desperate to get your puppy back on his lea—"

"Maz." Sol hissed, his fingers tightening on the phone so hard the metal creaked, and the sharp edges dig into the meat of his palms. He was shaking, his muscles straining with the need to physically stop her from talking. "Stop fucking speaking about J that way, or I swear to Merlin, I'm going to come through this phone right fucking now and throttle you with your own fucking tails!" Sol stopped, his neck prickling. He was being watched. He hadn't meant to shout at Maz in the middle of a crowded square, but... he had. And now everyone was staring at him, their mouths hanging slightly open. Heat crawled down his spine, shame coiling in his belly. Fuck.

"So prickly." Maz clicked her tongue, and then he heard the dial tone. But it was almost drowned out by the murmurs of the crowd around him. The soft whispers. The way everyone had stopped, and locked onto him like he was. . . like he was. . .

Sol's eyes caught on an electric sign next to the crosswalk signal. It was brightly lit, even in the daylight hours, and there was his face, staring back at him. Dark hair, dark eyes, glasses. Someone had even put in the effort to show a picture of what he looked like without the disguise.

Fuck. He was a *fugitive*.

His phone rang again. No. Not *his* phone, the other phone. The one that Soren had given him. He stuffed his device into his pocket, taking a moment to tug the black hood up over his head, and tried to slink off with people's eyes still on him. Once he felt like he was reasonably hidden, he answered.

"I told you," Soren's voice murmured smugly in his ear.

"Told me what?" Sweat trickled down Sol's back, the hair on the back of his neck standing on end. They were still watching him.

"How long do you think it'll take for one of them to get up the courage to try to catch you themselves?" Soren asked, not answering his question. "One hour? Two? Doesn't matter really, you've already been spotted. The heroes are on their way."

"Fuck," Sol hissed, ducking into the shadow of an alley as a car buzzed by, siren wailing. He needed to get the fuck out of there. And quick.

"Such language." Soren tsked. "You kiss your mother with that mouth? Oh. Right. She's dead, isn't she?"

"Fuck you." Sol moved deeper into the alley, hoping it would come out on the other side of the block. Or maybe he'd find an open back door to someplace. There was nothing. He'd have to go back out onto the street, and hope no one noticed him. He waited at the mouth of the alley, tucked back into the shadows, watching for when the foot traffic was at its thickest before he stepped into the crowd, keeping his head low so no one could see his face for the hood. "What do you want from me?"

"I told you. I want you to join my organization. And I'll have you one way, or another."

"Don't listen to him, Sol! He's just a stupid fucking—" J's voice was loud, enough that Sol could hear it, but far enough away that he could tell she was shouting to be heard above Soren.

"Shut up, or I'll put a muzzle on you, mutt." Soren

growled, and Sol heard what sounded like a back handed slap across a cheek. The loud smack of skin on skin.

"Why don't you make me you fucking—"

"Put J on," Sol pleaded, suddenly almost desperate for it. Like if he could just talk to J, everything in this fucked up situation would make sense. Like he'd be able to figure it all out.

"Ugh. Fine." Soren sounded like he was rolling his eyes as he pulled the phone away from his face. "He wants to talk to you. And you better behave yourself mutt, or I really will muzzle you."

J snarled, but the sound was close enough to the phone that it rumbled through Sol's ears, and Merlin, it was so beautiful. It felt like it'd been centuries, not just hours, since he'd last heard that.

"Lettie. Lettie." Sol whispered, the word like a prayer, a mantra, a small fragile thing that might break under too much pressure. "Are you all right? Have you eaten? I hope you got some sleep."

"I'm fucking *fine*, Sol. Worry about yourself," J bit out, but Sol could hear the relief in it. The softness that lingered at the edges that no one else had ever been able to hear.

"I'm so glad." Sol was choking on his own air. It got caught somewhere around his chest, lodged next to the bond that had gone silent. "I'm so fucking glad."

J scoffed.

The people around him jostled Sol a little. His fingers tightened around his phone to maintain the connection between himself and J. To hold on, just a little bit longer. "What if he's right?" Sol could hardly breathe the words, but they were there just the same. "What if these people don't deserve my help? What if they don't even *want* it?"

J inhaled sharply through her teeth, and Sol imagined her pulling her lip back from them, giving him that sharp expression that could almost be mistaken for a smile. "You don't actually believe that. Do you?"

"I don't know." Sol shook his head. "You're not here. And I don't know what I believe anymore. I just know—"

"Hey! I wasn't done fucking talking!" J shouted; her voice distant again. Someone had pulled the phone away from her. Their time was up.

"Three hours and twenty-seven minutes, son. I'll text you the address," Soren informed him, tone almost lighthearted. "You meet me there, in three hours and twenty-seven minutes, and give me your decision, or I turn your Lettie into my next beauty treatment. And do come alone, or I'll just slit Jericho's throat, and wash my hands of this whole thing."

Then the line went dead, and Sol was left standing in the middle of a bustling crowd as people shoved, and jostled, and tried to get wherever they thought it was that was so important while his life was slowly caving in on itself. While everything he loved, or cared about moved steadily out of his reach.

Someone bumped into Sol, knocking him off balance, and sending him sprawling into a puddle where someone had dumped their soda. It seeped into his jeans. They didn't apologize. They didn't stop to make sure he was all right. They didn't even turn around to look at him. No one did. They just kept hustling to wherever it was they were going, and Sol realized... *Soren was right*. These people didn't give a rat's ass about him, or each other. Not so long as those around them didn't have power, or money, or prestige. Not so long as they weren't famous, and on every billboard. The only thing that got this herd's attention was wealth.

And Sol thought, *fuck it. If this is how Mythikos burns, fuck it.*

CHAPTER TWENTY

Sol dropped his ringing phone into a bin on the way down the street. Pickle was trying to get in touch with him, she'd probably seen the advertisements with his face plastered all over them. The reward under his name was more than most people in Mythikos could hope to earn in a lifetime, even those who were fae. But he wouldn't need it anymore, the phone, he reasoned. He was done with Eventide. He was done with Dusk. He was done with *Mythikos*.

He still had three hours and fifteen minutes, but there was little point in wandering around checking the addresses Pickle had sent him. He knew where Soren would be, and he knew when he would be there. Sol didn't know if Soren would bring J along, but that didn't really matter either. Because so long as Sol agreed to join up, J would be safe.

A thought niggled at the back of his mind, the voice sounding suspiciously like J. It told him to go to one of their safe-houses, to tuck into their weapons cash, and arm himself to the teeth. It told him to go find J's blades, and come prepared. But Sol brushed it aside. It wouldn't matter if he were armed or not. Soren was going to get his way.

He would join up with the White Rabbit to save J, and maybe in the process finally get the recognition he deserved.

That thought sat sourly on the back of his tongue. Recognition. Acknowledgement. He didn't—he didn't think he *wanted* it, not from this city, not anymore. Especially if it was going to cost him so much.

Soren had taken the signs down, now that he'd made his point, every electronic billboard going back to advertising wrinkle creams, and new restaurants. Sol didn't think he was in danger of being taken in anymore, Soren had called the heroes off, but that didn't change much. He still couldn't afford to be recognized. He wandered listlessly through the streets, keeping his head ducked, avoiding all eye contact. Hoping against hope that the people around him wouldn't recognize them, and if they thought they did they'd just brush it off as coincidence.

Time passed. It dragged against him like the thorns on a rose. Not piercing, but sharp, and scratchy. Until there wasn't much of it left at all, and he knew he needed to make his way to the meeting spot.

47 mins

Sol wiped his sweating palms on his jeans, and ducked through the back door of the old factory. It had been built to make books, or paper, or something, before the world had gone digital, then refurbished into some kind of storage facility full of metal lockers, and garages to hide away the junk that people couldn't fit into their houses, but the smell of paper still hung in the air. The scent of rotten eggs or cabbage, or something just completely foul had seeped into the floors, and the walls, and lingered for decades, maybe even centuries. It would probably never go away. Things like that didn't. Like the apartment where Sol had grown up which had at some point in the last two hundred years belonged to a smoker, and when it rained still smelled of ash and stale tobacco.

"You're early," a voice called over his shoulder.

"Didn't have much else to do. You know, since I'm public enemy number one and all that." Sol titled his head to glance at the man from the corner of his eyes. He didn't have the energy left in him to whip around and glare at the big man who Soren had hired to make sure Sol didn't do anything stupid, like pull a gun. "Is he here?"

"Not yet." The man braced his hands on his hips looking so much like a disgruntled kindergarten teacher whose students had woken up early during nap time that Sol had to choke down a hysterical giggle.

Fuck. When was the last time he'd slept? Really slept? Sol scrubbed at his tired eyes, coughing around the laugh. "No. He seems the punctual sort."

The man made a noise of agreement in the back of his throat.

"Are we just going to stand here out in the open? Or does he have a particular unit he means for me to meet him in?" Sol ran his hands over his hoodie, pushing it back down into place, trying to make himself look at least somewhat presentable. No one wanted to do business with a slob.

The man grunted, jerking his head in a quick *follow me* gesture, and turned down one of the many halls to lead Sol to a storage unit deep within the warehouse. There was a thick lock on the door. Which might have been enough deterrent for someone who was just wandering through, and worried about getting caught. But Sol knew better than to think it was all the protection that Soren had in place.

"Is this where he hides the bodies?" Sol asked, only half as cheekily as he normally would in this kind of situation. It was hard to muster the bravado when he knew he'd been defeated.

The man fixed him with an unimpressed look, and moved to the wall beside the metal garage door to where a lit panel of numbers and symbols popped out of the cement blocks. It hadn't been there before. But now the faint glow of it was enough to sting Sol's eyes in the dark corridor. Several beeps later—twenty maybe thirty, Sol had lost count—the garage door gave a jerky rattle, like someone on the inside had banged their fist against it, but didn't move otherwise.

Sol turned from it to raise a dark brow at the man, but he just gestured to the door again as if Sol should know exactly what to do. He didn't.

With a huff, and an exaggerated roll of his shoulders, the man leaned in and gave Sol a hard shove. Pushing him toward what still seemed to be a solid metal door. Only, as his face got close enough to smash into the cold steel that would surely shatter his nose, the warmth of foreign magic pressed against his face, and he stepped through. Sol stumbled, his steps stuttering as his body tried to adjust from bracing for impact to trying to catch himself from falling off balance and into a potted plant.

He blinked, looking down at the rose bush. The white petals blurred in his vision. Sol took a breath, and forced himself upright to look around. Heat prickled at the back of his neck from the high evening sun beating in through thick glass windows. The air was heavy with pollen, and the dull dirty scent of flowers and topsoil. And everywhere he looked was a neatly trimmed, rose bush. Each laden in enough white roses that Sol, who knew exactly fuck all about gardening, recognized that they must have been maintained by magic of some kind.

"I knew you'd be early," Soren said, drawing Sol's attention to where he stood leaning against the open greenhouse door. He was letting in a soft breeze from the outside, but it did nothing to help Sol's sweating which had started in earnest. "I just didn't think you'd be this early. I haven't even gotten our supper finished."

"I'm not hungry." Sol pulled J's hoodie down over his hands, hoping to hide how they shook. What would Soren do to him now that he was here? Where *was* here? Outside the glass of the walls he couldn't see much more than a sprawling field. Grass, grass, grass and more grass. No trees. No other buildings. Nothing. But that didn't really mean anything. Not when Sol had gotten there by stepping through a garage door in a storage facility.

"Oh don't be silly." Soren moved away from the door, and Sol noted the picnic basket slung over his arm for the first time just as he shut the door behind him, cutting off Sol's view of whatever was outside.

"Where's Lettie?"

"Really, son, is that all you came for?" Soren pouted. Sol tracked his steps from the door to a wrought iron table that sat in the middle of a circle of more rose bushes. "To get your... I'm sorry what is Jericho to you exactly?"

Sol's jaw ached from clenching it so tightly, his teeth grinding together enough to make a squeaking sound. Fury simmered under his skin at the nonchalance. "Where. Is. Lettie."

The white painted wrought iron chair scraped loudly against the stone floor of the greenhouse as Soren pulled it out and sat, the picnic basket taking up residence on the table. "Maybe if you sit down." Soren nodded to the chair across from himself. "I'll tell you."

With stilted steps, Sol moved to the chair, making a point to drag it out as slowly as possible to extend the screeching of the legs on the concrete before he threw himself into it. "Where is Lettie?"

Soren ignored him in favor of unloading a plate of finger sandwiches onto the table.

"Are you not planning to tell me?" His stomach twisted with the thought of it. Maybe J was already gone. Maybe Soren had decided she was more trouble than she was worth, and all this was for naught. Or maybe the moment he'd stepped through that portal, Soren had everything he'd wanted, and had no more use for J.

"Let's share a meal first. You can hear my proposition, and then I might let you see your... significant other."

"I heard your proposition." Sol's hands were clutching at his jeans so hard his nails dug in through the fabric. Every word he was about to say crowded into his mouth, choking him with the weight of them, but what else could he do? "And I accept."

Soren stopped, his arm elbow deep in the basket, on the way to pulling out something else, maybe another plate of obnoxiously small sandwiches. J would have hated that. She always said food was not meant to be made in miniature. "You accept?"

"I accept." Sol chewed on the inside of his cheek hard enough that he knew a sore would form later. He wanted to tell Soren that he didn't think he'd been given much choice.

"What changed your mind?" Soren asked, almost pleasantly, extracting his arm from the picnic basket and leaning back in his seat, one knee crossing over the other. Relaxed.

Sol frowned, meeting Soren's gaze across the table. He wasn't going to answer that question. Not with words anyhow. Because Soren wasn't an idiot. He knew what it was that had changed his mind. He knew that Sol had been left with few other options. Not viable ones, anyway. He'd painted Sol into a corner.

"Oh who cares what it was?" Soren laughed, clapping his hands delightedly. "The point is you've accepted!"

"Good. Now can I see Lettie?"

"Later. Later." Soren flapped his hand, making to stand. "For now, let me show you around."

"Show me around where?" Sol stood too, following Soren to the door of the greenhouse again. A quick sweep of the space told him that there were no other doors, and nowhere for Soren to be hiding any prisoners.

"Wonderland."

Sol snorted, rolling his eyes, before muttering, "Can we stop the *Alice in Wonderland* metaphors? They're getting fucking old."

Soren took no notice of it, pressing his hand to the doorknob and holding it there for a moment before he pushed through into a wide open kitchen space, which rivaled even Reboot and Pickle's, where he deposited the basket. His heels clicked softly against the hardwood floors as he led Sol deeper into the house, and back to what looked to be an office.

"This is where you'll work," Soren said, pulling out the leather wheelie chair, and gesturing for Sol to come sit in it.

Sol stayed by the door, leaning against the doorframe. "And what will I do?"

"As my son, you'll be our front man. The face of my organization, of course. The heir to all of this." Soren smiled, gesturing around himself to the big house with the kitchen that was too large for one man, and the office that was decorated too regally for someone who wasn't much more than a criminal.

"And you can't do that... why?"

"Because I have other things to tend to. I need someone to deal with the politics of it all. The parties, and the socializing. You're good with people. I've seen how charismatic you can be, when you want to. You'll be the one to set the people of this city at ease."

"You said you'd help me—" Sol took a breath, forcing his

posture to relax. "You said you'd help me set things right. That we'd help people. So long as I let you keep running your... operation, behind the scenes."

"And I will! Whatever you want. I heard last year there was a bill you were trying to get passed, something about equal rights for Unseelie fae? You can do that with my connections. You can step out of the shadows. Don't you want that?" Soren held out a hand, palm up. An offering. A promise. A deal. All in one.

Sol did. He wanted it so bad his very marrow ached with the want of it. To be the face of a movement. To not be reviled, and hated, and seen as a criminal. To *matter*.

But at what cost? A voice that sounded oddly like J's asked from somewhere in the back of his mind.

What will you sacrifice for your movement? Another that sounded like his mother asked.

The answer was *anything*. Sol swallowed down a scream that threatened to crawl up his throat at the realization. He really *was* his father's son, wasn't he?

"Yes. That's what I want." Sol nodded.

"Good." Soren's face split in that Cheshire Cat grin again. "Then let's get to work."

CHAPTER TWENTY-ONE

GETTING TO WORK, AS SOREN HAD PUT IT, REQUIRED A LOT more new clothes than Sol would have thought it should. Soren hadn't waited an hour before he pushed Sol into a fitting for a new suit, and pair of dress shoes. Which was fine, Sol told himself. It was fine to abandon the hoodie that J had left behind. It was fine to abandon Dusk, and the 'villain costume' that he'd so carefully crafted. It was fine to move on.

Sol ran his fingers over the suit jacket. It had pinstripes which were appalling. Though maybe not as appalling as the fact that it was black. Just plain, black and grey. No ornamentation. No color. Not even a pocket square.

"The fabrics are what set it apart," Soren said with a shrug. "You don't need loud colors if you've got the right fabrics."

Sol stuffed his hands into his pockets to hide the twitching of his fingers. There were words lingering at the tips. And he needed to keep himself from saying them. From telling Soren to go fuck himself. From telling Soren that he didn't get to decide what Sol *needed*. Because that wasn't true, was it? Soren did get to decide, and he'd chosen this. "When will I get to see Lettie?"

"Later. Later. First, I have a meeting set up for you."

Sol wondered, not for the first time, how long Soren would continue to say, 'Later. Later.' How many more ways Soren would brush him off before he actually allowed Sol to see J and ensure that they were all right. There had been a call, right after Sol had agreed to join Soren, just a quick thing, which had seemed more like Soren bragging than him letting Sol check in on J. Just to prove that J was still alive, to keep Sol in line, he supposed.

"With whom?" Sol asked, his eyes jerking to watch the way Soren's line-less face moved. He didn't even have smile lines. Who didn't have smile lines?

"Just an old friend. You'll like them, trust me." Soren gave a little shrug. "Finish getting yourself ready. They'll be here soon. I'll meet you in your office."

Your office, Soren said, like Sol was already a staple. Like after a single day he'd risen in the ranks high enough to even warrant such a thing.

Then he was gone, disappearing through the door like a ghost, leaving Sol to stare at himself in the mirror. He didn't even look like himself. He'd asked if he could wash the dye out of his hair, remove the makeup, but Soren had said no. He needed to look normal. He needed to look *human*.

There wasn't much more to do with his appearance. Sol wasn't like J, he didn't have war paint, and he didn't ever do anything with his hair. So he finger combed it a couple of times, to make it at least not stick up just at the end of his part where his cowlick was. He fiddled for a moment with his hearing aid, hoping it would help him to hear what was going on elsewhere in the house, but the walls were too thick, and everything came to him muffled.

"Damn it." Sol ran his fingers through his hair again,

letting out a shaky breath. There was nothing for it. He'd just have to go and see who Soren's mysterious friend was. He made his way down the hall, stepping carefully so that the wooden floors wouldn't give him away. Hoping that he might catch a snippet of whatever they were talking about without Sol in the room. But just as he got within earshot, his shoe squeaked loudly, the toe catching on the floor.

"Ah, Soliel, come in," Soren called from the other side of the door.

Inside the office sat an older man, human, like Soren. His hair greying at the temples, and wrinkles lining his face. Not a face Sol recognized, which was surprising. Sol thought he knew everyone who was anyone in Mythikos.

"Soliel, this is Councilman Lennox." Soren gestured, and waited as Lennox held his hand out to Sol.

"Nice to meet you," Sol said automatically, taking the man's hand and giving it a shake.

"You look surprised." Lennox tilted his head, a look of amusement playing along the lines of his face.

"I thought I knew all of the members of the Council." Sol shifted back, dropping the man's hand, and leaning against the corner of the desk opposite him. There was a chair free, but he didn't think he wanted to sit in it. He liked having the extra height.

"Yes, I'm sure you did. But the human council members don't get quite as much press as the others." Lennox's words held none of the usual bitterness that accompanied such a statement. "Why do you think that is?"

Sol had some ideas as to why, but the question seemed rhetorical, and the man shrugged it off a second later and continued.

"Your father tells me that you have some changes you want to see made in the council. I'm here to help you get that done."

"Why would you help me?" Sol narrowed his eyes, letting them flick down over the man's expensively tailored suit, and his face that would have been kindly if he were not sitting in Soren's home. Sol saw Soren stiffen out of the corner of his eye, but Sol wasn't worried about him. He needed to know what Lennox's agenda was.

"Because I owe your father a favor." Lennox waved his hand as if the matter was simple as that.

Later, after Lennox had gone, and Soren and Sol were alone again, Soren rounded on him, brown eyes cold. His fingers wrapped so tightly around Sol's upper arm that they pinched.

"The next time I introduce you to one of my friends, you'll behave yourself," Soren hissed through his teeth, his face hard and dangerous. "Your job is to charm them, not to interrogate them. Are we clear?"

"Yes." Sol yanked his arm free, and headed back to his room, his skin burning from the bruising grip. Once there, he let himself breathe. He let himself assess what had happened. He was being provided an opportunity, a chance to change things. He needed to take that more seriously.

That's how it went over the next couple of weeks. Soren would bring someone around to the house, and Sol would charm them into doing whatever it was Sol wanted. He talked to politicians. To businesspeople. To officials. To anyone and everyone that could further his cause. He thought maybe it was working. Maybe he was putting a dent in the inequality that had been ever present in their city since long before he'd been born.

But he didn't leave the house, and the communicator on

his hearing aids didn't work within its walls, so there was no way to contact anyone outside. No phone. No magic. Nothing. He reasoned with himself. Told himself that that was all right. That leaving his team, his family, without a word was an acceptable loss in the face of all the good he was doing.

He asked to see J every day. And every day Soren said 'later, later', or 'maybe tomorrow', or 'soon'. And every time it sounded less and less like the truth, and more and more like a lie. But that was all right. The ache of missing J was all right. Because he was doing so much good. Wasn't he?

At least he thought he was. Until he came face to face with Oakfur for the first time in weeks. The man looked wrung out. Dark circles smudged beneath his eyes. His face had gone sallow, making his red hair look almost orange in the soft lights of the house. One of Soren's many henchmen stood on either side of him, forcing him down the hall as Sol made his way downstairs. They headed to a door just off the kitchen that Sol hadn't noticed before. When the door shut behind them, his gaze slid off of it. Whatever magic Soren was using to keep it hidden made it hard to focus even when Sol knew it was there.

That night, when Soren had finally gone to bed, and the house was quiet, Sol crept from his room. The first week or two that he'd been there Soren had kept a close eye on him. His room was guarded every evening. But eventually Soren had begun to trust him. Or maybe not trust him, but at least realize that whatever game Soren was playing, Sol was playing it with him, and playing by his rules. Or perhaps it was just the threat of violence against J hanging over his head that Soren thought would keep him in line. Sol didn't know, and he didn't care. The point was that Soren had loosened his hold on Sol, and Sol was largely left to his own devices once whatever business he'd been tasked with for the day was finished.

Quiet had settled over the house. Leaving room for Sol to move. To breathe. He slipped on socked feet down the stairs of the sprawling manor house, and into the kitchen. It took him a while, standing there in the dark, squinting at the wall to get his eyes to focus on the place where the door was, but eventually he found it. There was no lock. No code panel. Nothing. Just the door, and the metal doorknob. Like Soren didn't think Sol would even find out it existed, much less decide he wanted to enter.

The knob was cold in his hand, and Sol waited there in the dark, his heart pounding so hard he could feel it where his hand was wrapped around the metal. He held his breath, listening for a sound, movement, some indication that Soren or one of the henchmen was around. Some sign that he was about to be caught. A silent alarm to let Soren know that Sol was somewhere he wasn't supposed to be.

When none of those sounds came, Sol turned the knob and was surprised to find it unlocked. The hinges didn't make any noise as he pushed it open to reveal a set of barely lit stairs that led down into some kind of basement, or sublevel.

Sol peered down into the darkness, and then looked over his shoulder to make sure no one had entered the kitchen while he'd been inspecting the stairs. With no signs of anyone else, Sol forced his legs to move. One step, and then another, and another, until he was at the bottom of a long winding staircase that didn't seem to fit the structure of the house, standing in front of another door. This one didn't even have a handle or knob, just a sheet of metal to indicate that a person should push to enter.

So Sol did.

The lights ticked on as soon as he was in the room. A soft hum of electricity filled the silence that had surrounded him. There was nothing. It was just a room with a big sheet of glass on one wall that looked like a two-way mirror from those old cop dramas. But as he watched, Sol noticed movement on the other side, and his heart stuttered in his chest.

He stepped closer, pressing his face into the glass, cupping his hands around his eyes, and a scream lodged in his throat. A scream that maybe had been living there since he'd come to stay with Soren weeks ago.

The glass, it seemed, overlooked another room, or a warehouse, rather. And in that warehouse, from where he stood up above, he could see smaller rooms cut out in boxes, like movie sets viewed from the ceiling. No. Not rooms. *Cells.* Because every single one of them held a prisoner. Some poor soul that Soren had snatched and was draining the life out of.

He pushed against the glass, and the view shifted, showing the inside of one of the cells, perhaps the last view that had been shown. And there on a tiny daybed, her too-thin shoulders barely moving laid a little red-haired girl. Her fingers were curled tightly around a teddy bear, and an older woman sat in a chair off to one side of the bed, slumped over in sleep.

It was hard to see from the strange angle, but the hair, and the freckles, and the way Sol had seen them bring Oakfur down there left only one conclusion. This was Oakfur's daughter. The little girl he'd begged Sol to help, and Sol... *Fuck.* He'd failed her! Sol stepped back, stumbling over the long silk pajama pants Soren insisted he wear, and then he saw a face in the mirror. A reflection over his shoulder.

"I didn't think you'd find this place so soon." Soren's eyes had narrowed, gone cold and calculating as he assessed Sol. What he was looking for, Sol wasn't sure, but he did know he didn't want Soren to guess at the sickening twist of his stomach, or the hard beat of his heart in his chest.

"Where are they?" The question came out unsteady, Sol's

fingers moving along to the words even though he knew Soren couldn't sign. It didn't matter.

"They're fine. They're safe, and happy," Soren said flippantly.

"They don't look safe or happy." Something cold was settling into Sol's stomach. Something like dread. He had agreed to this, hadn't he? He'd agreed to ignore Soren's shady dealings in favor of furthering his cause. That had been the deal. But that was when he'd thought there were ten or twenty lives at stake. Before he'd known about the prison Soren had... somewhere, of literally hundreds of Fae that he was draining for their magic.

"Safe and happy are all relative, son."

"I can't do this anymore." Sol shook his head, his hair falling into his eyes. "I can't be a part of this."

"But look at all the good you're doing." A smile slashed across Soren's face like a wound. Cutting and sharp enough that it pressed cold against on his skin from several feet away.

"What good?" Sol bit back. "What *good* have I done?"

"We're changing the world, together." Soren held out his hand again, just like he had that day, all those weeks ago. But it wasn't an offer anymore, it was a command, a threat.

"No. *No*, you can't make me stay. You can't fool me again!"

"If you leave," Soren said, voice suddenly as icy as the press of that knife-wound smile, "I'll kill Jericho." He nodded to the mirror behind Sol, and Sol turned to watch the image shift again. To show J sitting with their back to a wall in one of those cells. Their eyes were blood shot, and red rimmed, but they didn't look like they'd sleep, their eyes peeled back almost forcibly to keep them awake. They waited and watched as their fingers twitched. "You're bonded, aren't you?" Soren asked, his eye lingering on the bite scar on Sol's neck. The one that had saved his life, and tied him to the person who mattered most to him not so long ago. "What do you think will happen to you when Jericho dies?"

"You wouldn't." But he knew better. He *knew*. Because it had always been 'later, later'. 'Tomorrow'. 'Soon'. Never now. Never when Sol was clearly drowning. The realization shouldn't have been a surprise. The surprise should probably have *hurt* more than it did. But Sol realized, Soren wouldn't ever give a fuck about him, or his goals to help the Unseelie. And he wasn't ever planning to give J back either.

"Do you want to test that theory?"

Sol swallowed, his eyes not leaving that image of J, curled up in the corner. There was a perfectly good bed they could be resting on, sleeping. But they weren't. They were sitting in the corner, watching the room like at any moment a boogeyman might pop out of the closet. Sol shook his head. He didn't want to test it.

"Good. Then go back to your room. We'll talk about this in the morning."

Sol nodded, his face almost close enough to the glass that he could press his forehead against it. His shoulders slumped before he turned, and started back to the stairs.

"And, Soliel?" Soren called, as if it were an afterthought.

"Hm?"

"I think I'd like it if you started calling me Father."

Sol's stomach gave a violent twist. He breathed through his nose, struggling to keep what little food he'd had at dinner down as Soren's voice echoed in his head.

I think I'd like it if you started calling me Father.

Sol reached the dimly lit stairs in five quick strides, and then he was running up them, his lungs burning.

CHAPTER TWENTY-TWO

Isolated. Alone. Behind enemy lines. That's what he was. And he'd done it to himself, he realized. It had been a trap, of course, not a particularly ingenious one, and Sol had walked right into it thinking he could outwit and outmatch someone who had been doing this for decades longer than he had.

His throat ached with dryness from running. His knees still weak with the aftershocks of the confrontation. Ears buzzing with the words Soren had said. Sol's back hit the door, and he slumped against it, letting his weight slide all the way down to the floor where he curled his knees to his chest. He reached up to pull his hearing aids from his ears, letting them drop to the floor. Soren hadn't taken them away and provided him an "approved" set, not like the heroes had, but they were useless in his compound. Sol couldn't get a signal out the few times that he'd been able to try. And after dealing with the static for a couple of days, he'd turned off the communication feature all together.

"What're you going to do, Soliel?" The words came out

mumbled, and muddied, like he was hearing them through a thick door.

Nothing. You're not going to do anything. You're useless. You thought you could come in here, and play his game, and win. You egotistical fucking moron. Who do you think you are?

He sat there for a long time, his head ducked into his knees, his knees pulled so close to his chest that it was almost hard to breathe through the pressure. His own voice ran through his head so fast and so angry that he could hear nothing else. The moonlight streaming in through his window shifted across the floor as the night wore on. Minutes ticking away into hours.

When Sol finally had control again, he was able to think through the constant berating of his own voice, to silence it in favor of counting his breaths.

In. One. Two. Three. Out. One. Two. Three. In. One. Two. Three. Out—

"Well, if I can't beat him at his own game," Sol signed to himself, the words slow but growing in confidence, "Then I'll just have to change the game."

He stood, stretching his legs out, forcing the blood back into them to quell any lingering trembling, and bent to pick up his hearing aids.

SOL'S office was as strangely unfamiliar to him as it had been on that first day. He had allowed himself in the weeks in between to grow accustomed to doing business the way Soren wanted him to. To meeting the people Soren thought were important. To playing by Soren's rules. But the fact of the matter was that Sol had never really had an office before.

He had had labs. He had had hideouts. He had had spaces that he called his own. But they were always temporary. They were always one button click away from going up in smoke when the wrong person came through the door.

The four walls covered in thick leather-bound books. The heavy wooden desk. The high back wheelie chair. These were all permanent. They were things that might go up in flames if Sol held a match to them, but it would take time, and there would be something to salvage in the end. There was never anything to salvage when Sol left one of his own places behind. Nothing to link him to where he'd been. But there was also so much of Soren left in this office. So much of Soren linked to this whole fucking house. That would be his downfall, Sol was sure of it.

His knuckles rapped on Soren's office door. It was across the hall from Sol's, and while Sol's reminded him of an old man's study straight out of a period film, Soren's was all minimalist modernity. Sleek monochrome furniture. No books. Just a big monitor on the desk, and three chairs. One behind the desk, and two in front.

"Enter," Soren said, not even looking up from whatever he was working on. Sol could see a bird's eye view of his own office in the reflection on the window behind Soren, but it flickered, then was gone. Not a mistake, Sol knew, from the look Soren leveled at him when he drew his eyes away from the screen. Soren wanted Sol to know that he was watching him. That every movement he made within the house would be carefully monitored and judged. Sol wasn't stupid, he'd always known that; this was a threat as much as Soren's words last night had been. "Can I help you with something, son?"

Son. The word grated against his ears, making Sol's eardrums almost ache. But aside from a tightening of his jaw, he allowed no outward sign of his discomfort to show. He couldn't appear weak. Not now.

"I have some suggestions for contacts I'd like to speak with this week." Sol tucked his hands into his pockets, his shoulders relaxing down a fraction more, his chin lifting a little.

"Oh?" Soren's hands folded in front of him on the desk, his eyes narrowing in interest. "And who did you have in mind?"

"We're trying to ensure equality between the fae, correct?" This was a gambit, a gamble, and Sol knew it. It could all blow up in his face and go horribly, horribly wrong. But he'd tried playing it safe, and it wasn't working. He'd been foolish to think that he could work within Soren's parameters and get what he wanted. That he could outwit Soren using his own rules on his own territory.

"Yes. That is what you're aiming for." Soren's face pulled into a small smile. Like he didn't quite buy into whatever Sol was playing at, but he was going to let Sol try it.

"Well, we can change the laws all we want, but we need to make sure the ones who are enforcing them are willing to uphold those new laws. And look at people differently than they have been. So I'd like to work with some Hero Alliance officials to create some kind of sensitivity training. I'll need to talk to a couple of captains, to see what they think would work best for their people."

"Of course." Soren nodded.

"I know you have ties to that leprechaun who used to be Lettie's captain. The one you sent the files through. Maybe he'd be a good place to start?"

Soren leaned back in his chair, his head tilting a little as if he were trying to sort out where Sol was going with this. He might know that Oakfur had told Sol about his daughter, Sol realized. He might know that Oakfur had said that Sol was the only one who could stop Soren. Or. He might not. Sol just had to hope it was the latter. He had to hope that Soren didn't realize that the power he held over Oakfur didn't make him loyal, it made him scared, and that fear could be used by someone else. Someone like Sol.

Sol's knees locked up as he forced himself to remain still under Soren's considering stare. Soren was looking for some hint of what Sol was planning. He was looking for some reason why he should deny Sol this. Maybe he was even giving some thought to just getting rid of Sol all together. But he wasn't saying anything. The cold of his stare lingered on Sol's face like a brand. Sol swallowed around bile, knowing exactly what he was going to have to do. He didn't like it. But he wasn't being provided options, and he was the only one who could.

"Please, Father," Sol said, his voice somehow coming out steady past the violent urge to vomit. "I want to continue to do good in the world." The words were hollow in his chest. All he could hope was that they didn't sound that way to Soren.

Soren was still looking at him with narrowed brown eyes, the expression so similar to one that Sol had seen in the mirror, it was a little terrifying. But Sol waited, palms coated in sweat where he hid them in his pockets, eyes never wavering from that searching expression. Soren didn't trust him, and that was fine. He didn't need to. So long as Sol got what he wanted out of this.

"*Please*, Father." He was going to throw up if he had to say it again. Soren wouldn't need to know what was going on inside of Sol because it would all come out, splattered across the white granite floors. Soren was testing him; it was clear in the tension between them. Wanting to know how long Sol would keep up the act before he broke character. Before he showed Soren the man beneath the subservient son he was wearing as a mask.

"Oh, all right." Soren laughed, leaning forward a little to brace his elbows on the desk. There was something keen in his eyes—suspicion, very likely—but Sol wasn't going to look a gift horse in the mouth. "If that's what you really want."

"It is." Sol forced himself to swallow the long, relieved breath that threatened to spill out of him.

"Very well then. I'll set up a meeting with Oakfur in the next couple of days, how does that sound?"

"Perfect." Sol bowed his head in faux respect, and turned to leave Soren's office.

"Son," Soren called just as Sol reached the door, pulling him to a stop. "Aren't you going to thank me?"

Sol breathed in deeply through his nose, forcing down the swell of bile that rose to choke off his breath. "Thank you, Father."

The door shut behind him, but not before there was a soft, pleased hum from Soren just over Sol's shoulder. Like he'd scored a victory. Like he'd mastered Sol in a way. It made shame prick hot and sweaty at the back of Sol's neck, but he refused to turn around. To rise to the bait. He breathed, in through his nose, out through his mouth, focusing on holding back the nausea that ripped through him like a virus.

When he was finally back in his own office, he pressed his hands into the top of his desk to get them to stop shaking, leaving little puddles behind on the wood where they'd been sweating. It took a few minutes, but once Sol found control again, he stood up, straightening his suit jacket, and set to work.

He didn't have long before his meeting to find where Soren had the cameras hidden, and he couldn't be too obvious about it. So instead of looking up at the ceiling in search of them, like some novice, Sol moved to the bookshelf and started picking through the titles on their spines. He took his time, pulling a couple of books here and there, pretending to read the table of contents, or the first page before putting them back.

The camera was hidden among the tomes. Tucked up in one corner of a shelf that could give Soren the perfect view of anyone sitting behind the desk. It was so small that if Sol hadn't been looking for it, he would have missed it and the listening device stuck beside it on the spine of a book that he was sure wasn't actually a book.

That's one.

But there had to be others. He wasn't foolish enough to think that Soren would simply rely on one camera, so he kept going. It took hours. Long past lunch time, and well on to when he was expected downstairs for supper. There was a soft knock at the door, and one of the burly men who usually escorted people in and out of the house, or stood guard at doors, ducked in, his shoulders hunched like he could make himself smaller than he was just by doing so.

"Your father said you were hard at work. So I thought I'd bring your dinner to you," he said, voice soft.

"Thank you. Just sit it on the desk." Sol waved over his shoulder, his eyes narrowing as he looked through the books on the right side of the door. Would Soren reuse the same trick? Or would he hide the other cameras somewhere else?

The tray settled onto the table with a soft sound, but the man didn't leave right away. The hair on the back of Sol's neck prickled with his gaze. Sol had ducked his head over one of the books. It was a law book. On the new world order put into place after the wars. Riveting stuff. All complete hogwash, as far as he was concerned. But fiction was always interesting.

"Can I help you with something?" Sol asked, not lifting his eyes from the book.

"I just—" The man stopped himself, his shadow shifting nervously out of the corner of Sol's eye. "I think you might find the section on technological fae theory really interesting."

Sol stilled, his shoulders growing rigged. Was he—was he saying what Sol thought he was saying? "I'll take that under advisement."

"You do that." The man's clothes made a soft shushing sound as he nodded. "My uh. . . My name's Hugo. I have. . . I have. . ." He stopped, taking a long inhale as if to calm his breathing. "I have a little brother who reminds me a lot of you. He's really into that stuff."

Sol shifted so he could look at Hugo just over his shoulder, watching the way Hugo's pale hazel eyes jerked about uncertainly. His brown face had gone a little ashen with whatever discomfort lay in his tone. And he had his hands tucked into the pockets of his slacks so deep Sol was surprised they didn't rip. But those weren't the things that told Sol what he needed to know. No. What told him what he needed to know was the patch of green scales that was almost hidden by Hugo's collar. The sharp fang that peeked out just a little when his mouth was closed.

"You're a basilisk, aren't you?" Sol asked, almost conversationally.

"Yes, sir, I am." Hugo bit down on his lower lip with the fang. Sol could see it cutting in, drawing a pinprick of blood.

"I see." Sol studied him for a long moment, trying to decipher his motives. "How old is your brother?"

"Eighteen." Hugo met Sol's gaze, held it, almost pleading. He wanted to say something else, Sol could see it. He inhaled like he was going to. Like he'd spill all his secrets at Sol's feet.

Then his eyes shifted to a space just over Sol's shoulder, and he stopped himself.

"I'll look into those books you suggested," Sol said, hoping he heard the promise in it.

"You do that." Hugo nodded. Then he was gone, leaving Sol to comb through the rest of his office, finding another camera just where Hugo had mentioned.

CHAPTER TWENTY-THREE

HE COULDN'T REARRANGE THE FURNITURE, SOL REALIZED, with a grumble. It would most certainly make things less complicated if he could, but he couldn't. Not without drawing attention to the fact that he was using this meeting to gain allies within the compound. What he could do, was figure out the line of sight each of the cameras afforded Soren back in his office—and whoever else was watching the footage, wherever else they were. So he took his time, lingering at the top of the ladder, flipping through pages in books that held little interest, and trying to figure out how to situate himself and Oakfur to best conceal what they were doing.

By the time Oakfur did arrive—three days later, not the expected two—Sol had worked out a plan of sorts. It wasn't perfect, but it was something. And in reality, nothing about the situation was perfect. Soren had gone back to having a guard posted on Sol at all times, so he hadn't been able to escape to the basement again to check on the prisoners, or try to figure out how to get to them. There had been no more meetings with any officials in the meantime. And any tools

Sol might have used to try to alter the communicators in his hearing aids had suddenly disappeared. Soren was no fool. He knew Sol was planning something. And while he seemed content to let it play out, he certainly wasn't going to make it any easier on Sol than he had to. The only bright spot was Hugo. He hadn't said anymore to Sol, but he met Sol's eyes every time they passed in the hall with a look of intent. Sol's first real ally within the walls of his prison.

"Do I need to be here to make introductions, son?" Soren asked, his shoulder leaning against the door to Sol's office. Sol really wished he'd stop calling him son, but he knew what Soren was trying to do. He was going to keep doing it, looking for little tells every time, until Sol broke under the pressure. Sol wasn't at all impressed by the tactic. Soren could do better. It mostly came off as petty.

"No, Father," Sol said through his teeth. "I think I can handle it."

"Very well. I'll be just across the hall if you need anything." As if Sol needed to be told. He could see Soren from his own desk, the light of his huge monitor reflected on his dull brown eyes, a constant reminder that Sol was under observation. That if he stepped a toe out of line, Soren would see it, and he'd wind up wherever the prisoners were, used, and sucked dry for the magic that hummed through him.

Maybe that would be better, he reasoned. *Then at least I'd know where they were.* But it wouldn't solve anything. It wouldn't get Oakfur's daughter, Hugo's brother, and Sol's Lettie back to them. And that's all he cared about now. If he couldn't save everyone in Mythikos. If he couldn't get his recognition that way. At least he could get it from the families and loved ones of the people who Soren intended to auction off. Get those people back home, and put a stop to Soren's tom-fuckery. Then he'd... well he supposed he'd fade back into obscurity.

A knock pulled Sol from those thoughts, dragging him back to the surface, and he smiled a little, standing from his desk. "Oakfur, nice to see you again."

Oakfur looked tired. More so than the last time Sol had seen him. The dark smudges under his eyes had turned into true bags now, dragging down against his cheeks, and making him look like he'd aged a decade in the days since. His hair was unbrushed, and his suit was unpressed. But he had made the effort to at least put one on, to try to look respectable. "Yeah. Nice."

"Come in and have a seat." Sol walked around the corner of his desk, gesturing to the chairs. He sat down in one, carefully placing himself on the edge so he could curl his shoulders around himself. He may not be able to hide all his movements, but it would be enough to obscure what he was planning. Soren had never used sign language with Sol, but that didn't mean he didn't understand it, and that was not a gamble Sol was willing to take.

Oakfur settled across from him with a wince, like he had bruised ribs—something Sol had seen enough times on J to recognize—and then slouched a little himself, seeming to mirror Sol's body language. "You wanted to talk about setting up a sensitivity program for dealing with Unseelie?"

"I did." Sol ducked his head to direct Oakfur's attention to his hands. His movements were quick, and perfunctory, if this didn't work, he didn't know what else he'd do. "Do you sign?"

Oakfur's eyes widened, his red mustache twitching a little as his jaw seemed to come loose. But he pursed his lips to keep from gasping.

"So what are your plans?" Oakfur asked out loud, but his hands moved slowly as if he were unused to forming words with them, and said, "Only a little."

"Well, I was thinking we obviously need to change not

only the way Unseelie are treated by our heroes, but also how they're seen. Maybe if they aren't seen as villains they won't be treated as such." Sol had memorized this speech. He could give it forwards, backwards, and in his sleep. He needed to be able to if he was going to hold two conversations at once. He'd have to keep his sentences simple, stick to common words. With a flick of his wrists, his fingers danced over the words, "We'll work with what we've got."

Oakfur nodded along, his face set into an expression of mild interest, but Sol could see the way he was following the motions he was making down at the level of his stomach. Hopefully away from prying eyes.

"I mean of course the source of the problem is the education system. Children in Mythikos are taught from a young age to see Unseelie as evil thanks to the history books. And then there's the media. But we're already working to deal with that." Sol kept his tone light, and casual, like he wasn't worried at all that he could make the changes he wanted to make. Like the conversation underneath it all wasn't dangerous, and likely to get them both killed. "They have Lettie."

"Of course." Oakfur let his head move up and down slowly as if he was following along with every word. Attention rapt on Sol who was pulling on his most charming smile. "How long?"

"So I suppose what we'll need to do is set them up with some Unseelie buddies. Not partners, I know that. But what if we put them in touch with one of the youth programs? Let them see some Unseelie who have never hurt anyone, who just need a little guidance. Then they could help each other, right?" Sol was starting to sweat. A long trickle went down his spine. "A little over a month."

"Yes, I…" Oakfur struggled, his eyes skittering around the room, his fingers moving sluggishly. "How long have you been here?" he signed before he closed his eyes tight to think, and say out loud, "I think that might work. I'll have to get in touch with some people at one of the youth programs. Maybe you know someone I can contact?"

"As it happens," Sol smiled, grateful for the opening, but the expression was tight on his face, like that one time he and J had tried mud masks, and they'd left them on too long as his fingers flew over the words, "just as long." He took note of the soft gasp from Oakfur, and pressed on to say out loud, "I have an old acquaintance that runs a soup kitchen. His name is Fizz. I can get you his address."

"I'd like that." Oakfur shifted in his seat, crossing one leg under the other so he could tuck his hands in between the spread of his suit jacket to ask, "What's your plan?"

"Wonderful. I'm sure he'll be happy to hear from you." Soren wouldn't find anything on Fizz. They'd kept him out of their operations at Eventide. All he ever did was provide a safe harbor for people who needed it, run errands, and collect weapons... of course. But Sol doubted Soren would understand what it meant that Sol was sending Oakfur his way. And even if he did, Sol was willing to gamble that Soren would sit back and watch, thinking he had it all under control. Besides, Fizz wasn't really who Sol wanted Oakfur to talk to. His fingers moved slowly, to make sure Oakfur understood the name he was about to sign. "I need you to speak with Ildri."

Oakfur's brows twitched upward for a moment, before he schooled his features. He bit his lip as if he wanted to ask some question out loud. Sol almost felt bad about blowing Ildri's cover at the alliance, but there wasn't time to worry about that, not now.

"Next on the agenda," Sol pressed on, covering for Oakfur's stumble, "I think will be ensuring adequate consequences for those who show discrimination. That's only fair, isn't it?"

"Definitely fair." The words came out a little choked, but Oakfur signed back, "What should I tell her?"

"I'd like you to go back to your superiors and discuss this with them. I'm sure between the lot of us we can come up with adequate punishments that would deter such behavioral problems. Don't you?" Sol titled his head, his cheeky smile back in place, dimpling his cheek. "Tell her where I am. Tell her I'll be in touch with her. Soon."

"Right. I'm sure. When should we get started?" Oakfur's fingers were twitching, and Sol could see a sheen of sweat on his palms. The nerves getting the better of him.

"As soon as possible, I'd say." Sol let out a breath, his shoulders relaxing further forward, and his movements small, "we're going to get your daughter back."

Relief washed over Oakfur so visibly that Sol turned his ear to the hall, to listen for Soren's door. To make sure Soren hadn't caught on and come across to demand answers right that very moment. "Thank you," Oakfur said aloud, on a breath.

"Of course. I'll get you that address." Sol reached over to his desk to grab a pen, and a piece of paper. He quickly scribbled down the address to Fizz's shelter, right there in plain view of the cameras, and held it out to Oakfur who took it with both hands like it was his salvation. "Now, I think you ought to get a move on. I have some other business to attend to, and you've got much planning to do."

"I do." Oakfur sounded unsure, but he stood anyway and walked with Sol to the door. When they reached it Oakfur turned back, his mouth opened as if he wanted to say something. But Sol gave him a sharp shake of the head, and it shut with a click.

"Hugo will see you out. Won't you Hugo?" Sol asked, turning to the guard standing just outside his office door.

"Yes, sir." Hugo ducked his head, and began to lead

Oakfur through the house. Sol watched them for a moment before turning to look at Soren through his office door. He was sitting behind his desk, his cheek perched lazily on one fist. When Sol met his eyes, Soren lifted a dark brow, and Sol gave him a double thumbs up and a big smile, before turning to head back into his own office.

STARING at himself in the mirror, his shaggy hair hanging in his face, Sol thanked Merlin that his hair grew out so quickly, and that J had convinced him last year to keep it longer. It made what he was going to have to do over the coming days less difficult to hide. Not easier to deal with, because wearing only a single hearing aid was a frustrating experience that left him consistently off balance, like someone could sneak up on him at any time. But definitely less difficult to hide.

The device he usually wore in his left ear sat in the drawer of his bedside table, disassembled, and waiting to be put back together. He'd done it after spending several hours combing his rooms for signs of Soren's bugs. There had been none. Soren seemed to want to afford him *some* privacy. And since Sol couldn't well leave through the sealed window, or the front door, and no one was allowed on the third floor, it seemed Soren was under the foolish assumption that Sol couldn't get up to any trouble there.

Finger combing his hair, Sol rearranged it so that it covered his left ear. He shifted the part just enough to hide his empty ear canal, but not enough that anyone would notice. And then he headed down to his office where Hugo was waiting outside, as per usual.

"Good morning, Hugo! Have you seen my father today?"

Sol asked, his voice light, even as the word father made something violent burn in his chest.

"He's out, sir." Hugo's eyes shifted to the office door across from Sol's which was shut for perhaps the first time in weeks.

"Ah. I see." Sol stopped in front of his own office door, his hand on the knob. There were cameras in the hall too. Listening devices everywhere. Everywhere except his bedroom. Another guard stood opposite Hugo, watching the pleasant conversation mildly. A woman. Sol had never spoken to her, but he recognized her as some kind of gargoyle. She didn't seem like she cared much for Soren or his business, but Sol wasn't foolish enough to think she wouldn't run right back to him with whatever she overheard. "You remember those books you recommended to me last week?"

"Yes, sir."

"Well, I had a recommendation for you. I just… oh. I think I left it in my room. Let me run up and grab it, all right?" Sol turned his dimpled smile on Hugo, and Hugo's brows pinched a little in the middle as if unsure what Sol was getting at. They had had a few of these conversations. The coded back and forth that could mean nothing, or it could mean something. They meant something, to Sol. And although he hadn't been able to vet Hugo as much as he'd have liked, he didn't have any choice but to gamble on the young basilisk.

"Uh, sure." Hugo watched Sol, as he made a show of jogging back to the steps, and up to his room again. Sol moved quickly, tucking the note with the list of things he needed to fix his hearing aid into the book, and pressing it tightly under his arm so no one would notice the addition.

When he was back in front of Hugo, he made sure he sounded out of breath, a rasping laugh leaving him. *Appear weak*, Ildri had taught him. *Let them underestimate you.* He could still envision her face hovering over him just after she'd put him on his ass on the mat for the fifth time in a row, her eyes glittering with mischief while Adelia clapped slowly. His heart squeezed at the memory. Merlin, he missed them.

"Sorry about that. Anyway, I think you'll find the chapter on the transference from solar based electricity to ambient magical powered devices particularly interesting." He thumped the book against Hugo's chest, and Hugo took it, his hazel eyes still searching Sol's for some kind of answer.

"I'll be sure to let you know, sir."

"Splendid!" Sol grinned, and then headed into his office to spend another agonizing day pretending to do whatever it was Soren thought he was supposed to be doing, all while wondering if J was dying under his very feet.

CHAPTER TWENTY-FOUR

"I read that section you told me about, sir," Hugo said, leaning against the doorframe of Sol's office as if he were afraid to enter without an invitation. Which was likely for the best. They couldn't appear too friendly. Not with Soren sitting right across the hall.

"Did you?" Sol asked, his hand motioning for Hugo to join him. Hugo hesitated for a moment, and Sol's eyes flicked over his shoulder to see Soren watching them closely from his own desk. "What did you think of it?"

"It was very interesting. I wrote some notes in the margins." Hugo finally moved to set the book down on Sol's desk. It sounded heavier than it had been when Sol had handed it over, but that could have been Sol's imagination. His fingers itched to check, the sensation crawling up his wrists like bugs. But he didn't. He just moved his hand to rest on top of the book.

"I'll have to take a look at those this evening."

Hugo nodded. He looked so young. Sol knew he wasn't, he knew that Hugo was probably about the same age as himself and J, but Hugo looked *so young*. So unsure of himself, that Sol was reminded that not everyone had been brought up in this life. Not everyone had received lessons on how to do this from the age of fifteen. Sol had to shake off the desire to give him a brotherly pat on the back and tell him that everything would be okay, because he honestly didn't know that it would be.

"I'll let you know if I have any other recommendations." Sol's eyebrows lifted in question. He was getting so damn tired of the double talk, but there was no way around it.

"Please do." Hugo bowed his head in thanks, and then turned to leave Sol's office again. Sol set the book to the side of his desk, tucked under a small stack of other tomes he'd been planning to take to his bedroom that evening under the guise of better educating himself to be Soren's heir.

"You're making friends," Soren said, his tone almost accusatory, from where he leaned against the doorframe, arms crossed over his chest in a forced position of laziness. Like he wasn't two seconds away from striding across the room and snatching the book to see what was going on. It seemed to be taking all of his self-control not to. His hands twitched. The muscles in his neck shifted. If Sol made it back to his room with the book without Soren accosting him, he'd be amazed.

"It's not like I have anything better to do." Sol shrugged, disinterested, and then, because he knew if he didn't change the subject Soren would find some way to get the book from him, he said, "Where were you the other day? I asked the guards, but no one would tell me."

"Did you miss your dear old dad?" Soren's tone shifted to something teasing, and although the word dad made Sol's teeth clench, he knew this was better. Better to keep Soren distracted from what Sol was doing. Even if it meant having to play this disgusting game of family.

"Of course I did, Father." Sol let his voice turn cheerful,

his smile dimpling even if it didn't meet his eyes. "Maybe next time I could go with you?"

Soren's eyes narrowed, his dark gaze flicking over Sol's face looking for a tell. He wouldn't find one, Sol was too practiced at this. When he found none, Soren pulled a smile onto his face, forcing it into the same brightness that Sol had leveled at him. "Yeah. Maybe. I'll have to think about it."

"Good. Thank you, pops." The word *pops* stuck to the roof of his mouth. Like something gloopy and disgusting. But he forced it out. Pressed it between his teeth like a child might sticky porridge.

"Of course, *son*." Soren's smile grew, dimpling in the same place Sol's always did. Then he said, "I'll let you get back to work," before returning to his own office.

Even with Soren gone, the tension remained. It sat like a weight across Sol's chest the rest of the day, making it hard to breathe, making his eyes jerk at every sudden movement across the hall. It would have been easy for Soren to demand to see the book, but it also would have been too overt, and Sol was starting to get the impression that Soren was enjoying this strange game of cat and mouse they were playing. That maybe Soren hadn't been challenged in a very long time, and he was testing his son to see if he were such a challenge. It didn't sit right with Sol. He hadn't minded it before. It had been *fun* before. Merlin, he had been so stupid.

There was nothing fun about this interaction now. Not now that he knew the consequences to his actions. Not now that he'd lost the person he cared most about. The rush of exhilaration he'd had when planning his confrontations with the White Rabbit, the thrill of an opponent who might outthink him, that was all gone. All that was left was the hollow ache in his chest where the bond with J had once been.

Still, by some miracle he held it together for the

remainder of the day, until he made it back to his room with the stack of books he'd had by his desk. The door shut perhaps a little harder than it should have, and Sol stopped, holding his breath, listening for any sign that Soren would come and investigate what all the ruckus was about. When he didn't hear anything in the hall, he let out the breath, his shoulders slumping against the door.

"It's all right, Sol. You've got this." Sol nodded to himself, moving away from the door and to the little side table by his bed. It had a single drawer, and it was much shorter than the ridiculous four-poster canopy that Soren had outfitted the room with. The bedding was grey, thankfully, but still, it was obnoxiously extravagant for a person who had spent the majority of the last decade of their life sleeping on a mattress on the floor. The pieces of his disassembled hearing aid made soft metallic clinks as he pulled them out, and dumped them on his bed, turning on the lamp on the side table to provide more light.

Dust flittered up into the beam of light from where he dropped the stack of books. The one Hugo had returned made a clinking sound as Sol dug it out from the bottom of the stack, and when he opened it he found that Hugo had cut the center out of most of the pages to create a little box for hold the tools, and parts Sol had asked for.

He'd been able to get everything which was surprising. Someone must have been looking out for Sol. His fingers shook a bit as he grabbed the little pair of tweezers, and set to work, his mind racing with everything he'd ever learned from Reboot and Pickle.

An hour later he sat still looking at the pieces of his hearing aid. His hands had started shaking from pinching the tweezers so tightly, and he was no closer to reassembling the damn thing into a usable communication device.

"Fuck... maybe I don't got this." Sol huffed, dropping the

tweezers back down onto the bed so he could scrub at his face. His eyes had long since begun to crust, and the tendon in his wrist was starting to ache. The clock was ticking too loudly from the other side of the bed, and Sol didn't even want to look to see what time it was.

If Pickle or Reboot were there, they'd have been done this little project and moved onto something else long ago. But he was so out of fucking practice, and he'd never been as good with technology as they were. He was better with people. With understanding their inner workings and how to get them to do what he needed them to. His tech knowledge was rudimentary at best when compared to theirs. But they weren't there. And there was no way for them to give him instruction.

"So it's up to me." Sol rubbed at his eyes one more time before picking up the tweezers again, and setting to work.

The clock continued to tick too loudly, counting down the minutes until Soren would expect him awake. But sometime early in the morning, when the whole city seemed to be holding its breath, Sol finally heard the crackle of something other than static coming from the little device. He picked it up, jamming it into his ear a little too hard, and practically choked on a sob when he heard music. Distorted by the bad connection, with plenty of static, and fuzz, but music, nonetheless. And not just music, no. It was Pickle and Reboot's song. The one they'd always danced to in the years since Sol and Adelia had left their home in Ilygroth.

It wasn't as good as hearing Pickle's voice, but it was so close that something like hope bubbled up in his chest, fizzling in that empty place where J's emotions had been sitting since the bond between them was formed.

"Pickle?" he asked, only half thinking that he would get an answer. It was the asscrack of dawn, after all. Pickle and Reboot would surely be sleeping. Even if they knew he'd be in touch, they wouldn't wait around for him. That's what the music was for. To act as a signal, something he could tap into when he was searching for them.

"Soliel?" Reboot responded, her words scratchy like she'd been asleep and had jerked awake at the sound of his voice. "Is that really you? I didn't... I didn't dream that."

"No. Mama. It's really me." Sol's eyes burned, itchy with unshed tears. "Merlin, it's so good to hear your voice."

"I'm so angry with you." But there was no heat to it. In fact, he could hear her choke on a sob herself. The words getting stuck in her throat along with the tears. "Don't you ever run off like that again, do you hear me?"

"I'm not making any promises." He laughed, but it came out sounding wet, and rough. It didn't matter. This was his mama. She could hear him cry. It wouldn't be the first time nor the last.

"Of course you're not, you little shit," Pickle said, the words angry, but the tone oh so soft.

Sol coughed over another rough chuckle, tucking his knees to his chest.

"How are you? Are you all right? Has he hurt you?" Reboot asked, worry lacing every syllable.

"No. Mama. I'm all right. I'm fine." Sol's breath shook on the exhale. He looked over at the clock. He had at most a half hour before Soren got up and started his morning routine, when he might overhear Sol talking to himself. He had to be quick. "But... but that's not why I got in touch."

"No, I don't suppose it is." Pickle sounded incredulous, and Sol could picture her rolling her eyes.

"I don't have long to talk. I've sent Oakfur your way, has he been in touch?"

"He has," Reboot said, and he could just picture her leaning back in her chair, her hands steepled as she went into all-business-mode. "He's told us about his daughter, and that they are holding Jericho at the same facility."

"Do we have anything on where that is? There's a display down in the basement here that allows him to check in on the prisoners, but I don't think he's actually holding them wherever I am."

"No leads yet, but Oakfur has gotten us a list of all the properties he knows Soren owns. There are more, I'm sure, but I'm beginning to see a pattern." Pickle's fingers tapped against something, maybe her desk? Merlin, he hoped not. He hoped they weren't in their office this late. He hoped they had at least retired to the couch.

"Okay, you keep working on that from your end. I'm going to see what I can find out from my end. Maybe the display will show me something. If only I knew his sche—"

"You've made a friend there," Reboot said, breaking his train of thought before he could go into a spiral.

"Pardon?"

"Your basilisk friend," Pickle clarified. "He reached out to Oakfur to ask where he could get the parts for your hearing aid. Apparently, they don't sell most of the stuff you asked for at his local store."

"Hugo?"

"Ah, that's his name." Reboot's smile warmed her voice. "Yes, Hugo. Maybe he can help you get a look at Soren's schedule."

"It's worth a shot." Sol nodded. "But I need you to keep working on things from your end."

"Obviously." Pickle scoffed, and then grunted which meant Reboot had probably elbowed her. "Just keep your head down, kid. We're coming for you."

"No. You're not. Not before I've got a way to get the others out. Are we clear?"

There was a long, unhappy silence on the other end of the

line, and Sol recognized it as them both gearing up to argue with him.

"I can take care of myself in here. I'm not leaving until we've gotten everyone out. Are we *clear*?"

"Fine," Reboot said on a breath.

"Good. Then I'll be in touch." Sol ran a hand through his hair. "And mama... Ildri?"

"Yes?"

"I love you both."

"Oh Soliel, we love you too. Stay safe in there."

CHAPTER TWENTY-FIVE

Everything was going according to plan. Which, Sol reflected with some aggravation, should have been the first clue that everything was going to go to shit. Because none of his plans ever worked out that well, especially when he had to have a hands-off approach.

"He's onto us," Pickle said, out of breath like she'd been running when Sol knew full well she'd been sitting behind her desk all day searching for blueprints of the building they thought Soren was using to hold his prisoners.

"Of course he's onto us. We knew that." Sol rolled his eyes, his fingers tapping against his leg where he sat on the bed, his legs crossed at the ankles.

Pickle huffed, a soft annoyed sound in the back of her throat. "No, I mean he's really onto us. He knows you've found a way to communicate with us."

"He can't have. I haven't given any clues, and I'm not sending any communications through my sources here anymore. Hugo and Oakfur don't even connect with you directly." Sol's fingers balled into a fist. He knew Soren would catch onto the fact that he was up to something, but Sol'd given no indication that he had been in contact with his people on the outside. He'd been so *careful*. "What makes you think he knows?"

"He's added extra security to the building. And they're there around the clock." Pickle was stressed, he could hear it in the tightness of her voice. But not only that, no, she was scared too. "Are you sure you don't have a bug in your room?"

"I check every day, Pickle, before we talk. And I don't write anything down that you give me. It's all in my head. There's no way he could know what we're talking about. It must just be that he's nervous about something else. Unless—"

"Unless he has someone on the inside of our organization." Pickle sounded like she was talking through clenched teeth.

"But our people are all vetted. You aren't even letting anyone outside of the inner circle work on this. You told me so yourself. There's no way—"

"There's no other solution, Soliel." Pickle let out a breath, and he could picture her shoulders slumping back in her chair. "Someone on our side is feeding him information. Maybe has been for a long time."

"How long do you think?" Something crawled under his skin, nerves making Sol itch all over. It didn't make sense that someone would betray them like that. They were a team, a family. His inner circle had been together for years. It made something unsettled and unhappy sit low in his gut.

The silence sat heavily between them. Pickle didn't say anything, like she was scared to accuse anyone. But Sol knew she had her suspicions. She was too damned observant not to. She'd noticed something, something he had missed, and that rankled more than anything else. Because how could he have missed it while Pickle who spent her time as a voice in their ears hadn't?

"Pickle, how long?" He bit out, his patience wearing thin as the itching grew more incessant.

"A little over a year, would be my guess," Pickle said quietly. "Likely about the time J came to us."

Sol pressed his lips together, his jaw so tight it ached all the way up to his temples. She couldn't be saying what he thought she was saying. He was sure of it. Because that would just be absurd. "I know you're not suggesting that Lettie is the spy."

"I'm not. Actually." Pickle's chair squeaked as she wiggled around in it. "But there does seem to be some correlation."

"Or there's no correlation at all and whoever it is just got the offer from Soren around then. It could mean nothing." Sol wasn't sure why he was arguing against the idea. She'd said she didn't think it was J, but there was still something about the suggestion that it had *something* to do with J that made his skin feel like it was too tight for his body.

"Or it could mean something."

"Or it could mean *nothing*."

"Soliel."

"Ildri."

Pickle let out a long breath, the sound so loud it made the connection crackle. "Fine. We won't talk about it. But I'll keep my ear to the ground."

"You do that."

"Don't be dismissive of this." Pickle warned, her tone serious. "This is a problem."

"I recognize that, but there isn't anything I can do about it from in here. It's not like Soren is taking meetings with whoever it is."

"Fine." He heard her shift again, likely running a hand through her long hair, if he knew her at all. "Have you gotten your hands on his schedule so you can snoop?"

"Not yet. Hugo is supposed to get me information on it

tomorrow. I don't know that he'll keep actual blueprints of a building though. That seems like a weird thing to have on hand."

"It does, but I wouldn't put it past him. Soren is a meticulous planner. He'd want to know everything he could about the buildings he's running his operations out of." She sounded begrudgingly envious of this, but Sol wasn't going to say that to her. He liked his eardrums intact even if they didn't always work the best.

"And how am I getting you these blueprints?" Sol snorted, rolling his eyes. "I doubt I'll be able to connect anything to his computer, even if I did have a device to put it on. I don't have any of your pixie dust, and all of his equipment is too new to have ports on it."

"You might be able to connect your hearing aid to it through whatever latent magic network he's using." There was typing again in the background, the sounds loud and pointed. Whatever Pickle had thought of, she was going to make it work.

"Might?"

"Well, it wouldn't be the first time we used them as a transmitter." The click-clack of her keyboard almost ate up her whole voice as she mumbled the words mostly to herself. "And by altering the left one to increase the signal output so you could get it through whatever wards Soren has set up, you've already done half the work."

"For sound waves, Ildri. We both know information is a whole different beast. Even if I can get it connected to his computer, which I may not be able to, I don't know that the signal will be strong enough to send data packets through."

"Well you won't know till you try, will you?" Pickle asked with an air of finality.

Sol sighed, his head hanging forward against his chest. Fuck. He missed when the only person he had to worry about catching him sneaking around was J. At least with J, Sol knew how they'd react. "Tell me what I need to do."

The following day rose too bright, and too early. Bass pounded against his temples from somewhere in the house. Likely Soren down in the gym doing his morning routine to that obnoxious music he liked to listen to.

"Fantastic. He's in a good mood," Sol mumbled to himself, reaching over to grab the hearing aid off the side table. Good moods with Soren were always a wild card, Sol had come to realize. It either meant he'd be overly attentive, wanting to spend time chatting with Sol like they were old friends and calling him son every other sentence, or he'd be in his office all day on video calls with his various associates. Sol personally preferred the latter.

Either way, it meant Sol couldn't linger in bed, and hide away from Soren. He had to get up, get ready, and make it look like he was a contributing member of the household, even if they both knew it was a farce. So he dragged himself to the bathroom and started getting ready.

He was just straightening his tie—a tie! Who wore ties these days?—when the knock on the door drew his attention away from his reflection.

"Come in," Sol called, straightening his tie a third time. It had to be Soren. No one else was allowed on the third floor. But Soren had never come to Sol's room before. And that knowledge sat like a bit of wriggling carp in his gut.

Soren pushed through, his steps slow and casual as he made his way over to the wall where Sol was getting ready.

"Your friend Hugo wanted me to give this to you," Soren said, holding out a book. It was the one Sol had used to ask

Hugo to get him Soren's schedule two days prior. The one that was about theoretical magic.

"Oh. Well, thank you for delivering it." Sol reached for the book, but Soren snatched it back, holding it a bit out of reach just as Sol's fingers grazed the cover, and that carp gave another dangerous wriggle. "Why didn't he deliver it himself?" Sol asked, although he was sure he didn't want to know the answer. There could be only one reason why Soren had that book in his hands instead of Hugo. Only one reason why Soren was in Sol's room when he never had been before, looking at Sol with his head tilted just so as if he were looking at a particularly obvious word puzzle that no one around him had understood quite yet.

"Hugo won't be returning to the house." It was casual. Too casual to not be a deliberate threat.

"Oh? And why not?" Sol pulled his hand back to tuck it in his pocket so that Soren wouldn't see the way his fingers twitched with nerves.

"He's gone off to visit his brother for a while." Soren paused, to let those words sink into Sol, and they did. They sunk into his muscles, weighing on his bones and sinew. Making his muscles burn with the need to run. But he wouldn't be able to. Because he was frozen to the spot. Just listening as Soren told Sol that the first friendly face he'd found in this place was going to suffer for helping Sol. "I don't think he'll be back anytime soon, I'm sorry to say."

Sol nodded, his tongue stuck to the roof of his mouth where it sat heavy, and sluggish. Not that it would have mattered if he could move it. There were no words to say to something like that. No pleading he could do to help Hugo. No deals he could make to get his friend out of this situation. Nothing. Just the slow realization that Hugo was gone, and Sol would be next very likely.

Soren held out the book again, letting Sol take it in a grip so weak he was surprised he didn't hear the thud of it hitting the thick carpeting under his shoes. "And son," Soren said, dipping his head, and tugging Sol in closer by their shared hold of the book, "I wouldn't go trying to recruit any more of my people if I were you. Unless you don't mind having more blood on your hands."

Sol's legs were shaking like they might give out on him at any moment, even as he locked his knees and forced himself to stand, even as he tightened the muscles so much they screamed. He couldn't fall, not when Soren was looking at him. Sol waited for Soren to say something about Oakfur, but he didn't. They stood there in that tense silence as the clock on his bedside table gave another soft *tick* in the quiet between them. Sol supposed it went without saying.

"You wouldn't want that, would you?" Soren asked, finally letting go of the book and stepping out of Sol's space, his hands moving to tuck casually into his pockets. He lifted his dark brows, like he legitimately expected an answer from Sol, but there was none. Even if Sol had wanted to bite back at Soren, he couldn't. His tongue was too heavy. His mind strangely silent for perhaps the first time in his life. Soren clicked his tongue. "Pathetic. This is where caring about people gets you."

Sol wasn't sure what happened next. All he knew was that when he looked up again from where his gaze had fallen to his feet, Soren was gone. He moved to his bed; his fingers almost white with how hard he was gripping the book. Opening it, he found Soren's schedule. A schedule that might mean absolutely nothing now that Soren knew he had it. Sol let out a long breath, stuffed it into his bedside table, and pulled out the other hearing aid.

He winced when he jammed it in a little too far on his way to the bathroom, locking the door behind himself even if he knew it wouldn't do any good, and turning on the shower to hide his voice.

"Pickle." Sol croaked, his hands still shaking where they gripped the marble sink.

"What is it, Soliel? What's wrong?" It was Reboot who answered, and Sol could have sobbed in relief hearing his mother's voice.

"He found out about Hugo. He's— Hugo's— I can't— There's—" Sol dropped to the floor, knowing full well he was going to wrinkle the stupid fucking suit Soren made him wear. He didn't give a flying fuck. His chest heaved with every too-quick breath, and the room was gradually starting to darken around the edges in his panic.

"Slow down, Soliel. And tell me what happened." Reboot's voice was soothing, as it had always been. Calming any fear. Smoothing over any ruffled feelings. Sol had always known that his mother would solve whatever problem he presented her with. He never saw her falter. And so long as she was there, he didn't have anything to worry about. But that was when he was a child and the worst he had to worry about was a scraped knee from where he and J had been running too hard down the crooked sidewalk of Ilygroth. This was so much worse.

"He found out about Hugo." Sol repeated, swallowing down the swell of terror and bile threatening to make the room go completely dark. "He said Hugo is visiting his brother. He said I have blood on my hands, Mama."

"Soliel," Reboot said, her tone serious, and stern. "This is not your fault."

"Isn't it?"

"It's not." She practically growled, and if he closed his eyes, he could envision that fierce look behind his lids, the one she always gave him when she was furious at someone for slighting him. "But this does mean we need to move up our timetable. We need the information on the holding facility by the end of the week. Do you think you can do that?"

Sol took a deep breath in through his nose, forcing the air into his lungs, making his racing heart slow into something more steady. "Yes, mama. I can do that." He didn't know how yet, but he'd figure it out. There wasn't any other choice.

"Good. We've gotten some information on the security hardware he might be using, thanks to our investigation, but nothing on what magic or software measures he may have in place. I don't want us going in there blind."

"Got it." Sol nodded, though he knew she couldn't see him.

Reboot let out a pleased little hum. "Stay safe, Soliel. I'll talk to you soon."

Sol closed the connection, and took another deep breath, running his fingers through his hair before he rose on still shaky legs, and forced himself to return to the day ahead of him. If nothing else, Sol needed Soren to at least think he'd bested him.

CHAPTER TWENTY-SIX

THE ONLY NOISE SOL COULD HEAR WAS HIS OWN TOO LOUD heart in his ears. There were no other sounds of life about the place, and Sol almost wondered if that meant Soren wasn't there anymore. But he wasn't foolish enough to let his guard down. Even if an early morning hush had settled over Soren's mansion, just as it always did Mythikos, it didn't mean anything. Because danger lurked in the quiet corners of Mythikos, and there was a threat to the silence of Soren's home. Like the White Rabbit was holding his breath just to see what Sol would do with the information he'd given him. Sol had to be careful. Very careful.

Sol winced when the door to his bedroom made a faint squeak that he hadn't noticed before. He held his breath, waiting for some sign that someone had heard. Some sign that Soren was coming to see what the noise was about. But there was nothing.

His bare feet were silent against the plush carpeting of the third floor and careful down the stairs to the second, skipping over the step he knew groaned any time too much weight was put on it.

A shadow moved at the base of the steps, and Sol tucked himself into the darkness of the stairwell, watching as one of Soren's guards crossed the landing. The gargoyle with the long dark hair was muttering softly to herself, her words nothing but a faint noise in his ears, hardly distinguishable from the sounds of the sleeping house. He waited, watching, until she turned her back on the stairs. Sol took the last couple of steps two at a time, reached down, and pinched a nerve in her neck, sending her to the floor.

He grunted under her weight as he caught her before she could crumple entirely, and wake the whole house. Pulling her around the side of the steps, he tucked her into a chair that he'd honestly never seen anyone sit in and just seemed to be there for decoration, then prayed to Merlin that Soren hadn't posted any others.

Sol followed the hall down to where he and Soren's respective offices sat. His own always had the door open, waiting, and welcoming for anyone who wanted to come in and talk, or snoop, or put bugs in place. Giving off the idea that he had nothing to hide, although Sol was sure Soren wasn't fooled by it.

Across the hall sat Soren's office door, closed tight, and no doubt locked to keep Sol out. But a lock wasn't exactly going to stop Sol. He knelt in front of the door, waiting for a moment as he listened for any sign of movement around him. There was none. Not even the faint settling of the house. Shaking himself, he returned to his task, pulling out the little tweezers and screwdriver Hugo had provided him with to fix his hearing aid. They weren't the best tools for this kind of thing, but Sol had been known to do more with less, so he set to work.

Sweat trickled down his neck as the seconds ticked by into minutes, and he wondered how long it would take the guard to wake up from her nap. It had been a long time since he'd pulled that pressure point trick. And never on a gargoyle before.

The tweezers fell from his jittering fingers, clattering to the floor. He froze, listening. More time slipped by, Sol's eyes squinting into the dark. But no sound came. He let out a breath, scooped up the tweezers, and set back to work. It was another painstaking few seconds that seemed to drag on into hours before the lock finally gave, and he was able to push through into Soren's office.

Sol scrambled to his feet, tucking the tweezers and screwdriver back into the breast pocket of his obnoxious matching pajama set. Soren didn't believe in sweatpants, and t-shirts, or thought they were uncouth. Or something like that. Sol didn't know.

His feet scuffed against the cold tile floor on the way to the desk. For perhaps the first time since coming to stay there, Sol was thankful that Soren was a minimalist prick. The moon shone in through the big window behind the desk, providing just enough light for Sol to drop down into the chair, and tap at the keypad built directly into Soren's desk.

The screen blinked on a moment later, so bright it burned Sol's eyes. He narrowed them, peering through the glare. It didn't do much for the headache already building, but it did help him to see the little box floating in the middle of the screen. Password protected. Of course he had the stupid fucking thing password protected. Why would anything in this entire situation be easy?

Scrubbing at his eyes to relieve some of the pressure, Sol took a breath. "What would he use as a password?"

His fingers drummed against the desk thoughtfully, eyes jerking from the screen to the door every few seconds as he thought. Then an idea struck him, and he scoffed to himself.

"He wouldn't. . . would he? That would be truly fucking stupid." But now that Sol thought about it, he could see Soren doing such a thing. The man was a narcissist, and he probably didn't think anyone would even get this close to his computer. Or connect him back to the name. Sol threaded his fingers together, cracked his knuckles, and then typed \/\/H1T3_R4BB1T.

The little box lingered for a moment too long, and Sol didn't breathe until the screen flickered again and he was presented with Soren's bare desktop. The man didn't even have a file folder marked 'files' on it. Just the empty wallpaper of the Mythikos skyline.

"That's going to complicate matters." Sol's fingers jittered over the trackpad, moving to the top corner to pull up the menu of devices the computer could connect to. There was no guarantee that his hearing aid was still putting off a latent magic signal. No guarantee that even this close it'd be strong enough to connect to. No guarantee that Soren's computer even allowed connections to outside devices.

A little drop down appeared, and the only thing on it was a string of numbers Sol recognized readily as his hearing aid serial number. He relaxed a little more, and clicked on it, telling the computer to connect. Then he waited as a little spinning wheel appeared beside the serial number, the computer deciding if the connection was strong enough.

When it finally connected, Sol had to bite hard on the side of his tongue to keep from giving a little cry of victory. Something sharp and metallic tainted his breath, but he swallowed it down. His finger skidded over the trackpad, sweat making the surface slick as he went to the bottom corner to open the menu. There was nothing to suggest that there were any files on the computer there either.

He pushed the cursor away from it to rest in the middle of the screen as Sol's eyes jerked back to the door. He held his breath so he could listen. Still nothing.

"Too much to hope that he'd make his files easy to find, I

guess," Sol grumbled, pressing the command keys Pickle had taught him to bring up the file directory. From there it was the work of trying every search term he could think of to find what he needed. The minutes ticked by, each change of the clock in the top corner making his eyes flick up to it, and making another bead of sweat slide down his spine.

He found the file he needed just as he heard shuffling in the hall. Dragging it from the directory to the little icon for his hearing aid Sol's fingers curled against the trackpad almost hard enough to dig his nails into the glass.

The shuffling got closer. The guard. The guard had woken up. Sol's gaze flew back to the little clock in the corner of the screen. It'd only been fifteen minutes between the time he'd left his room and the time he'd found the file. But the guard had already recovered. She shouldn't have already recovered. Or maybe it wasn't her. Maybe it was someone else.

There was a voice, whispered, and deep, out in the hall. Sol's hand lifted to his hearing aid, and adjusted it, wincing when it screeched loudly in his ear before settling at the new volume.

"Wren? Wren?" Someone else. Another guard, maybe? "Wren, you idiot, you fell asleep on the job, *again*."

Sol looked back to the screen, watching the progress bar as the file transferred to the hearing aid still sitting in his ear. He couldn't even contact Reboot and Pickle while the damn thing worked on the file transfer. He wouldn't be able to until he got back to his room and was able to readjust the internals to work for sound again. Fuck. He was so fucked. He was so royally *fucked*. They were going to find him, and they were going to tell Soren, and Soren was going to—

A soft ding came from the computer, and Sol's gaze flew back to the progress bar to find that it had completed the transfer. Hastily closing out of the menu, and sliding from the chair, he prayed the computer would go back to sleep before anyone could peek into Soren's office and notice. Once he was to the door, he poked his head out into the hall, looking both directions.

"What the fuck do you mean you just fell asleep? That doesn't make any sense." The other guard was chiding Wren. Sol moved into the hall, shutting the door behind himself with a soft click, and then made a dash for the back staircase that led down to the kitchen. If he could just make it there then he could go back up the front stairs, far enough away from the offices that the guard wouldn't even—

"What're you doing out of bed?" Wren asked, her tone grumpy from having been woken from her nice nap, or so it seemed. Sol fought down a wince from how loud it was in his ear. He hadn't turned back down his hearing aid. Fuck.

Sol turned slowly, making a show of rubbing at his eyes. "Huh? Oh. Just going to get some water from the kitchen," he mumbled hoping they wouldn't look close enough to realize his chest was rising and falling quickly from sprinting down the hall.

"Water?" Wren repeated.

"Yeah. Why? What's up?"

Wren's eyes narrowed on him; her lips pursed. "I'll escort you."

"Oh. Okay." Sol shrugged and turned back around toward the kitchen, the guard's heavy boots loud behind him.

SOL HAD SPENT an unreasonable amount of time in the kitchen, sipping his glass of water, trying to calm his rabbiting heart. He hoped if he made enough of a show of it, Wren would get bored and go back to patrolling the second floor. She never did. She followed him all the way back up to his room, and he could hear her still standing out there, shifting her weight from foot to foot, until his light had been turned off for a full hour.

The floorboards creaked under her, and Sol waited several minutes even after that before turning on his lamp, and disassembling his hearing aid again to switch it back so he could communicate with Pickle and Reboot.

The music was still going. Sol relaxed back onto his headboard, turning off the light, and letting himself just sink into his blankets for a moment. When he finally wasn't trembling with panic he said, "Reboot. Pickle."

"He's back! Reboot! He's back!" Pickle shouted into his ear, and he winced. "Sorry. Sorry."

"It's fine. Did you get the files?" If things went as planned, they would have traveled through the connect while he'd been making his way back to his room.

"We did," Reboot said her voice a little groggy from probably being woken up. "And we're already formulating a plan to come and get you."

Sol sat up, almost banging his head on the ledge at the top of his headboard. "What? No. I can't leave. Then he'll know something's up, and he'll— He said he'd kill Lettie if I left."

He was finding it hard to breathe suddenly, the air getting stuck somewhere in between his nose and his lungs.

"We don't have much choice," Pickle said, a frown in her voice.

"Yes, we do. You just leave me here, and we'll deal with my escape once we know everyone else is safe." The way Sol saw it, that was the only solution that would keep the people Soren held prisoner safe. Because if Soren knew Sol was coming for him, he'd kill them all, Sol just knew he would. "I can't have any of them dying just because of—"

"Soliel," Reboot cut him off sharply, "we don't have any

choice. He's got a blood ward on the building. If we're going to get past it, we need his blood."

"Which means we need your blood, kiddo," Pickle said, not unkindly, the words like a ruffle to his hair.

"But the victims—

"We'll just have to be quick about it." Reboot's tone left no room for argument. "We'll have to make sure that as soon as we get you, we're ready to raid his facility shortly after."

"How shortly?" Sol swallowed around a breath that wanted to turn into a manic chuckle. He needed to keep it together.

"A matter of hours." Reboot's voice was calm, and sure.

"That'll put us at. . ." Pickle's voice faded as her typing started up, fingers flying over the keys. "Seventy-two hours or less."

"Seventy-two hours for what?" Sol asked, rubbing his palms on the blanket draped over his legs.

"Or less." Pickle sounded like she was only half paying attention to the conversation now.

"Till we can come and get you," Reboot said.

Sol shifted on the bed, wanting to duck under the covers and hide form the conversation like he might have when he was little. "All right," he said in a tone that sounded more certain than he felt. "I'll be ready for you in twenty-four."

"Perfect." Reboot smiled. And then the music started up again.

CHAPTER TWENTY-SEVEN

TWENTY-FOUR HOURS. THAT'S HOW LONG SOL HAD TOLD Pickle and Reboot it would take him to get ready for extraction. It had seemed like more than enough time, sitting there in his bed thinking of how he didn't have anything he needed to bring with him. It had seemed like plenty of time when he thought about how desperately he wanted out of the compound, and how there wasn't anyone left for him to protect there.

But there he sat not even twelve hours later, staring down at a random book from the shelves—Sol thought it might have been on the history of magical security, but he'd largely lost track of the words—pondering how he could possibly be ready for what was about to come, when there was a soft knock at the door. He looked up from the page, his tired eyes struggling to refocus on the red hair that clung to Oakfur's face.

"Do you have a moment?" Oakfur asked, his voice thin and reedy, like it was coming from a throat that had spent the night screaming. He looked worse than Sol felt. Dark circles marring the pale skin around his eyes, hair unkempt, shoulders slumped forward as if the only thing keeping him upright was the starch in his suit jacket, and even that was a near thing.

"Of course. Please, come in." Sol gestured to the seats in front of his desk, and stood up to move to one himself, sure that this was a conversation they didn't want Soren to be privy to. But Oakfur didn't sit. He stood at the door, his toes just over the line between the light hardwood of the hall, and the dark hardwood of Sol's office. "Did you get in touch with Fizz? How's the program going?"

"I. . ." Oakfur paused, clearing his throat as he leaned his weight more heavily onto his right side. "I did. The program is. . ." Oakfur stared intently at Sol, his eyes seeming to try to get some message across that his words likely couldn't. "It's on its way."

"Oh. Well. Good." Sol nodded, forcing on a smile past the rabbiting of his heart which was starting to make his stomach churn with nausea.

Oakfur dipped his head, relaxing a little now that his message had been delivered, and then his fingers worked over the words, "On my signal. Run. To the front door."

"What signal?" Sol signed back, his jaw clenching to keep the words from flowing off his tongue. Oakfur's back was to Soren. He was in a blind spot for the cameras, but Sol knew that the silence that stretched between them, however small it might be, was suspicious. Soren would know something was up. Something was coming.

"I'll be in touch with you if we need any other ideas," Oakfur said, and then he offered Sol the first smile he ever thought he'd seen on the man's face. It was a tight, sad thing, but it reached Oakfur's bright green eyes, crinkling the crow's feet there. "I just wanted to stop in and say thank you, Soliel, for everything."

Sol blinked, his mouth falling open at the sincerity that

laced Oakfur's words, at the acceptance without an ounce of regret that sat along his shoulders. Oakfur was... he was about to... Sol swallowed thickly, and opened his mouth again to say something, *anything*, to stop whatever horrible thing was about to happen. But Oakfur didn't give him the chance. He ducked his head lower, in gratitude, and left before Sol had even formed the words on his tongue.

The chair nearly toppled in Sol's rush for the door, but by the time he got there Oakfur and the two guards flanking him were already at the back stairs, and making their way down. Sol's sweaty palms skidded against the doorframe as he kept himself from falling through it. Then he stood, straightening his suit jacket, hoping he hadn't left stains in his wake.

"What was that about?" Soren called from his own desk. His dark head was half hidden behind his computer screen, the light from it washing out the skin of his forehead.

"He just wanted to thank me for my help with the program." Sol forced the words past the breathless, sick lump that lingered in his chest. Like he needed to cough, but it was getting stuck somewhere between his lungs and his mouth. His throat spasmed with it, urging him to acknowledge the instinct, but he breathed around it. "I think I'm finally doing some good."

The wheels on Soren's desk chair squeaked a little as he pushed back from his screen so he could look at Sol, and offer him what was likely meant to be an encouraging smile. "So it would seem. I'm proud of you."

There was a lie in those words, and it made the air thick with tension between them. Sol struggled to draw oxygen in past it, but he forced himself to lift his chin, to meet Soren's gaze, to show no fear. "Thank you, father."

"Of course, son."

Sol's muscles screamed with the urge to cringe away from

those words. He tightened them, not letting any of the discomfort show on his face. Then he nodded, probably stiffly enough that Soren knew what was going on internally, and returned to his desk.

The front door, Oakfur had said. Which staircase would be the best way to get there? The front stairs would put Sol in the front foyer, a straight shot to the door, but would Soren have people posted there? Sol hadn't been downstairs that day to check. And would Soren think that would be the way he'd go? Or would he assume that Sol would take the back steps as those were narrower, where it was harder for someone to sneak up on him? Or would he assume that Sol would realize that Soren would assume that and—

The muted sound of an explosion shook the house, sending several of Sol's books toppling off the shelves around him.

"That must be the signal," Sol whispered to himself. He stood from his desk, sending the chair back into the shelf behind him, and paced quickly to the door. He didn't know what he'd been expecting, but it wasn't the empty hallway, the blare of an alarm echoing off the walls. Sol looked into Soren's office, thinking that perhaps Soren would try to stop him from leaving, but the man was nowhere in sight. All attention had been diverted to whatever was going on with Oakfur in the basement.

And with that knowledge—the knowledge of the sacrifice Oakfur had made—Sol finally got his feet under him and started running. The hard soles of his shoes skidded against the hardwood floor. Sol had never wished for his own gear more than he did in that moment as his shoulder slammed into the wall just beside the back stairs. He winced, his hand lifting to hold the aching joint as he stumbled down the steps. One heel caught on a lip, pitching him forward so quickly he almost rolled down the rest of them and broke his fucking neck. But he managed to catch himself in time, the skid of a sweaty palm on the handrail burning.

By the time he got to the bottom of the stairs in the kitchen, he realized his mistake. The kitchen. Where the door to the basement was. Fuck. *Fuck!*

Sol stumbled to a stop, just before he reached the bottom step, poking his head around the wall that kept anyone in the kitchen from seeing up the stairs. There were ten, maybe fifteen, of Soren's hired guards standing in the kitchen, their backs to the stairs as they watched whatever was happening in the basement. His heart hammering in his chest hard enough that it made his ribs ache, Sol stepped down onto the floor at the bottom and began to creep across the kitchen. He'd have to be fast, and quiet. There was no good cover until he reached the door into the adjoining dining room. He'd have to—

A pair of washed-out gray eyes fell on him, Wren's stance still enough that she almost resembled one of the faux gargoyles humans used to put on their buildings to ward off bad spirits. Sol's breathing was too fast, sweat pooling at the base of his spine, making his overly expensive dress shirt stick to him. He waited, wondering if she'd alert the others, wondering if she'd turn him in. But she just raised a brow, then flicked her eyes to the door ten feet from him.

He took one step, then another toward the door, their eyes still locked on one another. Just as he reached the door to the still dark dining room Wren held up a hand to stop him. He stilled, his eyes flicking over her shoulder to make sure none of the others had noticed him yet. They hadn't. They were still focused on something down in the basement. Something Sol couldn't hear for the loud alarm.

Wren held up three fingers.

Sol frowned, his brows raising in question.

Wren nodded her head to the room over his shoulder,

and held up the fingers again, then gestured to the men and women over her shoulder.

Sol blinked, then he got it. Three guards. In the foyer. It was a warning. He mouthed a 'thank you', and Wren shrugged it off, before turning her back on him again as someone behind her said something that he couldn't hear over the sirens.

He ducked into the dining room, eyes squinting as they adjusted to the dark, muddy light of a room without windows. It was difficult to avoid the chairs, and that stupid fucking bar Soren seemed to think he needed even if he never entertained. But thankfully the floor was carpeted, and that kept him from slipping anymore.

The dining room opened to a small receiving room, with a little settee, a bar cart, and a fireplace. Once there, Sol was able to take in a steadying breath, wipe his sweating hands on his pants, and back himself to the wall beside the open doorway. The alarm wasn't as loud there, but there was a ringing in Sol's ears that was making it hard to hear anything else. He reached up to turn his hearing aids down, hoping it would help, and it did a little. But the ringing stayed, making his ear drums ache. He'd just have to rely on what he could see.

And what he could see were the shadows of two muscular figures standing on either side of the front door, blocking the light from the windows that flanked it. He needed a distraction. Something to get their attention away from the door, and maybe tell him where the third guard was. Turning back to the little sitting room, he weighed his options.

There wasn't much. And fuck, he was already running out of time. He should have had his left hearing aid on him so he could check in with Pickle and Reboot. He should have been ready. But he hadn't been. He hadn't thought over how to escape at all in the last eight hours, because he'd thought he'd have more time! He didn't think they'd move this quickly. But they had, and now he was winging it in a way that he never had before. Sol's tightly wound control was quickly unraveling.

With no better options, he pulled a bottle of whiskey from the bar cart, headed to the fireplace to grab the box of long matches, and ripped his tie over his head. It was the work of seconds to stuff the fabric far enough into the bottle that it soaked up the liquor. Another peek into the foyer, and his eyes landed on a potted plant near the front staircase. It wasn't the best solution. It looked a little too green to catch like he needed it to. But he wasn't being given a lot of other choices, and Sol didn't have time to waste.

The tie smoked when he lit it, smelling more like burnt flesh than smoldering fabric, but Sol didn't let himself consider if that meant the silk was real or not before he pitched the bottle of whiskey toward the plant some feet away. His aim shot wide—he never claimed to be an athlete who could throw things with any kind of precision—but the burning fabric caught at the base of the wicker pot the plant was sitting in, and in seconds it had gone up in flames.

The two guards near the door ran across the foyer, but the third had stopped in front of the stairs, their eyes narrowed on the doorway where Sol had poked his head out to watch the chaos. Sol's breath caught in his chest, sure they would come after him.

Then the door flew open, banging hard enough against the glass panes on one side to crack them. Sun streamed into the foyer, blinding Sol so that he saw was the silhouette of a woman. Another flash, something that looked like it might have been a taser fired at the guard who had just begun to make their way towards Sol. Their steps stuttered, and then they hit the floor, drawing the attention of the other two who had been investigating the burning plant. They spun, but not before she fired again, sending them to the ground as well.

Sol squinted; his eyes finally able to adjust. Reboot was saying something, her mouth moving almost too fast for him to catch the words. But he thought it might be his name, over and over again. He stepped out of the little sitting room, the movement drawing her eyes, and then she was smiling that soft, relieved smile, the one she'd always had when he'd come home after a long night out with J, except a little sharper now for the elongated canines.

"Mama," Sol said, but if he hadn't felt the word leave his throat, he wouldn't have known he'd spoken at all.

Reboot's eyes jerked from his, her dark gaze narrowing on someone at the top of the staircase, lips pulled back over her teeth in a snarl. Sol didn't have to look to know who it was. Soren. He'd figured out what they were up to. Sol didn't wait. He ran across the foyer, grabbed Reboot's wrist, and yanked her out into the too-bright daylight, slamming the door behind them on their way.

He didn't stop running until Reboot yanked him into a vehicle, and someone slammed the door shut behind them. He didn't let himself breathe properly until the van was peeling away from the curb outside of Soren's compound, taking them to whatever safe house Pickle had set up for them.

CHAPTER TWENTY-EIGHT

"Well, that was a shit show," was the first thing Sol heard when he turned back on his hearing aid, Maz's irritated tone grating on his nerves more than it normally would. The ringing was still there, but it had dulled enough to merely be an annoyance and not a hinderance.

Rachel gave Maz a hard shove.

"What? It was!" Maz grunted, rubbing at her arm where the wraith had touched her, maybe leaving behind a lingering patch of cold.

"No one said you had to come," Reboot said, her hands reaching up to adjust her ponytail.

"Please. Like I'd let you guys come without backup when that leprechaun was in charge of the distraction." Maz scoffed, rolling her eyes. It didn't sound as fond as she perhaps meant it to, but Sol wasn't going to look too hard at that, because there were other things to worry about.

"Is he going to be all right?" Sol shoved his suit jacket down off of his arms, balling it up and throwing it into a corner of the van. "He sounded like—"

"We don't know." Reboot frowned; her tone soft as if she

thought she might scare Sol if she told him the truth. But she was going to anyway, because she had never lied to him, and Sol knew she wasn't about to start now. "He said he would create a diversion, he didn't say what kind. And he didn't ask for an extraction plan."

"There was—" Sol sucked in a breath, forcing himself to stay calm. It was a struggle. Such a struggle. "There was an explosion."

Reboot met his eyes across the space of the van. She'd sat up a little more so her ponytail poofed out strangely above her head where it was pressed back into the side of the van. But her dark eyes, the eyes she had gifted her son, met his without flinching. "He didn't ask for an extraction."

Sol nodded, swallowing around something knotted, and painful in his throat.

"We'll go back for him when everything is said and done," Pickle promised, her voice a disembodied thing where it came through the speakers of the radio. "For now, we have bigger problems."

"You were early." Sol started rolling up his sleeves to distract himself. It was only half working. He couldn't get Reboot's words out of his head. Oakfur hadn't asked for an extraction. Oakfur had looked at him like he was saying goodbye right before everything had happened. Oakfur had *thanked* him. Sol shook himself, focusing on the wrinkled fabric under his rough fingers.

"There was some talk that they were going to move locations this morning," Dominic called from the driver's seat.

"How did we hear about that?"

"Does it really fucking matter? The point is we did." Maz huffed, her arms crossing over her chest.

"Yes. It does fucking matter." Sol didn't look up from where he was rolling up the left sleeve. He wanted to fix Maz with an unimpressed look, but he was still trying to swallow around that lump in his throat, and he didn't want anyone else to see that.

"You think it was a way for him to force our hand." Reboot leaned forward, bracing her weight on her knees. "To flush us out."

"I wouldn't put it past him to decide he was tired of sitting around waiting for me to make my move." Sol shrugged. He had no proof of that. No proof at all. But it lined up with what he knew of Soren. "He had to know I was going to retaliate after he told me about Hugo. Now we're working on his timetable, not our own."

"Damn it." Pickle's voice crackled, and Sol could just imagine her standing from whatever desk she was behind to begin pacing the room. "We played right into his hands."

"We did." Sol sat back, banging his head a little on the side of the van when Dominic took a turn too sharply. "But it doesn't really matter now."

"What's done is done," Pickle said in agreement.

"Right. Fill me in on what we know. How long do we have?" Sol gripped his knees to keep himself from pitching forward at the next hard turn.

"A couple of hours." Reboot pulled a tablet from a bag under her seat and held it out to him. "The facility it just outside the city limits."

"Smart." Sol zoomed in on the aerial pictures to get a better look at the high rise that Soren had built amongst the trees just outside of Mythikos. It was modern, and sleek, with windows on every side, and taller than some of the ancient looking trees that surrounded it. But it was far enough from the urban sprawl of the main city that no one would be able to see the comings and goings. "Is this the only one?"

"The only one close enough to Mythikos to be useful for his operation." Reboot leaned forward, swiping her finger across the screen to show him a list of similar properties. "He's built places farther out too, all outside of the city lines, in every direction. We found ten total. We'll raid them all by the end of this."

"How do we know this is the holding facility?"

"I followed one of the buyers out there," Dominic said. "Apparently he doesn't do delivery."

"Typical." Sol snorted, rolling his eyes. "All right, what kind of security measures are we looking at? Outside of the blood warding that you needed me for."

Reboot leaned forward again, the screen switching to a schematic. "We don't know what kind of magic we're up against, but this is the tech security system he has in place. Key codes, alarms, that kind of thing."

"Pretty basic," Rachel said, her leg jittering like a five-year-old that had to go to the bathroom.

"We also have no idea how many people he has on the inside to act as security." Pickle sounded like she was still pacing, probably running her hands through her bi-colored hair. "If he's expecting us…"

"More than he likely had before." Sol hummed, his dark eyes looking over the schematics. "What are our numbers?"

"Probably not enough," Maz mumbled, but everyone ignored her.

"We've got at least three more vans on their way," Dominic called from the front seat. "Oakfur and Fizz found us some backup."

"How'd they manage that?" Sol wasn't sure he wanted to know.

Dominic smiled in the rearview mirror where Sol could see him, the expression all teeth. "Well, they are our record keepers, aren't they?"

Sol barked a laugh, perhaps the first laugh that had come from him in over a month, delight singing through his veins.

"How did Fizz convince Oakfur to recruit quote unquote *criminals?*"

"Fizz can be very convincing when he wants to be." Dominic chuckled.

"All right, tell me the plan." Sol leaned forward, his fingers tight around the tablet so that he could listen to whatever Reboot and Pickle had come up with.

THEY WAITED until darkness fell among the trees, the van idling somewhere off the road on a dirt path that Sol hadn't even seen until Dominic had turned onto it. Sol's leg jittered the whole time, so long that the muscle started to burn from the strain, and didn't stop until Reboot finally stood and said, "It's time."

Then he followed the others out of the van, and let them load him up with anything and everything he could need once they were inside. A taser strapped to his thigh, a knife hanging from his ridiculously expensive leather belt. Sol reached for the long katana that were sitting in the bottom of the duffle Reboot had packed, but stopped when a hand grabbed his wrist.

"Don't take anything you don't know how to use," Reboot chided softly.

"Lettie will be there. They'll know how to use them." Sol didn't have to see them to know that the blades were well-oiled, he could smell it lingering on the canvas of the bag. Someone had been taking care of J's weapons in their absence. Likely Pickle.

"Do you honestly think Jericho will be in any shape to fight?" The words clenched like a fist around Sol's heart, reminding him that while he'd been living in Soren's ridiculous mansion, wearing expensive clothes, eating expensive meals, being tended to like a pet, J had been elsewhere. Curled up in a cell somewhere, terrified for their life. Sol swallowed. "If you can't use it, don't bring it. You can't afford to be carrying things that might slow you down, and keep you from getting to Jericho."

Sol nodded, pulling his hand from Reboot's grasp, and turning to the group around him. He was grateful when no one said anything about his little moment. "Where are the rest of them?"

"I had them park in other places. We didn't want to chance Soren's people scouting the woods and coming across us all together." Dominic had bent down to tuck a little pistol into his boot. Sol hoped he didn't really intend to use it to shoot someone, but then he supposed he did already have blood on his hands, what was a little more?

"All right, everybody ready?" Reboot asked, holding out a new com for Sol. When everyone nodded, Reboot turned on her heel and led them through the forest to the massive building that housed Soren's current operation.

There were no guards stationed outside, which Sol registered as strange. He stopped for a moment, looking around the little group that had gathered behind him at the door, wondering how many of them felt the same creep of unease crawling up their spines at the lack of security. Maybe it was nothing. But maybe it meant that Soren knew they were there. Maybe it meant he was waiting for them. Maybe the security had been called off because Soren had already moved house.

"Soliel, we need to move," Reboot said, her voice a whisper over his shoulder.

"Right." Sol's shoes squeaked a little in the quiet of the clearing as he made his way up to the front doors. They were big, and made of glass, with a little keypad off to the right-hand side that didn't actually have any numbers. It wouldn't, if what Reboot and Pickle had said was true. Because it wasn't about numbers, it was about DNA, and Sol was the only one with the code. "How far is the control room once we're inside, Pickle?"

"It's toward the back of the building. But the whole first floor is mostly lobby. Once you get up to the second floor it looks like office space. You should be able to go right through to the security office after that." Pickle's voice was soft, like she was afraid to speak too loudly lest Soren hear.

"Office space?" Sol pulled the dagger from his belt, and nicked the tip of his finger with it to draw forth a little bead of blood. "What the fuck does he have office space here for?"

"Well, I imagine someone works here seeing to the needs of the ummm…" Pickle cleared her throat awkwardly. "The prisoners. That space is probably for those people."

"And the floors above?" The keypad stayed dark, but Sol felt like it was glaring at him.

"Mostly cells. Except the top floor which looks like some kind of executive suite."

"That's where he'll be," Sol muttered to himself, smoothing the blood over the tip of his finger before pressing it to the little pad.

"What?"

"Nothing." The doors opened, and Sol waved them through into the glass and marble lobby. "We'll split up," he said already halfway across the wide-open space. No one was there to stop them. No alarms sounded. Nothing. And maybe that should have been proof enough that Soren knew they were coming, but Sol wasn't going to flinch. Not now. Not when he was so close.

"I'll come with you to the control room," Maz volunteered, stepping up beside Sol as he made his way to the bay of elevators.

"I'll lead everyone else upstairs. Give us the signal once you've got the floor doors unlocked." Reboot waved to the others, and they followed her to the door that would open into the darkened stairwell. It would be a long climb, but it was safer than taking the elevator. At least until they were in total control of it. "Dominic, you're in charge of our people down here."

Dominic nodded, motioning for another kelpie and a vampire to flank the front doors. Sol didn't think Soren would call in reinforcements, but they couldn't be too careful.

"Rachel, you're with us too." Sol held the elevator door when it dinged, waving for Maz and Rachel to load up. "Pickle gave you a run down on the system, right?"

"She did." Rachel hopped into the elevator, a cocky grin on her face. "I'm an expert."

"I wouldn't say that," Pickle mumbled in Sol's ear. "But she's adequate."

"Hey!"

"Enough, you two." Sol grumbled, rubbing at his temples. Merlin his ears were still ringing. Would they ever stop? "I need to think."

Rachel and Pickle fell blissfully silent as the elevator made its way up to the second floor. Sol could see Maz in the reflection beside the front panel of buttons. She was backed in the corner of the little box, her arms crossed over her chest, eyes narrowed like she was expecting an attack at any time.

The elevator dinged, and the three disembarked slowly, but the room was as empty as the lobby had been. Whoever had sat in those tiny cubicles had long since gone home, leaving not even heat lingering on their computers.

"This way," Maz said. The floor was only lit by security lights, but Maz seemed to have no trouble picking her way through the partition-made aisles, her eyes never straying from the path like she wasn't even worried about someone lingering ducked under a desk where they may spring out at any time to attack.

A big clock ticked somewhere deep in the space, and Rachel jumped, letting out a soft 'eep', but Maz kept right on walking. Her chin held high; her spine unusually stiff. Sol frowned. There was something... off about her. There had been something off about her since he'd joined them in the van, but he couldn't put his finger on what it was. He shook it off, his eyes flicking from left to right with each new little office space they passed. But no one lingered waiting to surprise them, and they made it to the door that led onto a narrow corridor lit only by a red emergency sign unmolested.

The door shut behind them with a bang, and Rachel let out another undignified yelp.

"Calm down." Maz sounded like she was rolling her eyes, her steps measured across the tile floor to the singular door at the back of the hall. She stopped in front of it, her hand pressed to the knob. "No one's here."

"How do you know that?" Rachel asked. It sounded rhetorical, but Sol was wondering the same thing.

"We haven't seen anyone, have we?" Maz twisted the knob, and frowned when it didn't give right away. "Anybody bring their lock pick kit?" When she received no answer, she huffed. "Of course not. I've got to do fucking everything myself."

Maz knelt in front of the door, turning around to grab Sol's dagger, and started to work on the lock with it.

"Fuck. We don't have time for that shit, Maz." Sol sighed, running a hand down his face. "Inwards or outwards?"

"What?"

"Which way does the door open?"

"Inwards."

"Then get out of the way, and both of you cover your ears. Actually, you know what, go into the next room over. These walls look pretty thick." Sol lifted his hands to turn off his comm and his hearing aid, before squaring up. He waited until the light from the other room was extinguished by the closing of the door behind him, and then he took a deep breath and screamed. Not as loudly as he could have, but loud enough that it left his throat raw and aching. Loud enough that the pressure jolted the door open, so it banged against the wall on the inside. Loud enough to send himself stumbling back a few steps. Then he went to bang on the wall, and Maz and Rachel joined him again, rushing into the little control room.

It was dark, but Maz found a light switch, and Rachel sat down to get to work without a word while Sol leaned against a wall, breathing through the pain in his throat. It wasn't as bad as the last time he'd used his Voice, but he knew from experience that he probably shouldn't try to use it again. At least not any time soon. J was going to kill him.

"Okay, doors unlocked, elevators are yours Pickle. We're good to go." Rachel gave a little cheer.

And just as Sol was reaching up to turn back on his com there was a loud bang followed by a thump. Sol looked up in time to watch Rachel slump against the control panel, her blood coating the circuitry. Sol froze, the cold of a gun pressed to his temple pulling him up short.

"Don't turn that back on," Maz chided gently.

Sol's fingers twitched.

"Hand down, Dusk. We wouldn't want anyone getting in the way of your reunion with your father."

Sol nodded numbly, lowering his hand. He couldn't look away from Rachel. Was she even still breathing? How fatal of a shot did Maz take? He wasn't... he wasn't sure. He couldn't tell from this angle. Was she... was she *dead*?

"I wouldn't worry about her; you've got bigger problems." Maz snorted.

"Maz," Sol said slowly, trying to breathe around the smell of blood that seemed to be coating his throat. "What in the ever-loving *fuck* are you doing?"

"We're going to take a little trip, up to the top floor, to see dear ol' dad." She pressed the gun into his temple harder for a moment before drawing it away, and aiming it squarely at his chest. "Move."

Sol stood from where he was leaning against the wall, and turned his back on her to head back to the elevators, not waiting for further instructions. Once they were inside, he watched her in the shiny button panel, her white tails flicking out behind her in irritation. "You're not going to explain yourself?"

"No. I'm not. Use your bloody finger to touch the panel, it'll take us all the way up."

His finger had stopped bleeding, the blood dried into a brown stain, but he pressed it into the little empty space where a button should have been at the top of the pyramid, and the elevator started moving.

CHAPTER TWENTY-NINE

The doors opened with a ding, and Maz pushed Sol out into the big open office on the top floor with the press of the gun to his back. He heard the doors shut behind them, but the cold bite of the barrel still dug into the base of his spine. A reminder that Maz was there, and she wasn't letting him go anywhere.

"My. My. Look at you. My son!" Soren crowed, a smile slashing across his face in a cruel line that reminded Sol of a villain from a cartoon. He was standing in the middle of the room, big wooden desk behind him that would have looked ridiculous in any other space except for the one they were standing in. Windows on almost every side. Thick, plush carpeting. And Soren in his suit, looking more deranged than ever before, with J pressed into his side like they were old friends. J's lids fluttered, letting Sol know that they were still alive. *Alive. Alive. Alive.* But unconscious.

"You can go now, Maz. Take my exit to avoid the mess and let the boys waiting in my car know we'll be down shortly."

"Right." Maz snorted, sounding put out by the whole

thing, but she removed the pistol from where it was likely leaving a nasty bruise on Sol and made her way to a door across the room. Soren reached down, not taking his eyes off of Sol for a second, and pushed a button. There was a buzz, and Maz opened the door to head down the stairs without even bothering to look back at Sol. At the person who had once thought himself her friend.

Sol shook himself, jerking his head away from her retreating form to fix his gaze on Soren, and J again. Soren had pulled what looked like a straight razor from somewhere, and was running the flat of it down J's too pale cheek. Sol's palm itched for the taser, but he couldn't risk it. The sharp edge of the blade was too close to J's skin. He needed to get J away from Soren if he had any hope of using it.

"I am not your son," Sol said, once he was sure they were really alone, Maz's booted footsteps nothing more than a memory.

"Of course you are!" Soren barked a laugh, that manic slash of a grin on his face only seeming to grow wider. "I mean look at you! So smart! So resourceful! So manipulative! So cunning! So—"

"*So not yours.*" Sol's fingers clenched into fists at his sides, his eyes darting around for a way to distract Soren. To draw him away from his captive. If he could just keep him talking. Just keep Soren's attention on him, then maybe he could get close enough to get J away from him. Once that was done, it'd be all over. He just needed to keep Soren talking. "I am Adelia's son."

"Nonsense! You're mine! You've always been mine! Just look at you!" Soren's eyes crinkled to accommodate the smile on his face, turning them into crescents in a horrifying mirror of Sol's own smile. Soren was right, there was no denying the family resemblance. There was so much of them that was the same. So much of Soren that Sol saw in himself every day when he looked in the mirror. The freckles. The dimpled smile. But there were other things, things that went deeper than the skin. The need to be immortal, in some way. The need for validation, and recognition. The willingness to — *No*. Sol would never hurt other people to get those things. He would never use other people just so he could be a hero.

"No. I'm not." The cut on his index finger throbbed, but it was perhaps the only thing keeping Sol from completely losing his shit. The only thing providing any clarity as he took one slow step forward, hoping that in his irritation, Soren wouldn't notice. Or he would take it for Sol trying to assert his own dominance on the conversation. "I've never been your son. You gave up your son when you hurt my mother."

Soren threw his head back and laughed, his chest heaving with the motion, his neck and face turned a ghastly red color that almost hid the freckles on his cheeks as he shook J. J's head lolled like a rag doll, but a soft groan left their lips, and Sol's eyes snapped to them. *Alive. Alive. Alive.* J was alive. Maybe not for too much longer. Sol needed to hurry. He took another step forward, hoping Soren wouldn't see it.

Soren's head snapped forward, his eyes narrowing on Sol. He had noticed. Sol lifted his chin, daring him to say anything.

"You did this," Soren said, instead of acknowledging the slowly shrinking space between them. His hand lifted to stroke J's cheek in a mockery of the tenderness that Sol had always felt for them.

"Did what?" Bile rose from Sol's chest, burning like acid at his already aching throat. His voice sounded slightly ruined, even to his own ears.

"Made Colette Jericho the perfect little battery for my eternal life." Soren's eyes had fallen to J's face, seeming to linger over the way J's lashes brushed their cheeks, over the little scar along their jaw where J had been grazed in a fight not but a few months ago. The skin was still a little shiny. "You know that, don't you? Imagine what else you could do…"

"I didn't." Sol managed to choke the words out somehow, past the metallic taste of blood, and the burning of vomit that was traveling up his ruined esophagus. Why hadn't he taken a gun from the bag? There had been so many there. Why hadn't he grabbed one? Why the fuck had he thought coming into this mess with nothing but a dagger and a taser would be enough? He didn't want to kill anyone, no. But he'd known, hadn't he? He'd known that this was going to end in a showdown with Soren. He had to have known. But he hadn't brought a gun. Now all he had a taser he was too afraid to use lest he hurt J in the process. And… And his Voice. But one more full burst of that and he'd probably never speak again. His vocal cords would fucking rupture, and that'd be the end of that.

There was a crash somewhere on the floors below. His people smashing into one of the cages Soren used to hold his victims, probably. Sol couldn't hear it, but he imagined the fae inside sobbing with relief as their rescuers helped them from the wreckage. Sol wished he could see it. But he couldn't take his eyes off of J where they hung limp from his father's arm. Their long blond hair was matted to their face with the stickiness of dried blood from a wound Sol couldn't see.

"I didn't," Sol repeated, forcing himself to breathe, to calm down, to think. But there was still a ringing in his ears. And J was not even ten feet away. If he could just reach them. If he could just touch them.

"You did!" Soren snapped, giving J another hard shake that made their head snap up and down painfully on their neck. "A werewolf alone has strength, vitality, sure. I could charge plenty for that. Any human would be grateful to be given that kind of boost." Soren shrugged like these things meant nothing to him. Like they were concerns for lesser men.

"I didn't make Lettie a werewolf."

"No. You didn't." Soren met Sol's gaze again, his eyes were wide and wild now, something like victory in their depths. Like he'd cornered Sol, and he knew it. "But you made Jericho *special*. Don't you see? By bonding with a banshee…" Soren shook his head, releasing an awed, manic chuckle. "I could live forever off of Jericho's magic if I wanted to," he murmured to himself, his head turning back to J's lax face. "It's because *you're* special, Soliel."

"I'm not." Sol took another small step toward them. Nine feet now. So close. So close that Sol could see the subtle rise and fall of J's chest. They were breathing steadily, at least.

Soren's gaze snapped back up to Sol as if he'd just remembered he was there. "You are," he insisted. "I made you special."

"You didn't make me anything."

"I did!" Soren growled, the smile slipping a little from his face. "You're better than everyone else. And think of the things we could do, Soliel, together. We could remake Mythikos in our image! No more seelie, unseelie, bullshit. No more humans down in the mud. No more politics. Just us."

Sol cringed at the words, his shoulders hunching. How many times had he wanted that since he'd been a child? To abolish the lines between the fae. To make it fair for the humans. And it would be so much easier to do if he were in charge. He'd thought that, once or twice when he was young and naïve enough to think that one man could solve everything. He still thought it sometimes, when things were their darkest, and he hated everyone around him a little more than he hated his own circumstances. And Soren was seeing that now. Seeing all the dark, uncertain corners of his mind. He was determined to shine a light on all the things Sol kept hidden in the hopes that no one would realize how close he really was to just leveling the city. The answer was uncomfortably close. Or it had been, anyway, before J had come back into his life. Before they'd been a team again.

"Come on, son." Soren clucked his tongue softly, chiding. "Don't think I don't know what's in that head of yours. You're mine, after all."

Sol clenched his fingers tighter, letting the sharp sting of the cut on his index finger keep him silent, keep him grounded.

"Come be the Alice to my White Rabbit. Let's remake Mythikos into our own Wonderland. I'll even let you keep your... your Lettie. Provided you let me use them to keep myself young." Soren held out a hand, that grin curling the edges of his mouth so far that it ate up his face, making him look more Cheshire Cat than White Rabbit.

There was a moment—it wasn't a very long moment, but it was a big one—where everything fell silent. Like the first second after Sol took his hearing aids out for the night, when the entire world sounded like it was behind glass. A moment where Sol looked at Soren's hand, his *father's* hand, and his palm itched to take it. To bask in the warmth of his father's approval, and acknowledgement. To *be* special, the way Soren said that he was. This was his chance to finally put an end to the violence. To finally set things right. To make a difference, a real one. Alone, he was nothing. He was one man against a tide. But with Soren's network, with his money, with his power... All Sol had to do was take his—

"Sol," J groaned, their lids fluttering open to look at Sol from the corner of their eye, breaking the silence, and rooting Sol to the floor. He'd been stepping forward, he realized belatedly. Nine feet had turned to six. His hand outstretched to Soren's. Sol snatched it back, jaw tightening at his own traitorous impulses.

And Sol realized suddenly that this, *this* is how Mythikos would burn. Because Sol couldn't save it on his own, and he couldn't sacrifice J for Soren's help. Mythikos would burn in a blaze of glory, lit by the action of one man who would give up anything for the person he loved most. Even any hope of saving the city he'd been fighting for since he was a child. And if Sol couldn't get J away from Soren safely using the taser then...

Well. It was a small price to pay.

Fuck it. If this is how it all has to end. Fuck it.

Sol opened his mouth, and he screamed. He screamed so loud the electronics in his hearing aids screeched in his ears. The sound knocked J from Soren's arms, making J fall limp to the floor, their head knocking against the desk probably a little too hard. But they were safe. *Safe. Safe. Alive. Alive. Alive.* And out of Soren's grip.

And Sol didn't stop screaming. He took one step forward, and then another. The sound threw Soren back against one of the windows, the glass cracking like a spiderweb with Soren at the center. He didn't stop. Not until the glass shattered under the force of Sol stepping so close, he could reach out and touch it. Not until Soren stumbled back reaching out to grab Sol to try to steady himself. Not until he felt his vocal cords give way, blood thick and metallic coating his tongue. Not until there was nothing left. Only the ringing silence.

Soren's eyes were wide, blood trickling from his ears, and he was trying to say something, but Sol couldn't hear him. Then Soren smiled, wicked, and horrible, gripped Sol's arm tighter, let his balance lean back just enough...

And they fell.

CHAPTER THIRTY

Sol woke up—which was surprising enough—and when he looked around to figure out what had woken him, he found J at his side, their eyes narrowed into a cutting glare that Sol could practically feel carving a hole into his cheek.

That must have been it, then.

"Wh—" Sol stopped, coughing around the croaking, scratching of his throat. He opened his mouth to try again, but all that came out was something that sounded more like a broken speaker than a person.

"Don't try to talk, idiot," J signed, their hands moving pointedly over the sentence in anger. Their mouth was moving along to the words, but Sol couldn't hear what they were saying. He frowned. He realized he couldn't hear the beeping of the machine beside him either. Or the creak of the chair under J as they shifted.

"What happened?" Sol asked, ignoring the way his own fingers were sluggish, and clumsy from whatever they'd given him to dull the pain, and keep him under while he healed. Or at least that's what he assumed it was. He hoped he hadn't injured the nerves or tendons somehow. That would be a bitch and a half to come back from, especially since he wasn't sure how long it would take his throat to recover.

"You threw yourself out of a fucking window, that's what happened." J's lips curled back over what was probably a snarl, their movements growing more agitated.

"I didn't throw myself." Sol rolled his eyes. "Soren grabbed me."

"Sure the fuck looked like you threw yourself. And what the fuck were you doing using your Voice like that?" J snapped, green eyes alight with so much rage that Sol was honestly surprised his skin wasn't boiling under their gaze.

"I don't see where I had much of a choice, Lettie. He had a fucking knife to your throat." Sol huffed, dropping his head back onto the hard hospital pillow. J had probably picked it out, they were petty that way when they were pissed. Sol loved them so fucking much. "What was I supposed to do? Let him cut you open?"

"You had a fucking taser on you, you moron!" J shouted, but still managed to keep enough composure to sign along to it, so Sol would fully understand just how furious they were.

"If I shocked him, the current would have traveled through you. Plus! His body would have started jerking around, and who knows where that blade would have ended up. I couldn't take that chance."

"Couldn't take that chance, he says. Didn't see that bastard flattened like a pancake. Coulda been him." J muttered and leaning back into the chair. They didn't look as angry as they'd been when Sol first woke up, and he counted that as a small, but likely meaningless, victory. "And who the fuck asked you to come in and save me like that anyway?"

Sol laughed, the sound broken, and grating in his throat.

It made him cough. And then J was on their feet grabbing a cup of water and forcing the straw between his lips so hard the plastic almost cut him. Sol took a grateful sip just the same before settling back again.

"You did say I was your hero," he teased, letting his fingers linger over the words like a drawl.

"Oh, go fuck yourself." J snorted, but Sol thought they might have been blushing.

"Which ones today?" Sol asked, the words soft in his hands, as he fell back on their ritual, needing some normalcy now that things were over.

"He." J muddled the gesture a little, like he was mumbling, and Sol smiled softly.

"Okay." Sol nodded. "Now, can you stop being pissed at me for like, two seconds? Just long enough to thank me for saving your life? I mean how fucking ungrateful—"

"You fucking asshole! Don't you dare think you're off the hook for—"

"Boys. Boys," Pickle said when she came through the door, the words almost nonexistent in Sol's ears, but he could read her lips even from across the room. "There are other people in this hospital trying to recover. Could you please keep it down so they can rest?"

Reboot came in behind her, shutting the door as they made their way over to the bed. J rolled his eyes, and Sol could imagine he'd probably clicked his tongue in a soft tsk.

"Sorry, Pickle. I didn't mean to make him yell." Sol smiled a little. Pickle and Reboot both looked tired. Like they hadn't slept in weeks. But they were both whole, and uninjured as far as he could tell, and that was something. He really needed to stop winding up in hospital beds after big missions... "How long was I out?"

"Long enough," Reboot said, her eyes serious, movements

chiding. Sol didn't know how mothers always managed that. Even in sign, he could always tell when his mother was telling him off. It was a mystery.

"You had us all very worried." Pickle moved to sit in the chair beside J, but Reboot stayed at the foot of his bed, just looking at him. Drinking her fill like she was sure she'd lost him. Maybe she had. He didn't think he wanted to know what had happened when they brought him to the hospital. "What do you remember?"

"I just..." Sol paused, flexing around a sharp ache in his forearms where the words got stuck very much like they often did in his throat when he was upset. He nodded to his water, and J moved to grab it for him, holding it up to his lips until Sol had taken a couple of deep drags from the straw. "I remember Soren grabbing me, just after the glass shattered. And then I remember falling."

"You didn't fall very far." J signed almost dismissively. Not that he was trying to make light of what had happened, or make the trauma smaller, Sol knew that. Just that he didn't want to think about it. J had always needed to distance himself from things that hurt him. And as J reached to replace the cup on the little table, Sol saw the bandages on J's forearms.

"You grabbed me. Didn't you?" Sol frowned. There had been so much glass. And not all of it had detached fully from the frame. If J had grabbed him... Sol shook himself.

"Well what the fuck else was I going to do? Let you plummet to your fucking death alongside that dickhead?" J cocked his head, one blond brow raised.

"No. I guess not." Sol bit back a laugh. It was hard, but he didn't want to choke again, and he was sure his throat would thank him if he gave it a rest. "So... now what?"

J shrugged, getting up to refill Sol's water cup from the

pitcher, and Sol turned his attention to Reboot. She had been watching him through the whole conversation, her brow pinched in the center. She looked up from where she'd been staring at the bandages around his throat, and smiled a little.

"Now... We rebuild," she said.

EPILOGUE

THE KIDS WERE LOUD. ARGUABLY, SOL HAD ALWAYS KNOWN that children were loud, but he'd never really thought much about it when he'd been one himself. Now, faced with a playground full of screaming fae and human children, he realized what his own mother must have gone through with he and J.

Speaking of J...

Sol's eyes flicked around the turf that Oakfur had laid down for them some months ago when he'd decided that mulch wasn't good enough. Like they hadn't all grown up on mulch. But leave it to Oakfur to decide that his little girl deserved better. A little smile dimpled one corner of Sol's mouth when he spotted J, standing at the bottom of the slide, his hands held out, waiting for one of the little kelpies to slide down. Water was streaming down the plastic, splashing J's pants legs, but he didn't move. He just waited diligently for the child to build up the courage.

"He's good with them," Fizz said, clapping his hand down on Sol's shoulder hard enough to make Sol stumble a little.

"You sound surprised," Sol signed, not taking his eyes off of J.

"Not really." Fizz shrugged. "But I think Oakfur was."

Sol hummed, the sound a hoarse rasp in the back of his throat that made it tickle a little. He pulled a bottle of water from the picnic table off to his right, and took a long drag. By the time that was done, the kelpie child had gotten up the courage to slide down the slide, and J had caught them up, spinning them around, as they giggled delightedly, all signs of water gone with their anxiety.

"You know when Reboot said we were going to rebuild..." Fizz cocked his head, brows raised a little, but there was that sharp smile on his lips, the one that showed a row of pointed redcap teeth.

"You thought Eventide would continue on as it had been." Sol nodded thoughtfully. He'd known it couldn't. Or at least if it did, he couldn't be a part of it. Not if he wanted to live to see his thirtieth birthday. There had been a long discussion with J about it. About how Sol wanted to be a hero, but he didn't think he could deal with the blood on his hands anymore. J had agreed, likely on the basis that Sol had wound up in a hospital bed, fighting for his life twice in as many years. So, they'd decided on this instead.

"I thought for sure you'd at least continue the fight." Fizz looked back out to the playground full of laughing children. Unseelie children. Seelie children. Human children. All mixed in together as they should be. All ages. All races.

"I did continue the fight." Sol pursed his lips, thinking of how best to explain the choice he'd made. It had been almost too easy to make it. Oakfur had been left in a wheelchair after what he'd done to help Sol escape, and his daughter had lost her mother long before Sol's people had gotten to her. They needed a safe harbor. Someplace to recover from their losses, and build a new life for themselves. They needed counseling, and a roof over their heads away from the toxicity of Mythikos. And they weren't the only ones. "The fight just looks a little different now."

"You could have run for office, like Reboot." Although Fizz sounded like he didn't understand, Sol knew better. Fizz had known all along that the war for the Unseelie in Mythikos was never going to be about anything flashy. He'd known long before Sol did that it was going to be about quiet acts of kindness. Sol just hadn't been paying attention. "Isn't that what you always wanted? To be the face of change?"

Sol let out a long breath, his shoulders sagging a little. "It was," he admitted, but it rankled. He hated thinking about what an egotistical little shit he'd been. If he hadn't been, maybe Soren wouldn't have— No. He wasn't going to think about the similarities between himself and his father. Not again. "But I couldn't keep it up. It wasn't sustainable. I was letting Dusk consume me, and turn me into something I wasn't. Mama has a better time separating herself from the work. Besides... imagine Lettie being the spouse of a politician."

Fizz tilted his head, squinting a little as he watched J sit a little human girl on his shoulders, then take her hands and hold them out to either side, before spinning in a circle that would be sure to leave J with a headache later. He'd complain about it, Sol would make soft sympathetic noises and force feed him a couple of aspirin, and life would go on.

"No. You're right, I don't see it." Fizz laughed, shaking his head, and Sol turned his head to smirk at him. "He seems really happy here."

"He is. His parents' place isn't even a half hour up the road, and he gets to shift into a wolf and go running through the forest anytime he wants. It's good for him."

"It's good for you too."

Sol nodded. It was. He knew that. He hadn't felt so much like himself since he'd been a teenager. Since the day J had walked out of his apartment and ended whatever they'd had together. "There's a lot of healing still left to do, but this place... this center?" Sol signed, lifting his head to look at the buildings that surrounded the courtyard where they'd built the playground. It wasn't what he'd always imagined for himself—in fact he imagined a teenage Sol being almost ashamed of what he'd become—but this was better, he realized. Instead of pain, he and J were able to bring peace, and happiness, and hope when people needed it most. And Sol found that in doing so, he'd found all of those things for himself as well. "It's given Mythikos more hope than Dusk ever could."

Fizz smiled again, reaching over to pat Sol heavily on the shoulder before he stepped away to join the siren who was doing watercolors with some of the older children. Oakfur was there, his wheelchair pulled up to the end of the table, his daughter in his lap.

Water hit Sol in the face, and he jerked to glare at J whose fingers were ringing out the long braid he'd thrown over his shoulder. "Was that necessary?"

"Sure was." J winked. He leaned in to plant a kiss on Sol's lips, half apologetic, half smug. "What did Fizz want?"

"I think he was trying to tell me he told me so. Self-satisfied bastard."

"Has he heard anything from Maz?" J moved to stand behind Sol, wrapping his arms around his waist, and tucking his chin onto Sol's shoulder. There was water on his shirt seeping into Sol's sweater, but Sol shrugged it off.

"I don't think so. I think she knows better than to come back here." Sol leaned back into the warmth of J's chest. "I still can't believe she did all of that because she was pissed about you joining the organization."

"Jealous," J corrected. "You couldn't kill her if she did."

"I wouldn't really have a choice. Not after what she did."

Sol frowned. He wouldn't want to kill Maz, she'd been his friend too long, and the betrayal of what she'd done still stung. But he would if he had to, if it would keep the rest of his family safe. "How's Rachel by the way? Ildri said she'd started her rehab?"

"Good. I wish she'd do it here. We have the facilities now." J frowned, burying his face in the side of Sol's neck. Sol reached up to brush his fingers along the soft peach fuzz of J's undercut.

"She wants to be where the action is. She can't run Mama's campaign from here."

"I mean she could..."

"Let it lie, Lettie. We've got plenty of people to look after. Focus on that." Sol laughed softly, the sound still a little broken. J huffed into his neck, his breath ruffling Sol's hair, but he didn't disagree as they looked out over the little safe haven they'd built. Humans, and fae alike all together in one place, like it should have always been.

Yeah. Fizz had been right. Kindness really was the way to go.

ACKNOWLEDGMENTS

First off, thank you—the reader—for reading this, and hopefully enjoying J and Dusk as much as I did. I really appreciate it, and I hope you'll drop a review on GoodReads to let me know what you think.

If you loved this story, and these characters, as much as I did, please check out some of my other works!

Next, I'd like the thank my small hoard of beta-readers. You guys gave some excellent insight, and I really appreciate all of your hard work. And my editor Meg for turning this into a story worth reading.

And last but certainly not least, thank you to my writing community. Particularly, Tiss, Elle, and Jasmine who I have known for near a decade now—without you there would be no Lou. And to my other bookish friends, Candace, Nancy, Tanya, Jordan and Justin for being supportive and awesome.

ABOUT THE AUTHOR

Born and raised in a small town near the Chesapeake Bay, Lou Wilham grew up on a steady diet of fiction, arts and crafts, and Old Bay. After years of absorbing everything, there was to absorb of fiction, fantasy, and sci-fi she's left with a serious writing/drawing habit that just won't quit. These days, she spends much of her time writing, drawing, and chasing a very short Basset Hound named Sherlock.

When not, daydreaming up new characters to write and draw she can be found crocheting, making cute bookmarks, and binge-watching whatever happens to catch her eye.

Learn more about Lou and her future projects on her website: http://louinprogress.com/ or join her mailing list at: http://subscribepage.com/mailermailer

facebook.com/LouWilham
instagram.com/lou.wilham

Also By Lou Wilham

The Curse Collection
    The Curse of The Black Cat
    The Curse of Ash and Blood
    The Curse of Flour and Feeling

The Clockwork Chronicles
    The Girl in the Clockwork Tower
    The Unicorn and the Clockwork Quest
    The Rose in the Clockwork Library

The Heir To Moondust
    The Prince of Starlight
    The Prince of Daybreak

The Witches of Moondale
    The Hex Next Door

Sanctuary of the Lost
    Of Loyalties and Wreckage

Completed Series
    The Tales of the Sea Trilogy
    Villainous Heroics

Sneak Peek!

continue reading for a sneak peek of Lou's

THE GIRL IN THE CLOCKWORK TOWER
A STEAMPUNK RAPUNZEL RETELLING

LOU WILHAM

CHAPTER ONE
PERSINETTE

The washed-out, dilapidated buildings of the labor camp spread out beneath Persinette as she floated high above it all. Drifting down toward them, Persi bobbed lightly through the narrow alleys between one building and the next, her bare feet several inches off the ground. With not a soul in sight, an eerie silence blanketed the vast vacant camp.

A soft snap drew her attention. She spun to see what the sound was, and all at once the narrow alley was full of people. A sea of dirty, tired, gaunt faces swam below her, dirty arms reaching for her. What seemed like a million bony, pale hands grabbed at her ankles, to pull her down—down into that sea of frail bodies.

Persinette's green eyes jumped from one face to the next as they tore at her hair and clothes. She recognized them, all of them. She'd seen them all before, though never in person. They dragged her lower and lower into the pushing, writhing pit of dirty and too-thin bodies.

. . .

Persinette awoke with a start, her face sweaty and her breath coming in hard, shallow pants. A scream was on her lips, but she swallowed it down with a dry gulp. "Just a dream, Persi. It was just a dream," she whispered to herself, taking another deep breath to calm her racing heart. Even with her familiar room in the Tower before her, those faces still swam in her mind, each the same dirty, terrifying rictus she'd seen the first time she'd had the vision.

"Just a dream," she repeated. But a part of her asked *"Was it?"*

A shrill, angry noise broke the silence of the early morning, startling Persi and setting her heart racing once more. With narrowed eyes, she glared at the offending alarm clock on her bedside table. Beside it sat a piece of crisp parchment that seemed to glow in the soft morning light. In one swift motion of her freckled hand, she silenced the alarm and scooped up the paper. She rubbed at her eyes and read the schedule typed neatly on the page before her.

- 6:30 a.m.—Briefing with Agent Gothel
- 7:00 a.m.—Breakfast

After that, Persinette skimmed the rest. Other than the briefing with Gothel, nothing mattered; everything else was just trivial busywork. She dragged herself from the warmth of plush blankets and soft sheets to the washroom to prepare for her morning meeting.

After sixteen years of living in MOTHER headquarters, the long walk down the bustling corridors, the too-early meeting, the rush of passing MOTHER agents and automatons, even the hiss of steam as the door to the conference room opened—all of it was routine. When she'd first been brought to MOTHER at eight years old, it had all scared her, but Persinette found that over time, anyone could get used to almost anything.

"You're late." Even the guttural, admonishing voice of MOTHER Agent Gothel had become commonplace for Persinette. The slender, middle-aged woman with sharp features and even sharper eyes was standing at the head of the table, a clutter of papers strewn before her.

The doors to the room groaned shut behind Persinette, barely missing the long train of her skirt. "I'm sorry, Gothel," she murmured. Her long lavender hair fell into her face as she ducked her head and tried to make herself as small as possible. Gothel had never let an outright threat fall from her lips, but the implication was always there: the moment Persi was no longer useful to MOTHER, she would be disposed of, as so many others had been.

Gothel's eyes narrowed on Persinette before she seemed to make up her mind about something. "Now that you're here, sit," she ordered, gesturing to the seat across from her. The bustle of Persi's skirts let out a soft *poof* of air as she hastily complied. "We need an updated list of Enchanted in Province Four."

Gothel held out a file and Persi hurriedly reached for it, knowing full well what was inside. Still, she made a show of setting the file on the table, opening it, and flicking her eyes over population statistics, maps, and photographs of Daiwynn's fourth Province.

"We have provided you a map of the area and plenty of pictures. Any other information you may need is available upon request, of course." The agent's words were sharp and direct, as always.

Persinette's fingers conducted their obligatory flip through the pages of the file as she nodded and took in the information she'd been given. She dared not say a word, however. With Gothel, it was usually better to speak only when spoken to.

The agent gave her a moment before asking, "So, how long will this take you?"

Swallowing roughly, Persi took a moment to think. Whenever possible, she did her best to stretch out the length of time between the Collections she was involved with. She thought—however foolish the thought might have been—that by taking her time, she would give whoever she had a vision of—her target—the chance to get away. Still, even now, some annoying and logical voice in her head reminded her that these Enchanted didn't even know MOTHER was coming for them. Without that knowledge, they had no idea that they needed to run at all. She promptly told that voice to be quiet; she was doing the best that she could, after all. "A couple of months or so. Province Four is rather large," she said finally.

"You have six weeks," Gothel replied sharply, leaving no room for argument. Those cold, dark eyes narrowed on Persi as if perhaps she expected an argument. However, there would be none; Persinette saw no point in it. She would deliver what was expected of her in the time she was allotted, or else.

"Right, then. Guess I better get to work." Persi grabbed the file as she stood. She was already standing to head back to her rooms in the Tower, far away from Gothel's glare.

The agent's voice stopped her before she could push the button to open the doors. "One more thing, Persinette."

Persi licked her dry lips, almost afraid to ask the question. "Yes, Gothel?"

"They want you in the field this time."

"Excuse me?" Persinette's stomach did a sick drop toward the toes of her buckled boots. She'd been prepared for almost anything—just not that. "I can't go into the field, that's not my job," she argued. "My job is just to find the people. You and the Steps are supposed to go on Collections, not me."

Gothel shrugged her slim shoulders, not even bothering to lift her eyes from the papers in front of her. "Those are the orders," she said simply.

"But..." Persinette frowned deeply. "I'm not even trained to go out into the field! What do they think this is going to accomplish?" she demanded as she spun to meet Gothel's eyes again. The shock of those orders brought with it a rare instance of bravery and contradiction. Never did Persinette go against orders. Seldom did she even question them.

The corners of Gothel's mouth pinched with obvious disgust, her eyes narrowing. She seemed to find Persinette's sudden bout of courage neither amusing nor admirable. "They are hoping this will speed up your process and allow increased Collection rates as you will be out in the field able to disseminate any visions that may occur on the spot."

What Gothel didn't say—and didn't have to say—was that Persinette's limited results had finally begun to draw attention to her. The higher-ups in MOTHER had noticed, and if they didn't start seeing better results from her, she would be punished.

Persi nodded so quickly her teeth clacked together, then headed for the doors. Orders were orders, and Persi knew she didn't have much choice. She was going out into the field whether she wanted to or not.

"You may be outfitted with a stunning pistol, so make sure you get down to the firing range to practice," Gothel added as an afterthought.

Swallowing hard, Persinette nodded once more eyes fixed on the closed door before her, then smacked the button to open the doors. Out in the corridor, and out of Gothel's sight, she leaned against the cement wall to take calm her pacing pulse.

"Calm down, Persi. This might be for the best."

Even as she told herself so, a small, nasty voice that sounded eerily like Gothel reminded her of all the things that could and likely would go wrong.

It took her a few moments to silence the voice and regain control over her trembling knees enough to walk in a strangely robotic fashion back to the Tower. Each step was a struggle, but she focused on the click of her hard-soled boots on the tiled floor as she fled the probing eyes of MOTHER.

ALTHOUGH PERSINETTE HAD NOT BEEN BORN THERE, the Tower was the only place she'd ever really called home. The rooms that surrounded hers housed others of her "kind": fairies, pixies, werewolves, and even a troll or two. Each was given plenty of living space and the illusion of freedom, but Persinette understood the Tower for what it was—a prison. She and the others of her kind did not *live* in the Tower; they were *kept* there.

Once back in her quarters, she opened the barred windows just a crack. There was no way to get out past the bars—and at night the windows locked automatically—but at least she was able to let some fresh air in. Persinette slumped down into the oversized chair that was perched on the rug in front of the jam-packed bookshelf. She inhaled deeply, pressing the heels of her shaking hands to her eyes to stop the panicked burn of tears.

"Get ahold of yourself, Persi. You can do this," she scolded herself. The file—which she'd picked up from the chair and flopped across her legs—sat heavily in her lap as she continued to breathe in through her nose and out through her mouth until her eyes stopped burning and she was in control again.

When her hands were finally steady, she opened the file and let her eyes flick over the printed pictures. Perhaps this could be a blessing in disguise. Maybe she could make this work for her. She could finally have a chance to do something to help the Enchanted, perhaps even stem the flow of faces that regularly haunted her. She could warn them somehow, allow them time to escape before MOTHER reached them.

But how? she asked herself.

She would have to make it look like she hadn't engineered their escapes herself. Like those Enchanted simply decided to pack up and leave. As much as Persinette wanted to help, she also knew that if she were found out, she'd be sent to the camps right alongside those she'd help Collect. Then she'd be no good to anyone. Still, in spite of her fear, she had to help. She knew that with every fiber of her being.

Yes, but how can someone like you help? That nasty little voice asked.

She shrugged the voice off, but still she asked herself: *How? How? How?* Persinette sat there in that overstuffed armchair asking herself over and over until lunch time.

No solution came to her.

When, at last, the lunch bell rang through the halls, she pulled herself to her feet and headed down to the mess hall. Tray in hand, Persinette settled at one of the little tables with a few other Assets, her mind still focused on the single question. *How?*

"You're a train wreck, 11-24-10." The snide words and the sound of her Asset number turned Persi's stomach and ripped her from her thoughts.

A rainbow-haired man with a short, dark beard stood on the other side of the table, two ruddy, brown-haired men flanking him. His name was Agnes, and he'd never said more than a handful of words to her before that night. Persi shrugged, trying to come up with a lie that would explain away the mussed lavender hair and what must have been a vacant expression. Again, nothing came to mind.

Agnes sneered at her silence. He was beautiful, painfully so—but then, unicorns always were. "Oh look, cat's got the Seer's tongue. Maybe all those visions finally addled her brain."

Persinette opened her mouth to say something, anything to get him to stop, to get him to leave her alone, but she couldn't get any words past her lips.

"Pathetic." He snorted with disgust. The two men on either side of him let out soft chortles of laughter.

"I have to hit the shooting range after dinner," she blurted out suddenly.

A short hateful bark of laughter left Agnes. His eyes lit with vicious amusement at her obvious discomfort. "Is that so? Do you not know how to fire a pistol, 11-24-10?"

Persi floundered for words again. She'd seen Agnes's cruelty toward the others, but up to that point he'd ignored her. The longer the confrontation dragged on, the harder she found it to think at all. Her palms were sweating against the table, slicking the surface. Her mouth gaped—to retort, to cut him down, to show him she was not someone to be pushed around—but the well of words in her throat was dry.

Loud chuckles rippled through the little group. In a moment of sheer panic, Persi stood abruptly from the table and made a beeline for the door of the mess hall. The laughter only grew louder, following her as she ran. "That's right, run, 11-24-10! Get lots of practice running! Or they'll kill you out there!" Agnes shouted after her.

The words echoed behind her, her heart racing and her palms getting even damper.

Persinette thought of little else all evening. The memory of Agnes's words kept her awake more than the nightmares ever had, and at breakfast the next morning, she had to prop her head up on one pale hand just to keep herself from falling asleep in her porridge.

It took her till lunch to finally shake those words and focus on the task at hand once more. She still had not formulated a plan, however; all she had was a plan to formulate a plan. Which was…a start. Of sorts.

For a plan—or a plan for a plan—she'd need research.

Once she finished eating, she went down to the office that handled information requests. At the front desk sat a scowling young woman with bright blonde hair and sharp grey eyes that narrowed on Persi as she walked up to the counter. "What do you want?"

"Good afternoon," Persi said with a smile. She wasn't sure what she was hoping for—maybe a smile in return?—but what she got was a blank stare that left her feeling awkward and uncomfortable. "I, um, need to fill out a library access request form, please?"

With a cold look the MOTHER agent stared Persinette down for a moment longer before she wordlessly pointed to a rack of forms beside the window and promptly ducked her head back down to whatever she'd been doing before.

"Right. Thanks." Persinette forced her smile wider and looked over the rack for the form she needed. Once she'd found it, she filled it out at one of the longer, counter-height tables. She was so engrossed in the little boxes and spaces for explanation that she didn't notice anyone else in the room until someone peered right over her shoulder—Agnes.

"I don't think a book is going to teach you how to handle

a pistol," he said coolly. "At least not enough to keep you alive."

Persinette spun around, sending her long hair fluttering, and fixed Agnes with a look of sheer determination. She was going to do it. She was going to tell him off. This was it! She opened her mouth to speak and…and…and *nothing*. Nothing came out!

Agnes laughed coldly and shook his head. "I'll leave you to it then, 11-24-10. Good luck." He gave her a mock bow and strode off.

She stood there for a long moment, still trying to coax words from her mouth, but if any words had formed, the stubbornly refused to come out. Instead, Persinette's eye twitched, but she forced herself to turn back to the task at hand: getting into the library.

If you loved the first chapter of *The Girl in the Clockwork Tower*, you can grab your copy at Louinprogress.com/the-girl-in-the-clockwork-tower/

More books you'll love

Then check out more books from
Midnight Tide Publishing!

The Castle of Thorns by Elle Beaumont

To end the murders, she must live with the beast of the forest.

After surviving years with a debilitating illness that leaves her weak, Princess Gisela must prove that she is more than her ailment. She discovers her father, King Werner, has been growing desperate for the herbs that have been her survival. So much so, that he's willing to cross paths with a deadly legend of Todesfall Forest to retrieve her remedy.

Knorren is the demon of the forest, one who slaughters anyone who trespasses into his land. When King Werner steps into his territory, desperately pleading for the herbs that control his beloved daughter's illness, Knorren toys with the idea. However, not without a cost. King Werner must deliver his beloved Gisela to Knorren or suffer dire consequences.

With unrest spreading through the kingdom, and its people growing tired of a king who won't put an end to the demon of Todesfall Forest, Gisela must make a choice. To become Knorren's prisoner forever, or risk the lives of her beloved people.

Available now

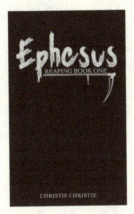

Ephesus by Christis Christie

As a soul lost before it could live, Ephesus was gifted a special role—he must collect the dead.

Ephesus has known no other existence than reaping souls, experiencing life only from the shadows. Remaining separate was easy, until the day he meets a unique little girl with an ability she should not possess.

But can friendships be nurtured when life and death aren't meant to mingle beyond the point of passing? Ephesus must navigate the world fulfilling his purpose while also balancing his newfound curiosity of the girl's life. However, when a threat arises, will it mean their ruin?

Available Now

Come True by Brindi Quinn

A jaded girl. A persistent genie. A contest of souls.

Recent college graduate Dolly Jones has spent the last year stubbornly trying to atone for a mistake that cost her everything. She doesn't go out, she doesn't make new friends and she sure as hell doesn't treat herself to things she hasn't earned, but when her most recent thrift store purchase proves home to a hot, magical genie determined to draw out her darkest desires in exchange for a taste of her soul, Dolly's restraint, and patience, will be put to the test.

Newbie genie Velis Reilhander will do anything to beat his older half-brothers in a soul-collecting contest that will determine the next heir to their family estate, even if it means coaxing desire out of the least palatable human he's ever contracted. As a djinn from a 'polluted' bloodline, Velis knows what it's like to work twice as hard as everyone else, and he won't let anyone—not even Dolly f*cking Jones—stand in the way of his birthright. He just needs to figure out her heart's greatest desire before his asshole brothers can get to her first.

COME TRUE: A BOMB-ASS GENIE ROMANCE is the romantic, fantastic second-coming-of-age story of two flawed twenty-somethings from different realms battling their inner demons, and each other, one wish at a time.

Available Now

CPSIA information can be obtained
at www.ICGtesting.com
Printed in the USA
BVHW072113030622
638872BV00004B/111